I0451721

*This book is dedicated to freedom fighters around the world.
We may never know the battles you face
to secure the freedom of others.*

*"Enslave the liberty of but one human being
and the liberties of the world are put in peril."
William Lloyd Garrison*

Journey to Freedom

ESCAPING THE DARKNESS

JOURNEY TO FREEDOM

A novel by

Debra Shelton

Escaping the Darkness is a work of fiction.
The events that take place within these pages are based in
historical fact. While the names of well-known people, places,
and actual events may be real, the characters are fictitious.
Their experiences are a composite of survivor stories.

ISBN 978-1-7327892-0-3

CHAPTER 1

Northeastern DRC

The decrepit Rover skidded to a stop inches from the uniformed man who stepped into the middle of the rutted track that passed for a road in most parts of the DRC *(Democratic Republic of Congo)*. The thirty ish, hard-looking African worked a hand-rolled cigarette between his full lips. An assault rifle rested across his forearm like he was cradling a baby. The menace in the man's eyes dared Jean Pierre to try something—to give him an excuse to demonstrate what his 'baby' could do. Experience told him the soldier could swing the gun into position and firing off a clip in a matter of seconds without hesitation or remorse.

"No sudden moves, Jackson." Jean Pierre whispered in French to the young driver next to him. "Let them see your hands." He resisted the urge to wipe the stray lock of hair out of his eyes and push his sunglasses back up on his nose. Instead, he raised his own hands and placed them on the top edge of the windshield frame to show he was unarmed. The open-topped 4x4 offered little protection to the two occupants.

Eight more men stepped out from the screen of palms, brush, and tall elephant grass that lined the road on both sides. They all wore the same nondescript, camo uniform, red beret, and black, dusty boots. Ammo belts crossed their chests and most gripped machetes at their sides. Jean Pierre couldn't miss the dark stains on the long steel blades.

They ranged in age from fifteen to twenty-five or so. All looked seasoned and grim. Their black faces expressionless. Were they friend or foe? He looked for identifying insignias. There were none.

With twenty-five years of chasing stories across the globe, Jean Pierre knew he needed to reassure the armed men he was not a threat. Making nice would hopefully buy him time to figure out what it was they wanted. Nervous sweat trickled from his armpits down his sides to gather at the waistband of his Levis. He sucked in and let out a deep breath to calm his rattled nerves. This could go so wrong, so quick.

He worked up a smile and raised his fingers. "Bonjour *(Hello),* my friends." He motioned to the cardboard wedged in the corner of the glass frame and said to them in French, "As you can see from the placard, I'm a journalist and authorized by your government to be here."

In a mix of French and Lingala, Jackson hissed from the side of his mouth, "They're not Congolese."

Jean Pierre figured as much. With three or four rebel groups roaming the eastern border of the DRC, he couldn't hazard a guess as to which faction these men belonged to. "I've been in Kinshasa covering the elections and flew into Goma this morning to cover the Mt. Nyiragongo eruption."

The leader rolled the cigarette between his lips, from one side to the other. "Get out," he ordered between clenched teeth, yellowed from too much nicotine and not enough toothpaste. The man spoke in barely discernible English.

Jean Pierre eased out of the passenger side. Knowing Jackson's limited English, he repeated the command in French and hoped the young man complied.

The leader swung his weapon around and directed it at Jean Pierre, then motioned to the ground. Jean Pierre's heart beat a quick tattoo against his ribcage. With his hands still raised, he worked himself down to his knees. The broken kneecap he received in Somalia a year earlier screamed in protest. From this viewpoint, he had a close-up view of the muzzle of the Kalashnikov AK-101.

Jean Pierre had no doubts the decade old weapon was still deadly. He wasn't sure if the acidic whiff of rotten eggs came from the gun, its handler, or the dark specks of suspicious residue on the barrel. His nose twitched at the smell.

Lord, I hope you're watching this. We may need your help here.

A filthy-smelling bandana came down over Jean Pierre's eyes, effectively cutting off any light. He resisted the urge to pull the blindfold away and kept his hands raised. The gun was still close, too close. He could feel its menace.

"Please," Jackson begged. "I see nothing. I know nothing." Taunts and snickers peppered the beating that followed. Jean Pierre cringed at the sickening sound of bone being crushed. Jackson cried out in pain, then was silent.

The stakes just got higher.

It's all my fault. He'd seen the fear in Jackson's eyes when he told him he wanted to go up into the Virunga Mountains, ostensibly to cover the breaking story of the eruption. *He's here because of me. I have to do something before they kill us both.* "Look, I have francs. Congolese francs," he pleaded, knowing they'd do what they wanted and take the money, anyway.

"You. Up."

Jerked to his feet, Jean Pierre staggered as his hands were wrenched behind his back and secured. The skin at his wrists pinched between the tight bindings that would quickly cut off his circulation. He flexed, easing the nylon rope by a fraction. Adrenalin sent his brain into overdrive. Would these rebels recognize the transitional government? Probably not, but he had no other options. "We're under the protection of the MONUC." *(United Nations Organization Mission in the Democratic Republic of the Congo)*

Someone laughed. Was it Cigarette Man? Something solid cracked against the side of Jean Pierre's bad knee. Sharp pain exploded. He staggered to keep upright. A hard blow to his kidney sent a stab of fire radiating out from the point of impact. He crashed to the ground. *Oh, God...*

Before he could complete his plea, hands grabbed his upper arms, and he was tossed into the Rover. Another flash of pain shot through the back of his head as the metal edge of the wheel well connected with his skull. Pinpricks of light flickered behind his eyelids threatening to pull him into the darkness of oblivion. He fought the urge to give in—to succumb to the unfolding nightmare. The light stayed. He realized one eye was uncovered. He looked up at Cigarette Man. "Please," he begged.

A rifle butt slammed into his temple. Oblivion won. He fell into the void.

CHAPTER 2

The rain beating down on the metal roof was deafening. Like being inside the base drum at a throw down between Smashing Pumpkins and Foo Fighters. The noise did nothing to ease Jean Pierre's raging headache, but at least he was alive—for now. In slow motion, he laid his head back against the steel side and tried to straighten his right leg. He grimaced and sucked in air as pain shot up his thigh. His kneecap was shattered for sure—which pretty well eliminated any chance of escape—even if he could figure out where he was.

His hands still tied behind him, his fingers felt the raised Corten steel ribs against his back and rough wood under his butt. A container? He moved his good leg across the floor. It connected with nothing. The air felt empty, like there was nothing filling the void.

"Jackson, are you here? Please, mon ami *(my friend),* say something." His only answer was the staccato hammering of the rain. He released an anxious sigh as he remembered Jackson's cry and the sound of his bones being broken. "Je suis désolé *(I'm sorry)*".

Guilt wrenched his soul. He'd coerced the young driver with a promise of a month's worth of pay for a three-day trip, knowing the man was desperate to feed his family. Jean Pierre's need to learn more about the mining operations in the area and their use of slave labor had caused him to be reckless. Now he may have cost the innocent young man his life.

Time crawled like a patient lioness creeping up on her prey. The unknowns played out in his mind. The rebels could have left them in the bush, taken the Jeep, his camera equipment, his precious laptop, and the wad of francs he had in the zippered pocket of his duffel. Why had they bothered with him? The value of the vehicle and equipment would fund their covert operation for months. Robbery was the norm in this part of the world. Hijackings and taking hostages were happening more frequently in central and northern parts of Africa as the ebb and flow of insurgencies, rebellions, and the struggles for power seemed to ignite the continent.

Jean Pierre covered them all from the Rwanda genocide of '94 and the embassy bombings in '98 to the First and Second Congo Wars. The latest had been the crises in Sudan and Ethiopia. Africa was his specialty. He'd ridden across the Sahara desert on a camel and walked the slums of Nairobi. He interviewed Idi Amin just before his death and shared a meal with The Lord's Resistance Army. His piece on the kadogos *(child soldiers)* won him a Pulitzer in 2004. He was used to his press credentials getting him out of tight spots and into the office of presidents and dictators. These guys didn't even ask who he was, and he wasn't sure he was going to get a chance to tell them.

In the solitary darkness, Jean Pierre lost all concept of time. It seemed like days had passed since he'd caught the plane from the capital. The early flight was short, the landing nerve racking. Once on the ground, he spent a couple of hours on the streets of Goma negotiating for a Jeep and driver, and another hour bumping over the rough track that passed for a road here in DRC. His stomach confirmed he had missed a few meals, and the small amount of saliva he was able to work up did nothing to quench his parched throat.

Trying not to dwell on the sandpaper feel of thirst, he thought back to the last time he'd been subjected to a blindfold. It was when he managed to secure an interview with Saddam Hussein. The dictator was in hiding but couldn't resist an opportunity to shout to the world his innocence. Jean Pierre was brought to a secret location blindfolded and a dark bag placed over his head. Then, he was a 'guest' of sorts. Now he was someone's prisoner.

A loud clanging and the groan of metal interrupted his recollections. He wasn't alone. Voices and the tramp of booted feet echoed on the wood floor as they came toward him. The pungent smell of unwashed bodies filled the surrounding air. Were they going to execute him? He thought of his beautiful wife and children. Their faces flashed before his eyes.

Betta, my love, I'm sorry. You asked me to only cover the elections and leave, but I wanted one more story.

Globetrotting the world chasing the latest newsworthy scoop had been his life. Up until two years ago, it was what he lived and breathed—then he literally crashed into his future. He was at Lake Victoria Lodge in Tanzania, recovering from a rough stint in Somalia. After consuming the most delicious meal he'd had in months, he stood and turned to leave the table when his injured knee gave out. Before he could catch himself, he was sprawled on the ground, the most beautiful woman he'd ever seen pinned beneath him.

"Oh, pardon, mademoiselle. I'm so sorry!" He struggled to his feet and helped her up.

A lovely blush flushed her mocha-tinted cheeks as she smoothed out and tightened the knot on her kanga *(wrapped skirt)*. "No problem, sir. It was my fault. I was just coming to ask if you enjoyed your meal." She pushed the scrap of matching cloth that held her dark curls, back into place.

He looked into her gold-flecked eyes, mesmerized. "It was completely my fault. Please give the cook my compliments. It was an unexpected pleasure and so is meeting you." The French gentleman in him couldn't resist the urge to capture her hand. *Fingers missing?* The realization gave him a jolt, but didn't stop him from drawing it to his lips.

With a small gasp, she pulled her hand away and hid it behind her back. "Thank you, sir." She gave a slight bow of her slender body, backed away, and vanished inside.

***

The rattle of a lock and the scream of steel hinges interrupted his memories. Jean Pierre felt the floor shudder with the tromp of several pairs of feet. He tensed—every muscle and nerve on alert. Would they beat them again? *God help me!*

Without warning, a boot connected with his ribcage just above the bruised kidney. Air whooshed from his lungs as the sound of something snapping confirmed he would be adding broken ribs to his list of injuries. "Please…"

A fist slammed into his face, cutting off his plea. His brain registered the stench of tobacco and sweat. Would they kill him now? Cigarette Man and his crew were certainly capable of murder. He gritted his teeth and growled at his inability to defend himself. If he weren't tied, he'd do some damage of his own. For now, he could only wait for them to get bored. Jean Pierre prayed for unconsciousness. His prayer wasn't answered.

After what seemed like an eternity, they yanked him to his feet. He hung in their grasp, unable to stand on his own. A groan escaped his lips as the battered muscles along his side screamed. They began to drag him face down. His arms wrenched up and back, carried the full weight of his slack body. His shoulders threatened to pull from their sockets. Fire hot pain shot up his side and across his chest. "Aww," he groaned. "Please, I can walk. Just get me on my feet."

No response. He tried again in French. A sudden rush of fresh air bathed his sweaty face, but did little to relieve the hammering of his heart. Before he finished his plea, the toes of his Merrells dropped off the wood floor to plow furrows in the mud.

The rain had stopped. The jungle dripped with the smell of damp earth and the fragrance of flowers. Daylight and the shifted blindfold allowed him to see the ground a couple of feet below him. It moved under him as if he were on a conveyor belt. He caught a glimpse of a green camo leg and high-top, mud splattered boot. These guys weren't Congolese army, but the uniform meant they were probably part of one of the larger and more well-connected rebel groups that controlled the Nord Kivu sector.

Jean Pierre ran the list of known groups through his pain-infused mind. There were four acronyms that stood out, Laurent Nkunda Batware and his RCD *(Rally for Congolese Democracy)* troops, the UPC *(Union of Congolese Patriots),* RCD-Goma, and the FDLR *(Democratic Forces for the Liberation of Rwanda).* The letters alone didn't mean much, but the groups they stood for were notorious for humanitarian abuses that included murder, rape, and slavery. Their propensity for violence and the savagery they resorted to was mind boggling.

The different rebel factions survived on the backs of slave labor in the gold fields, and the cobalt, coltan, and diamond mines. He'd foolishly thought the eruption of Mt. Nyiragongo offered a nice cover for the real reason he had stayed and headed north. It was a chance to investigate and do an exposé on the brutal conditions laborers worked under so that the world could have electronics, cell phones, and expensive jewelry.

Before he could chastise himself for getting into this situation, his arms were released, and he crumpled face first into the muck. The bandana fell back over his eyes. Laughter surrounded him as he spat mud and grimaced in pain. With his hands still tied behind his back, he struggled to gain his good knee. Indignation fueled his efforts until he managed to get himself upright.

As bad as the condition of his body, it was the dark that was the most frightening part. The inability to see left him defenseless and vulnerable—two things he hated. If he could just see his captors and his surroundings, he'd be able to figure out how to get himself out of this situation.

Maybe it's better I can't see to identify them. Maybe they intend to let me go, and that's why I've been blindfolded the whole time.

A spark of hope ignited. He began to think how he would survive this when he was picked up again and carried forward until his feet bumped the edge of a solid lip. He felt a difference in the air. They were inside. Without warning, they released his arms. He landed face first again. Unable to prevent the impact of his nose hitting the hard floor, he felt a gush of blood. With a grunt of determination, he pushed himself to his knees, trying to favor the damaged one.

"Get him up."

Voices murmured, and a hand helped him to his feet. Before he gained some balance, his head was jerked back and the smelly bandana pulled from his eyes. By reflex, he squeezed them shut against the light, then squinted and blinked through his lashes. So much for keeping their identities hidden.

A shaft of light fell across a tall, gaunt man sitting behind an ancient table. He leaned in and rested his long-fingered hands on the scarred surface. A uni-brow made a dark, bushy line above deep-set eyes that emanated evil. Or was it death? Jean Pierre's skin prickled with dread and something else he couldn't identify.

"So, Mr. Fontaine," the man began in accented English. He picked up a laminated card Jean Pierre recognized as his press credentials. "It says here you are a member of the French press and an Associated Press affiliate." He let the card drop and picked up a sheet of wrinkled paper. "And according to your travel permit, it looks like you're under the protection of the MONUC."

He let the paper drift back to the table's surface as if it meant nothing, and steepled his hands. "Here in Nord Kivu it would be better if you were under *my* protection. You see, Mr. Fontaine, I run this sector now." He swept a long arm out to include the soldiers that stood at attention around the small, cluttered room. Jean Pierre's eyes followed the motion and rested on the man from the roadside ambush. A cigarette still dangled from his lips. Unlike the others, he leaned against a stack of bulging bags piled along one wall. The cigarette shifted from one side to the other. He smirked and brought a booted foot up to rest on a dented, red jerry can.

Jean Pierre's attention jerked back to the thin man when his fist slammed down against the table, threatening to split it in two.

"I am Bonaface Muteko, but people here call me y'Imana Igipfunsi or 'God's Fist' in English. Do you want to know why they call me God's Fist?" He stood up, leaned over the still shuddering table, and raised his bony-knuckled fist to eye level. "I rule with an iron hand. No one is allowed to question my authority because God put me in charge. I am educated. They are not. I am superior. They are not. I have been chosen to rule the lives of those under my protection."

Without pausing, his rant subsided and his tone changed. "I'm sure you've heard of Laurent Nykunda Batwana and the Rally for Congolese Democracy. Batwana was my compatriot for many years until he forgot the reason for the fight. He has become weak and ineffective. I, Bonaface Muteko, am the new power in Nord Kivu." His eyes took on an odd glint, and he looked down his hooked nose at Jean Pierre. "Soon, because of you, the rest of Congo and Africa will know me and God's United Coalition Army."

The puzzle took shape in Jean Pierre's mind. This screwball warlord wanna-a-be needed him alive to make himself famous. Nord Kivu was remote and if Muteko wanted the rest of the DRC to sit up and pay attention, he needed press.

Feeling like he finally had some leverage, Jean Pierre ignored the pain in his side and knee and worked to stand straight. It cost him, but he managed to pull himself vertical so that he stood an inch or two taller than Muteko. The height advantage and the thirteen kilos *(thirty pounds)* he had on the man gave him a measure of confidence. In reality, it meant nothing, as Muteko was in complete control. Jean Pierre mustered up his courage and pushed his chin against his shoulder to wipe the blood from his mouth. "So you expect me to sing your praises to the world, yet you have me beaten, tied up, and left without food or water. Seems like an odd way to get my support."

Muteko eased back down into his chair, shrugged his thin shoulders, and smiled. "That was unfortunate. My lieutenant here was a little overzealous. He apologizes, don't you, Gerald?"

Gerald took a long drag from his cigarette and blew a smoke ring in Jean Pierre's direction. "Sorry."

Jean Pierre looked back at Muteko and decided to go for broke. "I need a doctor, water, food, the latrine, and these ropes off me. Once that's taken care of, we can talk about your story." He held his breath. Had he pushed too hard too soon?

Muteko pursed his lips, leaned back, and looked at the tin ceiling. "You will write a piece that will make those dogs in Kinshasa take notice." He looked at Jean Pierre. His eyes hooded and calculating, he pushed out his bottom lip and wagged his head. "I will grant you what you've asked for because, you see, Mr. Fontaine, I am not a harsh man—firm and decisive, but not harsh. Ah, but you will learn all about me soon enough." His sudden smile never quite made it to his eyes.

Gerald stepped away from the stockpile, crushed his cigarette under his boot, and moved up alongside Jean Pierre. In an instant, a long-bladed knife was in Cigeratte Man's hand, the thin tapered length honed to a sharp, deadly edge.

I'm a dead man.

Jean Pierre closed his eyes, tightened his gut, and prayed.

CHAPTER 3

Jean Pierre wheezed and coughed. He couldn't seem to get a full breath and the lack of oxygen was making him lightheaded. He put a hand against his chest, thankful the knife he thought was going to be used to kill him had freed him instead.

The commander had kept his promise so far. He was escorted across a busy compound and pushed into a small thatched-roofed hut. It was dark inside. The only light came from the doorway behind him. A rank smelling bucket sat in one corner announcing its purpose. Against the far wall squatted a metal-framed cot with a thin bare mattress sprouting tufts of cotton.

A boot to his backside sent Jean Pierre staggering the few steps to the cot. He landed on his injured side and laid there. Before the door shut, a tin plate of runny ugali *(maize mush)* was plopped down on the dirt floor. A plastic carton of cloudy water accompanied it. The wood-slab door slammed shut, effectively blocking the light. Jean Pierre heard a bar drop into place on the outside and the rattle of a lock.

He eased off the bed and crawled to the food. Using the wall for support, he picked up the jug and took a long, deep gulp. Cloudy or not, it tasted like pure ambrosia. He poured a little in his hand and washed the mix of blood and mud off his face, then used a little more to clean his hands of at least the first layer of grime. Pushing the plate in front of him, he crept back to the cot and leaned against the side, too tired to pull himself on top.

The only light came from the cracks around the door, leaving his meal in semi-darkness. It was just as well, if the smell was any indication. He bowed his head. "Heavenly Father," he prayed. "You see me and you know where I am, even if I don't. You've always worked things out for your good and I'm sure this time will be no different. But, God, could you let me in on your plan this time? I'm kinda hurting here and I think I need some help if I'm going to get out of this one. And thank you for this food, such as it is."

Another fit of coughing interrupted his words and caused him to grimace and grab his chest and side. The plate teetered, threatening to spill its meager contents in the dirt. He saved it and using his fingers, he shoveled in the lukewarm mush.

His belly full and his thirst satiated, Jean Pierre gave thought to his predicament. Broken ribs were a given. A punctured lung? Possible. The kicks to his kidneys worried him as well when he noticed blood in his urine. This was the most precarious situation he'd ever found himself in because of his current health issues. He chastised himself for being so stupid and not letting his boss know what he intended to do when he left Kinshasa. Would he now pay the price for that stupidity with his life?

He dropped the empty plate to the floor and pulled himself up onto the lumpy cot. His long frame meant his feet dangled over the end and the breadth of his shoulders covered the width of the narrow cot. It felt good to lie in relative comfort and peace.

His body wanted nothing more than to rest, but his mind would not give in to the temptation. He needed to figure out an escape. He went over several potential scenarios. He could break away from his captors and make a run for it through the jungle. He snorted at the ridiculous idea. Without help, it would be impossible on a gimpy leg, with no idea where he was or how far-reaching Muteko's power extended.

His was a solitary job. Working alone meant taking risks alone. He'd been in a few scuffles and nail-biting situations over his career, but he always managed to either talk his way out or to outsmart the other guy. Still, he was no fool. He knew more times than he could count that he'd kept God's angels busy pulling him out of danger. He could only pray they'd come to the rescue this time.

At this point, his only option was to go along with Muteko and trust God to get him out of this mess. Jean Pierre looked at the positive side. Who knows, maybe he'd get a marketable story out of all this. Still, guilt sat on his shoulder. He wasn't supposed to be here. He'd promised Betta he would head home after covering the elections. In fact, no one knew where he was. If Jackson didn't make it back to Goma, well… the thought chilled him.

The light seeping through the cracks around the door dimmed. It had been hours since he was first dragged into the rebel compound. Jean Pierre began wondering why Muteko was leaving him alone for so long. He used the time to think about his family.

His beautiful wife, Betta, was the love of his life. He literally fell in love when he landed on top of her that fateful evening at the lodge in Tanzania. That was twenty-three months ago. It took ten and a half months to convince her to marry him. She'd been through a lot—kidnapped and held hostage for six and a half weeks by a Rwandan NRMD *(National Revolutionary Movement for Development)* commander who brutalized her. The fact that she escaped by herself was a testament to her strength and God's mercy. She'd also survived being shot and having two of her fingers chopped off after an attempt to run. What amazed Jean Pierre most was her ability to forgive.

He remembered when she finally told him her story as they walked along the shoreline of Lake Victoria. While rage boiled up inside him at what she had endured, she was at peace.

"Out of that nightmare, God blessed me with two beautiful children. Cyrus Munianeza has nothing. He's a wanted man with no future." She smiled at the twins playing in the waves. "How can I not forgive him? Don't get me wrong, I think the man is contemptible and I have to admit I still harbor some hate in my heart for what he did to me and so many others. I'm afraid I'll be working on that for the rest of my life, but I need to forgive him if I want to move forward."

She flashed a radiant smile at him. "For their sakes." She nodded toward the children. "I can't dwell on the past. They deserve the best of me."

Jean Pierre thought of the kids. Being a father to twelve-year-old twins was challenging. Still, he relished the opportunity, having quickly fallen in love with Mercy Grace and Andre Freedom. He couldn't imagine life without them or their mother. When Betta told him she was pregnant four and a half months ago, he was over the moon. His thoughts turned to his career. It was time to make some changes.

If I get out of this, I promise you, Betta, I'll...

The door flew open and Jean Pierre was hauled to his feet before he could stand on his own. "Easy, fellas."

The two soldiers quick-stepped him out and marched him across an open area to a shaded cabana structure where Muteko lounged, sipping from a sweating bottle of Coke.

Jean Pierre couldn't help but lick his parched lips. Where'd this guy get a cold bottle of anything here in a place where refrigeration was pretty much non-existent?

As if Muteko read his thoughts, he reached down and pulled a second Coke from a small cooler at his side. "Care to join me? I have a runner who delivers ice once a day. Unfortunately, it doesn't last long so I enjoy it while I can."

Jean Pierre took the bottle, unscrewed the cap, and pressed it to his lips. In a few quick gulps, it slid down his throat like a cool, refreshing shower on a sweltering day. He was sure nothing could taste better. The sugar rush sharpened his senses almost instantly. He handed the empty bottle back to the warlord. "Merci *(Thank you)*."

Appearing the gracious host, Muteko motioned to the plastic chair across from him. "Please, I'm sure you'd be more comfortable sitting."

Jean Pierre tried to show his indifference and remain standing, but his injuries protested much too loudly to ignore. He eased himself down onto the weathered seat, stained brown where the rain had puddled, and worked to keep his face impassive. "I still need a doctor."

Muteko quirked his bushy eyebrow and nodded. "That is being taken care of, but you must understand medical care is difficult to come by in these mountains. In the meantime, I think we will get started on my article."

He snapped his fingers. A soldier standing nearby produced Jean Pierre's laptop and camera bag and placed them on the table. He eyed both. They looked undamaged. Feigning indifference, he made no move to open the computer or the bag. Hope flashed. Maybe he'd be able to get a message out somehow.

Muteko leaned forward. "You want to live, you will need to write."

CHAPTER 4

Xavier Mwena was in his element, directing his team to the various tasks that needed to be accomplished before the Médecins Sans Frontières *(Doctors Without Borders)* team arrived. His organization, French Alliance for Children's Relief or FACR, often provided the logistical component when setting up their temporary hospital in a crisis area. The eruption of Mt. Nyiragongo had devastated the mountainous area on its southwestern slope, leaving an estimated hundred and eighty thousand people homeless, injured, or dead.

Xavier knew the majority of the people affected were his fellow countrymen. Trying to escape the genocide in Rwanda in 1994, over a million fled across the border into Zaire. Twelve years later, many remained unable or unwilling to return to their homeland. Although Zaire became the Democratic Republic of Congo, the country changed only in name. Poverty, disease, and wars over the mineral-rich land haunted the poor souls who inhabited it.

Xavier looked around, satisfied with the progress they'd made. Three main tents were up and a dozen smaller ones were being erected to provide the medical staff with sleeping quarters. He looked at his watch, a gift from Maria on their tenth wedding anniversary two years earlier. "Time to call home." He smiled and hurried off to the small mud-block house he had designated as administrative headquarters.

"Hey, Boss, the first load of medical supplies just arrived. Where do you want them put?" Xavier turned to the short man scurrying up to him. Xavier was only five feet, six inches, but next to Gabriel he felt like a giant. The little man's baggy cargo shorts reached almost to his high top florescent green Nikes. His white t-shirt with the red FARC heart logo hung on him like a dress.

"Gabe, the hat." Xavier motioned to the backwards baseball cap perched on top of a tangle of auburn curls. "You know the rules, hats and t-shirts worn so people can see who you represent."

"Sorry, Boss. It's not like a short white guy's going to blend in around here. Now you're a whole other story. If you untucked your shirt, wore a stained pair of jeans, and got rid of the professor glasses, you'd look like all the other black dudes."

"Dudes?"

Gabe swiveled the red hat around and pushed it back so he could see from under the bill. "Yeah, that's my new American word. It means man or guy. I like the sound of it—dude."

Xavier laughed and shook his head. Gabe's fascination with all things American kept the French crew guessing about what he'd come up with next. "Okay, so which *dudes* are guarding the shipment?"

"Peter and Henri offloaded about a dozen heavy crates. They've got a couple of dudes waiting to help move them."

Medical supplies—any kind of supplies for that matter— were precious in the Virunga Mountains. The closest towns were Sake to the west and Goma to the south, but it made no difference when you had no money to buy anything.

"Those crates are worth a fortune on the black market. You best lock them up in the container where we can keep an eye on them." Xavier looked at his watch again.

Gabe grinned up at him. "Time to call Madam Marie? Say bonjour *(hello)* for me and tell her to give little Annie a tickle from her Uncle Gabe."

"Why don't you come with me and tell her yourself?"

"Don't mind if I do." Gabe quick-stepped to keep up. Xavier unlocked the door, and the two entered the semi-dark of the thatched-roofed building.

He pulled the satellite phone from his pack, extended the foot long antenna, and checked his watch again. Between two forty-five and three o'clock in the afternoon was the best time to pick up satellite reception. He was eager to talk to Marie. He'd been gone four days already and was missing her and the children. With any luck, they'd be home, and he'd get to speak to all of them.

Xavier pressed the phone to his ear and waited for the static to clear.

"Marie Mwena à l'appareil *(Marie Mwena speaking)*."

He closed his eyes and smiled. "Bonjour, sweet lady. How are you?"

"Oh, Darling, I'm so glad you called. You got an email today from an orphanage in Zambia. They confirmed that they have a girl there named Precious Mwena, and she has the same birthday. Do you think it's her this time?"

Xavier sucked in a deep breath. His heart beat quickened. Could the impossible have finally happened after all these years of searching? He'd started the search twelve years ago while he laid in a refugee hospital recovering from a gunshot wound to the head. A phone call from his best friend informed him that a gang of genocideers had murdered his family back home on the farm. His father, brothers, aunt, uncle, and niece had been slaughtered. All except for his little sister Precious, his baby niece Felecie, and her brother Emmanuel. The three children seemed to have vanished without a trace.

The hours Xavier spent searching turned into years of contacting dozens of refugee camps in Rwanda and the surrounding countries, but he had turned up nothing. With millions fleeing, records during the genocide and civil war were sketchy at best. He never gave up looking. When the refugee camps closed down, he switched his focus to orphanages in hopes that somehow they made it to safety.

Marie was the one who suggested broadening his search to include Zambia, Uganda, and Kenya. She never lost faith that he would find at least one of them.

"Xavier?"

Brought back to the present by his wife's sweet voice, Xavier cleared the lump in his throat. "It sounds promising. Did they give you any more details? Is she Rwandan? Does she remember her family?"

"Yes, yes, and yes! Oh, Darling, I think it's really her!" she cried. "They're supposed to send a picture and they want more information to confirm you're really her brother. When can you come home?"

Xavier's mind was in a whirl. He wanted to jump in a vehicle and head down the mountain to catch the first plane out of Goma. How could he leave now? After all, he was in charge, and a team of doctors was arriving in the morning. They expected everything to be set up and ready for them to see the scores of patients injured as a result of the eruption.

"I have at least another week here." He turned to eye the little man next to him. "Maybe Gabe can run the show for a while once everything is in place for the doctors."

Gabe puffed out his chest and crossed his arms. "I'm your man."

Xavier knew Gabe was capable, just not as much of a stickler for following the rules and paying attention to the details as he was. Could he really leave his friend in charge? A surge of excitement began to grow. "Let me think about it." He glanced at his watch again. Two minutes left before their satellite window closed. "Are the kids there?"

A scuffle of passing the phone and then a tiny voice chirped, "Papa, when are you coming home? I miss you."

It was Xavier's youngest, Annie. His heart melted at the sound of her sweet little girl voice. At four, she was his princess. Her older sister, six-year-old Margarette, and her two brothers, Gift and Paul, were past the cuddling stage. He'd miss it when his baby girl outgrew the hugs and tickles.

"Hi, Sweet Girl. How's my ma petite fleur *(my little flower)* today?"

Before his daughter answered, the static drowned her out, then the phone went dead. Xavier groaned and glared at the phone in his hand. "Why can't this thing last a little longer? Remind me to order a new battery pack when we get back."

Gabe's shoulders slumped. "Aw, man, I wanted to talk to Annie. I thought up a new joke for her."

"Guess you'll have to save it for tomorrow." Xavier folded down the antenna, secured the phone back in the charger base, and shoved the whole thing back in his backpack. "Come on, let's go help Peter and Henri and I'll tell you my news."

They stepped out into the sunlight. Xavier turned to padlock the door.

"Ah, Boss." Gabe backed into him and made him drop the key.

"Hey, give me a little room."

Gabe didn't move. "You might want to turn around."

Xavier grabbed the key from the dirt and stood. "What are you…" The words died on his lips as he turned into the barrel of a gun.

The two men wore uniforms of sorts, but were definitely not DRC Army. Both carried assault rifles. The man with the cigarette dangling from his mouth pressed the barrel into Xavier's chest. "Back inside."

Xavier turned and fumbled with the lock. He hadn't had a gun pointed at him in a very long time. His heart pounded and his hands shook. In an instant, nervous sweat beaded across his forehead. Who were they and what did they want?

A beat up table, chair, filing cabinet, and Xavier's cot filled the ten by ten space. A shove from behind sent him sprawling across the cheap bed. Gabe landed on top of him. The flimsy frame groaned under the sudden weight and threatened to collapse.

Gabe rolled off him, a strange look in his eyes. Was it fear? Exhilaration? Gabriel Bourdair was an adrenalin junky and loved extreme sports. Would he think having a gun shoved in his face exciting? *God, don't let him do something stupid.*

Xavier sat up and focused back on the gun-toting rebels. Had they heard about the medical supplies? Was that what they were after? He was working up his courage to ask when Gabe stood up, flipped his hat backwards, and planted his hands on his hips.

"Hey, dudes, what's with the artillery? Want a Coke? We've got a couple in the cooler." As if they'd answered, the little man strolled over to the metal ice chest, pulled out twin soda bottles, and held them up. "Nothing like a cold drink on a hot day."

The men looked at each other; one lowered his weapon and took the offering. He unscrewed the cap and took a deep swig of cola. The other took a long drag on his cigarette and blew out a cloud of nicotine-tainted smoke.

Xavier coughed from the acid stench.

Without saying a word, the soldier dropped it on the concrete floor and ground it out with his boot.

When he didn't make a move to take the other Coke, Gabe shrugged his shoulders and opened the bottle. "Your loss, mon ami *(my friend)*."

In the moment it took for the surreal scene to play out, Xavier mustered up his courage. He stood and in a voice more calm than he felt; he said. "The guns aren't necessary. If you need some assistance, we'd be glad to help. That's what we're here for—to offer aide, nothing else." He put his hands out in a show of peace.

Cigarette Man jerked his head and gun toward the door. "Let's go."

Xavier started to comply when Gabe spoke up. "If someone needs help, we'd better grab some supplies. Boss, why don't you get your pack and I'll carry the medical kit." He gave Xavier a look that said to just play along and follow his lead and then ducked under the table to grab the first aid duffle.

"Yeah, sure." Xavier stepped over and shouldered his backpack, aware of the weight of the satphone inside. *Smart thinking, my friend.*

Gabe stepped out, followed by one of the men. The pressure of a gun barrel in his side spurred Xavier forward.

"Move!" Cigarette Man ordered.

Xavier grabbed a wide-brimmed hat off the hook next to the door and settled it on his head as he stepped out into the afternoon sun. Although there were plenty of neighboring huts and people around, the foliage on this mountainside grew thick. He doubted anyone would notice or question them leaving with the soldiers. Even if they did, most would be too afraid to intervene. They'd seen too many beaten or cut down when they got in the way of the area rebels.

He left the lock hanging on the iron rasp, something he'd never do. *God, let Henri or Peter notice.*

In less than twenty paces, the jungle that covered the Virunga Mountains enfolded them.

CHAPTER 5

Xavier was completely lost. His sense of direction went off course within minutes of entering the jungle. He patted the lump under the front of his shirt. The compass Marie had given him in 1995 at the onset of his first mission trip to Lebanon rested against his chest.

"So you'll always be able to find your way home to me," she said as she hugged and kissed him goodbye.

"Find me, too. Papa. Find me, too." Little Gift pulled on Xavier's pant leg. The five-year-old was as much his son as if his blood ran through his veins. It took time and patience to bring the spirit back to the little boy who had watched his parents killed during the Rwandan genocide. With lots of love, Gift had blossomed into a happy, healthy, mischievous little boy.

"I'll be home soon," he muttered under his breath, and prayed that it was true. He buttoned his shirt at the throat to further conceal the compass.

The amount of green around them was mindboggling. Every shade imaginable was represented in the dense foliage. Xavier became hyper-alert to every noise outside of the swish of the machete in one of the soldier's hands. This was, after all, the home of the famed mountain gorilla. Would they have a warning if they stumbled onto one? He'd read the big males, the silverbacks, reached heights of over six feet standing upright, and weighed in at between one hundred eighty and two hundred twenty kilos *(four hundred and five hundred pounds).*

A scream rent the air, followed by a shower of leaves and twigs. Xavier ducked. He wanted to run, but the way was blocked by Gabe in front of him and Cigarette Man behind him. A gun poked into his back.

"Keep moving!" Cigarette Man ordered.

"But…" Xavier stumbled forward and put a hand on Gabe's back to steady himself.

In answer to his unspoken question, Gabe waved a hand above his head. "Chimps sounding the alarm. Don't worry, Boss, they don't have guns."

In the dank humidity and semi-darkness of the canopy, their clothes soon plastered themselves against their bodies as if they'd showered fully clothed. They had been walking single file for a couple of hours through heavy foliage and rough terrain. Sunlight dappled the trail as it found a path through the foliage. Xavier was ready for a break. He imagined a cool drink of water, a shower, and a hammock, when the jungle opened up to a bizarre landscape.

The green forest had been laid bare, pushed back to expose the raw, brown earth beneath. Men moved in and out of the gaping hole bored into the mountainside. Bulging bags rested across bare, brown-skinned, sweat-glistening shoulders as they staggered across the open area to a waiting truck where others relieved them of their burden. While Xavier watched, another truck backed in alongside the full one. Several boys jumped from the top of the stockpiled bed to the wood slat rails of the other and scrambled to the empty bed to catch the next bag hoisted up to them. They never missed a beat—heave, catch, pile. The rape of minerals from the fertile belly of the earth moved like the well-rehearsed assembly line Xavier had once witnessed at a munitions manufacturing plant in Turkey.

Like a busy termite mound, three or four dozen men scurried from one place to another while armed soldiers watched from strategic vantage points. As busy as the area was, Xavier was surprised at the lack of noise. Oh, there was the rumble and clang of machinery, but the sound of human voices was reduced to the grunts and groans of the workers as they delivered their burdens. An air of oppression hung in a dense fog over the area. Were these men prisoners? If not, why the armed guards? A chill ran across his back between his shoulder blades as a new question entered his mind. Why were they brought here?

As they crossed the compound, Gabe glanced back and caught Xavier's eye. He tipped his head to the dark hole of the mine entrance. Out staggered several ragged, bone-thin teens escorted by two armed soldiers. Hands came up to shield their eyes as if they hadn't seen the light of day in a very long time. The youth, second from the front, swayed and collapsed, bringing down the two behind him. A commotion broke out as the guards waded in to pull them back to their feet. The shoulder butt of a rifle connected with one of the young men's legs. He cried out in pain. The dozens of men laboring around them gave the disturbance a quick glance, then lowered their eyes and quickened their step.

"Get them out of here!" shouted the cigarette-smoking man leading Xavier and Gabe across the compound. He spoke in Kinyarwanda, Xavier's native tongue.

Xavier gave no indication of having understood. Being able to speak the language may come in handy later. He kept his ears and eyes alert.

As they drew closer and in line with the emaciated teens, Xavier locked eyes with one young man as he lowered his hand from his face. Shock caused Xavier to stop and gasp.

Emmanuel?

The soldier behind him shoved him forward. "Keep moving."

Xavier pulled his eyes away. Could it really be his young cousin? Emmanuel, alive? He hadn't seen the boy since Xavier had left the farm in Kamena thirteen and a half years ago. The youngster was eleven when Xavier took off for Rwanda's capital, Kigali. That would make him twenty-four, but the man looked at least six or seven years younger. Maybe he was wrong, maybe the poor kid just looked like Emmanuel.

Xavier's mind raced as they were led past the trucks and down a rutted road to a clearing. Several mud block structures squatted around the perimeter. A thatched, open-sided kitchen dominated the area, if not in size, then in activity. Several dozen soldiers lounged in the shade eating ugali *(maize mush)*, and what looked like stewed tomatoes and fried plantains. Xavier's stomach growled. They'd missed the noon meal, and it was early evening now.

Gabe must have heard the sound. He grinned back at Xavier. "Hey Boss, you're a little loud, ain't ya?" He turned back to the Cigarette Man. "We got time to grab a plate of food? You know we work better when we have full stomachs."

The lean, bushy-haired soldier ignored the request and kept moving.

Never deterred, Gabe asked again, "Come on, dude, five minutes to eat isn't gonna kill anybody." When he didn't get any reply, he shrugged his shoulders and kept going.

A breeze swept across the open space, chilling Xavier's body beneath his sweat-dampened shirt. He looked up to see dark, swollen clouds churning overhead. He harrumphed and followed without comment, wondering how much farther they were going.

His thoughts returned to Marie's news. Twelve years. Was it possible he'd finally found Precious? The picture in his head was of a tiny nine-year-old with big brown eyes and a mischievous smile. From the first time he laid eyes on her, there had been a special bond between him and his only sister. While their mother lay dying after giving birth to her, Xavier, the oldest of her four boys, promised to always look after his new baby sister. He'd kept that promise for nine years, but by the time he reached his twenty-second birthday, he felt he couldn't stay on the farm any longer. He realized he wasn't a farmer. That was his brother, Theo's, passion. Mixed emotions surfaced at the thought of the giant young man. Theogene Mwena radiated charisma. People were drawn to the natural leader, including their father. It took some time before Xavier would admit that jealousy played a big part in his decision to move away from the farm and start a life in the city.

It was a decision he would regret for the rest of his life. He should have been there. A muscle worked along his jaw. God had helped him with his anger over the senseless slaughter of his loved ones and his countrymen. With time—and Marie's help—he found peace, but guilt still rode his shoulder. Ever since he learned of the murder of his family and all the other Tutsis men from his village, he'd felt ashamed for having not been there to fight alongside his father and brothers.

I should have been standing there with them, defending the women and children—keeping Precious safe.

His mind in the past, he didn't notice the root that angled across the path like a gnarled finger and went down. His backpack crashed beside him, the satphone tumbling out in plain sight.

Xavier reached to jam it back into the depths of the bulky pack. A foot came down on his hand.

"Leave it," ordered Cigarette Man.

The pressure on his hand increased until Xavier cried out, "Okay, okay."

His hand free, he drew it to his chest and straightened his glasses with his other hand. He was about to explain when Gabe interrupted.

"Hey, how'd that get in there? I wondered where I put it." He reached down to pick the satellite phone up. He grunted as he was knocked sideways off his feet and sent sprawling next to Xavier.

"I said leave it!" Cigarette Man growled.

With a jerk of his head to the other soldier, he pulled another hand-rolled cigarette out of his shirt pocket and pressed it between his lips. A gold lighter came up to ignite the twisted end. Xavier clearly saw the design on the side of the casing. It was a circle of rope encasing stalks of grain, a cogged wheel, and a basket with the words Umbumwe, Umurimo, Gukunda Igihugu *(Unity, Work, Patriotism)* below the knotted cord. He recognized the seal adopted by the Rwanda government in 2001. How would a rebel soldier in the jungles of the DRC get an expensive gold lighter from the presidential palace of the neighboring country?

"Get up and keep moving."

A boot to Gabe's leg pulled Xavier's attention away from the lighter.

"Ease up, dude, we're moving, okay?" Gabe scrambled to his feet and rolled his eyes at Xavier.

The gesture conjured up a memory of Pawulo, Xavier's best friend. He was always rolling his eyes at Xavier's clumsiness. With a jolt, he realized the man who had saved his life all those years ago, died in a refugee camp not too far from where they were now. Sadness squeezed his heart as he stood up and shouldered his pack. It was lighter now that the satphone had been confiscated.

Another twenty feet and they stepped into a small clearing. Two identical huts stood side by side. Xavier noticed the thatched roofs were in need of repair and the mud blocks that made up the walls were crumbling in a few places, but the wooden doors seemed solid. A stout wood bar rested across their flat fronts, secure in hand-hewn holders. The rusty rasps sported newer, heavy padlocks on each, ready to thwart any attempt at escape. Were they going to be held prisoners in one of these dismal looking abodes?

They traveled past the shelters without stopping. Xavier breathed a sigh of relief. At first, he didn't notice the man sitting under a small thatched cabana nestled against the thick foliage. The smell of food drew his attention to the remnants of what looked like ugali and stew congealing on a plate in front of a thin-faced man in an officer's uniform. A half-drunk bottle of Coke rested at his elbow. Xavier's mouth watered.

Cigarette Man halted and pushed the two men forward.

"Well, Gerald, it looks like you found us a couple of doctors. Good work." The man's English was decent, although heavily accented.

Xavier was about to tell the man that they weren't doctors. A loud cough and elbow from Gabe stopped him.

"Gentlemen, I am Commander Bonaface Muteko. You can call me Commander or God's Fist if you prefer. I hope your trek through the jungle wasn't too taxing. It seems we are in need of your services. I'm afraid I have no money to compensate you, but I think allowing you to leave when you're done will be compensation enough, don't you?"

Gabe and Xavier looked at each other. What were they getting caught up in? Xavier decided their best option was to go along and hope the commander was true to his word. Looking at the assault rifle resting on Cigarette Man's—Gerald's shoulder, he realized it was really their only option.

God protect us.

CHAPTER 6

Jean Pierre laid on the sagging cot, an arm resting across his forehead above his swollen right eye. His breathing was labored and ragged. Dreading the pain that accompanied his bouts of coughing, he tried to concentrate on slow, shallow breaths.

When the rattle of the padlock announced the arrival of someone, probably Gerald, Jean Pierre opened his good eye but didn't move. Let them carry him out. He hurt too badly to care.

The stale smell of cigarette announced his visitor. Gerald's frame filled the small doorway, then moved to the side in the cramped room. A man and boy entered. The late afternoon light silhouetted their forms so that Jean Pierre couldn't get a good look at them. He closed his eye again.

"Muteko kidnapping more reporters?" he asked.

"Doctors, for you," replied Gerald.

Jean Pierre eyed them from under his arm. One was on the small side, black and sporting a floppy hat that hid his face. The other was white and not a kid like he first thought. He stood taller than a dwarf and had regularly proportioned limbs. The short man reminded him of someone from the Twa tribe except for the color of his skin and the fact that he wore a baseball cap over shaggy hair. A long t-shirt extended over a broad chest and fell almost to his knees.

The room had no windows, and with four of them in the tight confines, what light there was coming through the door was diminished.

Gerald blew a puff of smoke into the stifling air. "See to him." He nodded toward Jean Pierre.

"We'll need our bags and a light," the front man announced.

Without a word, Gerald stepped past them through the door. Seconds later, a backpack and a green duffel were tossed inside. The short man was handed a kerosene lantern and a single wooden match. The door slammed shut. They heard the bar slide back into place and padlock being secured.

Jean Pierre struggled to sit up, his hand pressed against his side. He gasped as the pain sparked a fire bolt through his body.

The black man advanced and fell to his knees in front of him. "It's okay, just sit there."

Jean Pierre's head came up at the same time the other man got the lantern going. "Xavier?"

The man pulled off his hat and Jean Pierre found himself staring into the face of his long-time friend and the best man at his wedding. "What… what are you doing here?"

Xavier looked as shocked as Jean Pierre felt. "They grabbed us thinking we were doctors. FARC is setting up a hospital camp a few hillsides over for Médecins Sans Frontières. They were coming in to help those injured in the eruption." He laid his hand on Jean Pierre's shoulder. "What are *you* doing here?"

"I'll tell you all about it, but first I need your help. Too bad you really aren't a doctor. I think I've got a punctured lung and maybe some internal bleeding. I think there might be a problem with my right kidney. There's blood in my pee and my side is distended and hard."

"Gabe, bring the light closer. Oh, this is my right-hand man, Gabriel Bourdair meet Jean Pierre Fontaine."

Gabe held the light up with one hand and extended the other. "The boss has talked about you and how you got him and Marie out of Rwanda after the genocide. Good to meet you."

The two shook. Jean Pierre was surprised at the strength in the little man's handshake. "I wish we could have met under better circumstances."

Gabe dropped the light a little closer to Jean Pierre's face and whistled. "Looks like you had a bad day at the rodeo, dude."

Jean Pierre chuckled. "If that means I look a mess, yeah, I had a bad day. A few, actually."

"Gabe here likes to think he's American." Xavier began rummaging through the medical bag. "We can wrap your ribs and give you some morphine for the pain, but I'm afraid that's the extent of my medical knowhow. You, my friend, need a real doctor."

"I was afraid you were going to say that. I don't think Muteko is ready to let me go just yet."

Shadows danced as Gabe swung the lantern around to take in the small room. "How long have you been his guest in these fine accommodations?"

"I don't know, probably a day or so. Before that, I was locked up in a steel container. I've been unconscious for most of the time. What day is it?"

"Saturday, the ninth," Xavier answered as he helped him sit up. Jean Pierre sucked in a breath as he eased off his shirt.

"Whoa, dude, you're almost as black as my friend here." Gabe brought the light in closer. "But a lot more colorful."

All three men looked at the dark mottled bruising that covered most of Jean Pierre's right side. The discoloration extended around his waist, across his back, and down into his waistband.

Gabe laid a hand on Jean Pierre's leg. He shuddered and let out a low groan. "Did I forget to mention a busted knee?"

Gabe jerked his hand away. "Sorry, Dude."

Xavier clenched his jaw. "Why'd they do this to you?"

"It was Gerald's way of introducing himself, I guess. Once Muteko found out who I was, he decided to hire me as his press agent." Jean Pierre saw the confusion on Xavier's face. "He's holding me prisoner while I write a news article about him taking over Nord Kivu."

Xavier worked the four-inch wide ace bandage under his arms and around his tender chest. "He said he'd let us go after we took care of you."

Jean Pierre tried not to flinch when his friend touched the skin right above his kidney. "I wouldn't count on it, mon ami *(my friend)*. The man is smart enough to know kidnapping a muzunga *(white foreigner)*," he looked at Gabe, "and a black doctor could get him hanged."

The wrapping secured, Xavier sat back on his heels. "Gabe will give you a shot of painkiller. It will probably knock you out for a while, but I need to tell you something before he does." He smiled. "I think I've found Precious."

"What? How? Where?" Jean Pierre laughed and flinched.

"I don't know the details yet. It looks like she's in an orphanage in Zambia. Marie was telling me about it when the satphone went dead." Xavier sobered up. "Another thing… I think I saw my nephew, Emmanuel."

Jean Pierre knew the story of how Xavier's family were all killed in the genocide. His father and brothers gunned down at the church while protecting the women and children inside and his aunt, uncle, and niece at the family farm. The bodies of his nephew, little sister, and baby niece were never discovered. It was hoped they had escaped.

"Wait a minute, Emmanuel is alive, and you saw him? Where? When?"

Gabe broke in. "Hey Boss, why didn't you tell me about your sister and nephew?"

Xavier got up and settled next to Jean Pierre on the cot, careful of the damaged leg. He looked at Gabe. "I didn't get a chance. Cigarette Man—Gerald—interrupted, remember? It was while we were passing through the mine site that I think I saw Emmanuel. He was one of the boys they were bringing out of the mine. At least I think it was him."

Jean Pierre was happy for his friend. The search for his little sister had been a long one. The news about his nephew was an unexpected shock. How did the boy get here? What was he doing working in a gold mine? Was he a hired hand or one of the thousands forced into slave labor underground?

While the questions rattled through his mind, Jean Pierre felt the prick of a needle. Gabe was pushing the contents of a syringe into his arm. He blinked, the room began to move in slow waves, and he felt himself sinking into the nice warm comfort of the cot beneath him. The face of Betta, his belle femme *(beautiful wife)*, danced before his eyes.

CHAPTER 7

Tanzania

He watched from the shadows, determined to see for himself if what he heard was true. Was she really living just across the border? The embers of obsession stirred to life at the thought.

Normally, he avoided towns and villages like Chumwe. He never knew when someone might recognize him as Commander Cyrus Munianeza, the officer who ordered the slaughter of hundreds of Tutsis *(Rwandan ethnic tribe)*. Wanted for years by the police and The International Criminal Tribunal for Rwanda. Concealing his identity had become second nature to Cyrus. Caution and instinct kept him alive. Hatred and greed sustained him. But today he would take the risk. He would learn if she was alive.

The sound of children's laughter floated down the street. Two little girls in bright green and purple plaid uniforms, white socks, and black Mary Janes skipped past within feet of his hiding place. A group of boys kicked a tattered soccer ball, shouting challenges and insults at each other. The ball rolled to his feet. He gave it a hard kick back into the street and eased further into the shadows.

Cyrus assessed the children with an experienced eye. They all looked healthy, and would bring a handsome sum from the Nguvu ya Giza *(Dark Force)*. For the past nine years, he had been a procurer of children.

He'd pick a cluster of three or four isolated huts with lots of kids running around. His ruse was to pose as a representative for a new Christian NGO *(non-governmental organization)* that was taking children into their care to educate them and offer them a better life. A magnetic sign slapped on the side of his SUV, and a nice shirt with a fake logo embroidered on the front made him look official. It was an easy ploy in rural areas, where parents were desperate to see their children get an education that would take them out of poverty.

Cyrus would approach the parents with gifts of meal, sugar, oil, and weave an elaborate tale of a new boarding school that was taking in poor, disadvantaged children. Any that showed reluctance were told the children would be brought back for a holiday twice a year, and during their month-long stay, the family would be supported as well. After a tearful goodbye, the children willingly went with him, a small bundle of belongings tucked under their arms. Delivery was made to one of Nguvu ya Giza's many clandestine transit points throughout central Africa. Cyrus' commission generally set him up for at least a month or two before he had to go out on another hunting expedition.

A few months earlier, he had moved his hunting grounds to the crowded streets and alleys of Kibera, the largest slum in Nairobi and the second largest in all of Africa. The decision had proved profitable. Thousands of children lived in the squalor, many alone, surviving on what they scavenged from the garbage piles that festooned every space not already occupied. He'd get their attention with a handful of sweets. Hunger and the promise of a hot meal provided the ruse to entice them away from their surroundings. This also proved to be a more profitable lure, as there were no parents to pay off.

The girls were easier to manage. Scared and docile, they obeyed his orders without much trouble. The perfect age was ten to twelve, but sometimes he got special requests for children as young as three, and as old as fifteen. It was the older ones he had to be careful with, especially the boys. They could be hard to control, and Cyrus knew leaving marks meant getting a lower price.

Today, he wasn't interested in grabbing a kid or making a profit. Today, he was on the hunt for information. The dirt street grew quiet, the schoolchildren having hurried home to their afternoon meal and chores. Few cars passed in this rural section of town. Chumwe was the wrong size town to chance snagging a kid from, anyway, too small to go unnoticed and too big not to have a police presence. Besides, that wasn't why he was here. This was personal. He rubbed the scar that dissected his lip. A scruffy beard and mustache covered most of the damage.

Cyrus was about to give up for the day. His stomach growled its protest at the lack of nourishment. He took a swig of

Ibanga. The bottled banana wine was much better than the local beer made from bananas. He drained the container and lit the bent end of a cigarette. He would wait twenty minutes longer, then look for a bar or bottle shop where he could buy some food and maybe get some information.

Pushing off the wall, he hesitated as two children came into view kicking a stone between them. Further back, a woman strolled at a more leisurely pace. Across the dusty road, the pair drew even with Cyrus' position. He took a step back, pulled the bill of his hat down over his brow, and took a deep drag of the cigarette pursed between his lips. Pressed against the concrete block wall, he eased to the corner and chanced another look at the children.

He studied their faces. The girl had the promise of beauty in her delicate features. A crown of tiny plaits secured with little colored beads that matched her uniform framed her heart-shaped face. His eyes settled on her chest where young breasts were just beginning to swell into womanhood. She would bring an exceptionally high price at market.

The boy had a darker complexion, and stood a head taller with long legs on a skinny, adolescent frame he had yet to grow into. His face was shaped like the girl's except with a squarer jaw and chin.

The boy must have sensed his stare. He stopped in mid-laugh and lifted his face to look at the figure leaning against the side of the building, then glanced back behind him.

My God, he looks just like me at that age. Same jaw line, deep-set eyes, and broad nose. Even the shape of his ears are the same. Cyrus reached up and ran a finger along the rim of his ear.

He pressed back to give himself a minute to think. He did a quick calculation in his head and gasped. "My son?" He scratched his scruffy chin and smiled. "My son!" he marveled.

Before he had time to digest the revelation, he heard her voice.

"Mercy, Freedom, slow down. It amazes me how you two can have such energy after a long day at school."

The voice took shape as a slim, beautiful woman stepped into view. One long, slender mocha-tinted arm raised to steady the basket balanced on her turbaned head. The other supported a plaid vinyl bag against her stomach. In profile, she was even more stunning than he remembered her. He drank in the slant of her golden eyes, the elegant sculpture of her nose, and the full graceful curve of her mouth. His gut twisted in nervous agitation. His nerves thrilled at the sight of her. Twelve and a half years and she still made his blood run hot. Twelve and a half years since she had escaped from him.

He sneered. "I told you, you were mine, Pretty Thing."

Cyrus followed at a distance, making sure he kept his head down and ducked out of sight every once in a while. He was taking a chance she would notice him, as there were few people on this particular road at this time of day. He couldn't stop himself from glancing up to watch her hips sway as she glided down the road. Everything in him tightened. His mouth watered. He had to have her. He needed to see where she lived and come up with a plan.

He stopped. From across the road, he watched her follow the two kids through a small door inside an ornate, iron-picketed gate. Curved stone walls on each side held back flowering shrubs and date palms. Manicured flowerbeds ran the base of the walls in a riot of color. Smooth cobbles surrounded the elaborate LVL inlaid on the driveway entrance. Cyrus read the swirling flow of letters that graced a metal sign, "Lake Victoria Lodge. Well, Pretty Thing, seems you've up and got fancy on me."

As dusk settled, he noticed a late-model Toyota Noah van pull up to the gate and honk. A uniformed guard swung the gate open. Cyrus caught a glimpse of lush grounds and well-kept cream stucco buildings with tiled roofs. He also noticed at least a half-dozen people strolling or lounging on the expansive patio. The gate closed. He recognized the rasp of a slide arm and the firm clank of a lock secured in place.

"No good," he muttered to himself. There were too many people, and the place seemed well protected. As nice as it was, they might even have one of those new warning systems that raised an alarm at the local police station, or worse yet, a couple of guard dogs.

He turned and walked back toward town, hands in his pockets and head down in contemplation. He thought about the boy. Could the kid really be his son? A strange pride overcame him at the thought. Undoubtedly, he had offspring scattered across several countries, rape being one of the side benefits and weapons of civil war, genocide, and the slave trade. They meant nothing to him. He never stuck around long enough to find out names or be a father. Today, seeing the boy churned up something in him he couldn't identify.

He wondered about the girl. She looked younger than the boy by only a year or two. Could Pretty Thing have gotten herself pregnant right after having his baby? The idea of some other man having his hands on her stirred up a rage that had smoldered in him ever since she managed to escape. She was his. He slammed a fist into a passing wall and kept walking, oblivious to the angry scrape across his knuckles. He'd promised her he'd get her back, and he meant to keep that promise.

With new determination, he stepped into the first bar he came across, dropped into a chair, and ordered a drink. He had all night to come up with a foolproof plan. He swirled the swill they called liquor and conjured up Pretty Thing's face. "This time you won't escape. And neither will my son."

CHAPTER 8

Betta smiled at her son when he looked back at her. She couldn't get over how quickly time had passed. It seemed like only yesterday she had held them in her arms for the first time, uncertain about the future. Now here they were twelve years later with a wonderful life filled with so much happiness. She placed a hand on her stomach where another new life was changing the contour of her abdomen.

Another blessing among so many. First, God had orchestrated her escape from that murdering madman, Commander Cyrus Munianeza and his squad of killers, and then he led her to Rukuramigabo Refugee Camp. It was there she met the three women who became her new family.

Betta's heart swelled with love for the women who had risked their lives to protect her. There was Royal, whom she now thought of as her mother and who the children call Grandmother, along with Claudette and Sonia, who always treat her like a sister and love her unconditionally.

After the genocide that took nearly a million lives, including her father's, she never imagined she would have a home and family again. Yet God had provided both. The day Tom and Gwen McMillian offered her a job as head cook at Lake Victoria Lodge, Betta's heart stirred with renewed hope. Although content and happy, it took many years before the nightmare of her captivity receded and she quit looking over her shoulder for the scarred face of her captor.

I have Jean Pierre to thank for that. A smile spread across her face at the thought. *My Frenchman.*

She remembered the day he literally fell on top of her when his knee gave out. He was embarrassed, while she was flustered. The next day, she bumped into him again as he was coming out of her kitchen. The tall, handsome stranger had a round of her chapatti bread in each hand and honey dripping from the corner of his mouth. A mischievous smile spread across his face as he caught the sweet liquid with his tongue. Betta stared at his lips. If she had given in to self-indulgence, she would have reached out and touched them.

"Pardon, Mademoiselle," he said around the bread in his mouth, "I can't seem to get enough of this delicious manna from heaven."

Brought back to the moment, she slid past him into the bright, cheery kitchen. "There's plenty more where that came from, Monsieur. Guests can have as much as they want." She poured him a glass of ice tea. "If you'd like to go sit at one of the tables outside, I can bring you a couple of my pasties *(called pastries in other parts of the world)*. I was just about to take a batch out of the oven."

The curly-haired Frenchman took the offered glass and grinned. "A beautiful offer from a beautiful lady." He bowed and headed out the open doorway, his wide shoulders almost touching the framework on either side.

Royal came in as he walked out. "That is one fine specimen of a man. Mm-mm." She waved a corner of her apron in front of her flushed face. "Now Royal could have done with a man like that thirty years ago. Yes sir, mighty fine."

Betta busied herself pulling a sheet of golden, sugarcoated pastries from the oven, hoping the older woman wouldn't notice the blush that she was sure tinted her cheeks. Royal loved nothing better than playing matchmaker. She claimed she was responsible for Sonia and Joseph's marriage and half a dozen others over the years. Betta and Claudette presented her biggest challenge.

"I hadn't noticed, but he does seem to love my cooking." Betta placed a couple of hot pasties on a pretty, flowered plate.

"Hadn't noticed, huh? Isn't that your Sunday katanga you be wearing? And those pretty ear hoops Miss Gwen gave you last Christmas? I suppose you's all dressed up just 'cause it's Tuesday and the sun be a shinin'." Royal chuckled and waddled over to catch the door, as Betta's hands were full.

"He's a guest." Betta tried to act indifferent as she stepped past Royal. "I treat all the guests the same."

A snort of disbelief followed her out. As soon as the door closed behind her, Betta shifted the tray of pasties to one hand and plucked a beautiful, bright pink hibiscus to lie on the tray. Happy with the display, she strolled out to where the guest tables edged the sand beach. The Frenchman was staring out across the water and didn't appear to notice her.

"Enjoy." She settled the tray on the table and turned to leave.

"Could you... I mean, will you please join me? I hate to eat alone and I'd enjoy sharing this beautiful sunset with you." His blue eyes pleaded his case.

Betta hesitated. She hadn't been comfortable around men in a very long time.

A beguiling smile crinkled the corners of his eyes with easy familiarity.

"Thank you. I could use a bit of a break and the sunset is especially beautiful tonight." She settled into the chair opposite the small wooden table, forever careful to hide her mangled hand in the fold of her kanga.

They sat in companionable silence except for the moans of pleasure that escaped around the edges of the treats he devoured in a few quick bites. "Heaven, pure heaven. Tom and Gwen told me they had a gem of a cook. Thank goodness my job has me here for a few weeks." He patted his flat stomach. "Not overindulging is going to be extremely difficult, I'm afraid."

Without thinking, Betta brought her scarred hand to her face to hide her blush of pleasure at his praise.

Before she could hide it again, he reached out and gently stroked the stubs where two of her fingers had been. "Your badges of courage."

It wasn't a question, but a statement. She laid the hand in her lap and covered it with the other one. "I've never thought of my missing fingers that way. They've always been ugly reminders of the nightmare I lived through."

"The nightmare you endured and overcame." His voice was gentle and at the same time firm. "Many survivors are broken, ghosts of their former selves. They exist but they don't live."

"How can you know?"

"I can hear Rwanda in your voice." Jean Pierre looked back out across the water. "I'm a photo journalist. I was there from the beginning to the end. The things I saw will haunt me for the rest of my life, but the world needed to know what genocide looks like. I'm not sure I really captured the ugliness and hate. I only provided the images and wrote the words that I pray will act as a deterrent and reminder of the inhumanity man is capable of."

He understood. Few white people did.

He turned back to smile at her, admiration in his eyes. "Be glad you survived, but even more importantly, be proud you've thrived." He reached for the flower. "May I?"

Betta gave a shy smile as he worked the blossom under the edge of the scarf that wrapped around her face and circled behind her head to hold her hair back. The fragile whisper of unseen wings fluttered across her heart. A contented smile came to her lips. She breathed in and sighed. How did he know she loved wearing her favorite flower in just that spot?

She reached up to touch the petals. "I have been extremely blessed over and above anything I could have imagined." She looked at the beautiful tropical surroundings, lush with brilliant colors and rich textures. "God saved me and brought me to Eden."

Jean Pierre nodded in agreement and laced his fingers behind his head. "I envy Tom and Gwen. This really is a paradise. I haven't had a vacation, let alone a home, for many years. I could get used to this."

"Surely you have a home in France."

The Frenchman eased forward and rested his forearms on his denim-clad thighs. "I have a base in France, but not a home. My work keeps me on the move. For the past decade I've lived out of a duffel bag and backpack."

"That sounds exciting, if not lonely." Betta couldn't imagine ten years of wandering. The forty-nine days she was forced to march with the militia were more than enough for her. Her heart craved home and family.

As if on cue, her children burst through the gate, followed by Claudette. Before Betta got to her feet, Mercy collapsed on the arm of her chair and Freedom encircled her neck from behind. Claudette waved and headed toward the kitchen with fresh fruit meant for the next day's breakfast.

"Freedom, Mercy, I would like you to meet Monsieur..."

The man rose to his feet and reached behind Betta to shake Freedom's hand. "Jean Pierre Fontaine." They shook, Freedom giving him a speculative look and a polite, "Sir."

"I like a man with a strong name and a firm handshake. Let's people know he means business."

Freedom grinned and stood taller. Betta could tell her son was pleased to be called a man. He constantly reminded her he wasn't a child anymore. At ten, his arms and legs were knobby and gangly, as he had yet to put on any muscle.

Jean Pierre took Mercy's fingers and bent to place a light kiss on the back of her hand. She giggled shyly and ducked her head.

"Vous êtes aussi jolie que ta mère."

"What does that mean?" Mercy asked.

Jean Pierre looked from Mercy to Betta. "I said you are as beautiful as your mother."

Unsettled by the compliment, Betta pushed Mercy from the chair, got up, and gathered the tray.

"It's getting late. Children, say good night to Mr. Fontaine."

Mercy went to stand next to her brother. "Good night, Mr. Fontaine," they responded in unison, then headed off to the small cottage tucked in the trees.

As Betta turned to leave, Jean Pierre touched her elbow. "Thank you for the dessert and for the company. They were both delightful, but you forgot one thing."

Betta turned back to look at him, trying to think what she could have possibly forgotten. Seeing to the needs of the guests held first priority at Lake Victoria Lodge. "Pardon me, Sir. I'm afraid I don't understand."

"Your name. You know mine, but I don't know yours." He smiled an easy grin that Betta found rather disconcerting.

She blushed and smiled back. "Nywebe Betta."

Before she knew what he intended, he took her disfigured hand and raised it to his lips. "Thank you, Miss Nywebe, for a lovely evening."

Flustered, Betta pulled her hand away and tucked it out of sight. "We'll be serving breakfast from seven to nine." She walked away. "Sleep well, Mr. Fontaine."

That was almost two years ago. Her world had changed so much since then. She dropped the hand from the basket on her head and placed it on the roundness of her belly. A deep contentment flooded her soul and brought a smile to her lips. Everything was right in her world now. The twins were healthy and happy. She had a good job, a nice home, wonderful friends, and an adoring husband. The one thing that pushed against her happiness was the long days when Jean Pierre was away on assignment. Setting up Betta's Bakery had occupied her time during Jean Pierre's first long absence. The wedding present he so proudly presented to her was now up and running, and she was back to missing her husband.

Her smile eased to a firm line as she considered the talk she was determined to have with him when he came home from Congo. She would just have to convince him to limit his traveling so he could be home more than a few days a month. She needed him here with her. The new baby and the twins needed a full-time father.

She started to bow her head to talk to the swell beneath her kanga. The basket wobbled. A steadying hand and straightening of her spine kept it in place. She pressed the bag in her other arm more firmly against her stomach. "Don't worry, baby, your papa will listen," she whispered. "He loves you so much." She looked up at the two walking in front of her. "He loves us all so much." She hoped it was enough to give up his career for.

CHAPTER 9

Northeastern DRC

Xavier paced the small room, three steps forward, three steps back. He always thought better when he was moving.

Gabe slouched against the far wall. "Boss, you're wearing a rut in the ground."

The three had been locked in the hut for a couple of hours. There wasn't any distinction around the door. Xavier had to assume dusk had settled in. The rain had come, dumping a deluge of water on the area. The thatch above them proved less than adequate as streams poured through, soaking whatever they landed on.

He stopped to look at Jean Pierre. The man didn't look good. His normally dusky skin color was a sickly shade of gray. His lips had a blue cast to them as if he wasn't getting enough oxygen. His labored breathing and the swelling along his side and belly worried Xavier. He decided he needed to press the issue with Gerald the next time he came by to get Jean Pierre to go meet with Muteko. He didn't have long to wait.

"Look, he needs a hospital, or he's going to die. I'm sure your boss doesn't want that kind of attention. Let me talk to him. He needs to know how serious this is."

Gerald took in the man on the cot, then looked at Gabe. "You stay here." He pushed Xavier toward the door. "Let's go, Doctor Man."

Xavier stepped outside and took in a deep breath. The rain had cleared the air, scenting it with the aroma of damp earth and fresh eucalyptus. Gerald pushed him forward, lifting his chin to indicate the path they'd walked in on when they first arrived. Xavier led the way through the tangle of undergrowth. Wet fronds slapped his legs, soaking his jeans.

When they came to the larger compound, it surprised him to see the same amount of activity as when they were marched through earlier. Dim bulbs on rickety poles around the perimeter cast yellow rings of light on the area. He looked for the boy he'd seen before, the one he thought was Emmanuel. Was he filling a plate at the kitchen? Maybe he was using the latrine.

Gerald gave him a shove and pointed to a large, square, low-slung building with a tin corrugated roof. His head lowered, Xavier let his eyes search the area as he marched in front of Gerald. There were probably sixty men engaged in various tasks across the compound. Some worked with ankle chains attached to the man next to them, others were guarded by armed soldiers. At the door, Xavier swept the area one last time, desperate to catch a glimpse of his nephew. The skinny youth of earlier was nowhere in sight.

Inside, a single bulb illuminated the room. Xavier heard a generator humming outside the window at the back. Bonaface Muteko sat at a makeshift desk, his legs draped across the corner and crossed at the ankles. Again, he was drinking a Coke. The man seemed to have an endless supply of the American soft drink.

He took a long swig and gave an exaggerated sigh of pleasure. "Gerald, you were supposed to bring me the journalist, not the doctor."

The soldier shrugged his shoulders and leaned against the wall. "They drugged him."

Xavier took the opportunity to step forward. "Commander, you brought me here to take care of the Frenchman. We've done all we can under these conditions. The man has internal injuries, and a punctured lung. My guess is that lung has collapsed and his belly is filling with blood. If we don't get him to a hospital in the next twenty-four hours, he's likely to die."

Twenty-four hours might be an exaggeration. Xavier didn't know. His friend looked terrible enough on the outside for it to be true. If his insides were in the same shape, he might not be lying. He hoped his ploy might get a better and quicker response.

Muteko brought his feet down and leaned forward on the tabletop. "What's your name and where are you from?" he asked in Kinyarwanda.

Without thinking, Xavier answered in his native tongue. "Mwena Xavier, I live in France."

"Rwandan, huh? I thought so. Don't see many Rwandan doctors in the Congo jungle."

Xavier could have kicked himself for the slip. Now they knew he understood what they were saying. *Stupid, just stupid!*

He tried to cover his mistake. "I was born in Rwanda, but have lived in France all my life. I'm a doctor with the French Alliance for Children's Relief." He pointed to the insignia on his shirt pocket and silently asked God to forgive the lies. "If you can spare a couple men to take us back to our camp, we're equipped to care for Mr. Fontaine there."

Muteko huffed and took another swallow of cola. "Mr. Fontaine hasn't finished his work for me yet. Maybe in a few days."

Knowing Jean Pierre's life was at stake, Xavier mustered up his courage and slammed a palm on the scarred tabletop. He pushed his glasses up his nose and leaned in. "Don't you understand that man doesn't have a few days. Your goons here," he gestured to Gerald, "beat him to within an inch of his life. If he doesn't get help immediately, you'll be responsible for his death."

Gerald pushed away from the wall and stepped between Xavier and the table. He wagged a finger in his face. "Not a smart idea, Doctor Man."

Xavier stood there, letting his indignation cool. When the commander didn't say anything after thirty seconds or so, he began to sweat. *What have I done?*

Muteko tossed the empty bottle toward a plastic crate that sat on the floor across the room. It bounced off a pile of bulging sacks stacked along one wall and rolled to the edge of the crate. "You are either very stupid or very brave, Dr. Mwena." He rose from his chair and, with fingertips spread on the table's surface, he leaned in. "I am God here. I decide who lives and who dies. My soldiers are loyal because I promised them they will share in the riches we are pulling out of the ground. I am called y'Imana Igiphunsi *(God's fist)* for a reason. You think you can make demands of me?" His voice took on a menacing tone. "I care nothing about you or the Frenchman, so do NOT make demands of me!"

He snarled at Gerald. "Get him out of my sight."

The soldier swung his rifle around and pressed the barrel against Xavier's forehead. "Move, Doctor Man."

His eyes traveled down the barrel to where Gerald's finger rested against the trigger. Xavier swallowed a hard lump that instantly rose up in his throat and raised his hands in surrender.

"Okay, I'm going." He complied as quickly as he could. Two minutes later, they were back at the hut. Gerald unlocked the door and shoved him inside. He landed squarely in Gabe's lap.

"Didn't go so good, huh?" Gabe pushed him off.

Xavier dusted his hands off and rested his back against the end of the cot. "You might say that." He rubbed his hands over his head. "I blew it, Gabe. We were in deep trouble before, but now…" He tucked his head to his chest. "I'm sorry."

Gabe reached out and rested a hand on Xavier's raised knee. "You tried. That's what counts. Besides, Boss, ain't you always preaching at me how God's in control. You think He doesn't know what's going on?" He shook Xavier's knee. "Hey, what would Marie tell you to do?"

Xavier raised his head and sighed. "She'd pull me down on my knees and we'd pray."

Gabe stood up. "Well, there you go. You know I ain't much for praying myself, but I've seen your prayers get us out of jams before. Remember Sudan?"

Xavier nodded, remembering when they got caught between the SPLA *(Sudan People's Liberation Army)* and another rebel faction outside of Darfur. Pinned down on a desolate stretch of road, Xavier prayed for deliverance. Not ten minutes later, a military convoy rescued them without anyone getting so much as a scratch. Their vehicle, on the other hand, was a total loss—shot up and set on fire.

"Yeah, that was pretty intense." He smiled at the memory of Gabe trying to high-five a tall Sudanese soldier.

"Ya' think it would work again?"

Xavier turned around on his knees, reached up, grabbed one of Jean Pierre's feet and looked up at Gabe. "Well, are you going to join me or what?"

The little man shrugged, eased down on his knees next to Xavier, and placed a hand on Jean Pierre's other foot.

Xavier closed his eyes. "Father God, you know the situation we're in. You know the condition Jean Pierre's in. We need your help in a mighty way. I've felt your hand of protection.

I've seen your army of angels. I know you can do what seems impossible. Lord, I'm asking you to give us a miracle." Xavier was about to say "amen," when a new thought entered his head. "And God, if that's Emmanuel out there, help me get him out, please."

"Yeah, and God, we could sure use some food about now," Gabe added.

Xavier smiled. "Amen."

A groggy Jean Pierre echoed Xavier's "amen" and struggled to sit up. "How long have I been out?"

Xavier looked at his watch. "Most of the evening. How do you feel?"

"Like someone beat me up real good." Jean Pierre tried to smile. "I'm hungry."

"That makes two of us." Gabe got up, marched to the door, and began pounding. "Hey, we need some food in here. Can you dudes hear me? We're hungry."

Fifteen minutes later, they heard the bar being pulled and a key working the padlock.

"About time," Gabe grumbled.

The door opened and a young man stepped in, three plates balanced in his hands.

Xavier jumped to his feet. "Emmanuel! Is it really you?" Xavier took the plates and handed them off to Gabe.

Emmanuel put a finger to his lips and spoke over his shoulder to the soldier standing outside the door. "I'm supposed to wait and take the plates back to the kitchen."

The soldier nodded. "Ten minutes." He closed and secured the door.

"Uncle Xavier?" Overcome, Emmanuel fell into Xavier's arms. Sobs punctuated his words. "I thought I was dreaming when I saw you walking across the compound." He pulled back and put a calloused hand on Xavier's cheek. "I thought you were dead like everyone else." He broke down and began weeping in earnest, his bony shoulders shaking.

Xavier pulled the young man back into his arms. Tears flowed freely as they clung to each other. He hadn't laid eyes on a single family member in almost fourteen years. He had no idea anyone was left. Overwhelming gratitude swelled inside him.

Gabe cleared his throat. "Boss, we don't have much time."

Xavier didn't want to let go, but Gabe was right. He pulled two empty crates closer to the cot so Jean Pierre would be included in the conversation. The three wolfed down the food, not bothering to taste it.

"How did you get here? Why are you working for Muteko?" asked Xavier around a mouthful of ugali.

"I don't work for y'Imana Igiphunsi." Emmanuel sneered and spat in the dirt. "He is not God's Fist, he is Umubi *(evil one)*. I was taken many years ago from a refugee camp, me and six other boys. I was fourteen. We were given guns and taught to fight."

A haunted look covered his face. "I resisted and was beaten. When I refused to raise my gun and fire at a poor terrified man, they shot me in the arm." He pulled a tattered sleeve up to reveal a round, smooth scar. "I still refused, and they put a gun to the head of my friend." His lips trembled and his eyes begged for understanding. "I shot the man to save my friend. We were forced to fight or be killed." His voice grew strained and his face took on a haunted look. "I shot many men after that. Then one day about a year ago, Muteko came, and my friends and I were sold to him. We live down in the mine. In the darkness we pick at the walls and load the rock into buckets to be hauled up to the surface. Every fifteen hours, we are allowed to come out and have a meal. Five days a month, we switch places with those above. I just started my five days. If you had come yesterday, I would never have seen you. I was working near the kitchen when one of the soldiers ordered food for you. I volunteered to carry it and here I am."

Xavier took in Emmanuel's face. Sunken eyes stared back from a gaunt face of dark skin stretched over a skull of angled bone and hollowed cheek. His thin t-shirt did little to conceal the ridges of his ribcage. Xavier knew he was hearing the short version of the hell Emmanuel must have lived through. His heart ached for the toothy, knob-kneed kid he remembered who loved to sing. Would he be able to return to a normal life after what he'd been through?

I'm not leaving here without him. That much I know.

He gave Emmanuel's bony shoulder a squeeze. "We're going to get out of this." He looked at the others and back at his nephew. "All of us."

Gabe handed his empty plate back to Emmanuel and looked at each man in turn. He leaned forward and used a conspirator's whisper. "We can't count on anyone coming to rescue us. I think it's up to us to get ourselves out of here. Manny, you're our eyes and ears out there. Pay attention, especially to the truck schedule. Gerald took our satphone so Muteko probably has it. You need to see if you can find out where it's being kept. Try to be the one to bring our meals so we have a chance to talk."

A puzzled look skewed Emmanuel's face. He asked, "Who's Manny and what's a satphone?"

Jean Pierre chuckled. "You're Manny. I'm Jean Pierre, and this is Gabe. Xavier, maybe you better describe your satellite phone to him."

Xavier was just finishing his lesson on the satphone when the door opened. Emmanuel gathered the dirty plates, secreted them a thumbs-up, and headed out the door.

The men settled in for the night. Xavier struggled to get comfortable on the hard-packed floor. With his backpack as a pillow, he laid back and stared into the dark. He wondered if they'd been missed yet. In the chaos of the arriving doctors and hundreds of injured looking for aid, Henri and Peter might not have had time to grow overly concerned with his and Gabe's absence.

As if the other man had read his thoughts, Gabe whispered into the dark, "They're looking for us, Boss. You can count on it."

The long night passed. Jean Pierre moaned and sighed in his sleep. Xavier and Gabe came up with and rejected idea after idea. They were outnumbered and outgunned. While the soldiers were trained killers, they knew that neither one of them had ever even held a gun before. It seemed hopeless until Emmanuel showed up with their meal and fresh water the next morning. Jean Pierre was awake, the painkiller having worn off.

Xavier turned from placing a damp cloth on his friend's forehead. "Good. We need to talk," he said as his nephew stepped into the room.

Emmanuel gave him a warning look and shifted his eyes. Gerald stepped in behind him, a wicked grin on his face and his assault rifle resting across his arms. "Commander Muteko wants you."

Xavier stood. Gerald shook his head and nodded his chin toward Jean Pierre. "Not you—him."

CHAPTER 10

Jean Pierre clenched his jaw in anticipation of the pain maneuvering himself down onto the plastic seat in front of Muteko's desk, would cost him. The room swayed for a second. Shards of pain as sharp as glass pierced and stabbed at his innards. Muteko paid him no mind as he shoved the black HP laptop and Nikon camera across to him.

"We will continue our interview." The commander leaned back in his chair, hands laced behind his head. "Now where were we?"

Jean Pierre tilted his head and looked at him through his good eye. Could the man be serious? He took as deep a breath as he was able, opened the computer, and powered it up. He had already recorded two hours of Muteko spouting off about his rise to power. "You had told me about your split with Laurent Nkunda Batware and the RDC."

"Ah, yes. My comrade, Nkunda, is now a loser in more ways than one, wouldn't you say?"

Jean Pierre knew Muteko was referring to the first presidential election back in July. Nkunda had run along with thirty-two other candidates. The hotly protested results led to the DRC Supreme Court ruling that there would be a run-off election. Allegations of voter fraud erupted in violence across the country. Things were so volatile UN Secretary-General Kofi Annan publicly voiced his concern.

Nkunda wasn't even close to the front runners—incumbent Joseph Kabila, and Jean-Pierre Bemba. His 2005 indictment by the Congolese government for war crimes and his long history of human rights abuses didn't win him any popularity contests. Muteko had been his second in command for many years. Both were power hungry, greedy, and full of self-importance. A falling out was inevitable.

What really irked Jean Pierre was the fact that both men claimed to be Christians appointed by God. Nkunda was even an ordained minister. How could a man who killed without discretion and made children into killing machines represent the God that Jean Pierre knew?

"Did you hear me? You're not typing." Muteko smacked a hand down, startling Jean Pierre.

"Yeah, I was just wondering how you think this article is going to help you. The people it's directed at know you. They know your history and reputation. One story coerced from a journalist, beaten and held prisoner, isn't going to do much to change their minds."

Jean Pierre dropped his hands back to his lap. He may have just signed his death warrant, but he didn't care. He wasn't going to cower to this tyrant anymore.

Muteko's eyes narrowed. His lips thinned into a hard line, then curved into a sneer. "You show courage for a man who's life I hold in my hand—courage or stupidity." He stood, came around the makeshift desk, and towered over Jean Pierre. "Before we are through, you will understand." He shrugged his shoulders. "Or maybe you will die before then."

Jean Pierre was looking up at Muteko. Out of the corner of his eye, he saw Gerald approach. His senses dulled from the drug and his injuries, he didn't react quick enough to avoid the attack.

***

The door crashed open and Jean Pierre was thrown into the small room like so much garbage. He crumpled to the floor and lay unconscious. Blood dripped from his broken nose and began to pool under the side of his battered face.

"Oh, my God!" Gabe exclaimed.

Xavier fell to the side of his friend. "Help me get him on the bed."

The two managed to drag and lift Jean Pierre's body to the low cot. He moaned. One eye fluttered open. "Am I still alive?"

Xavier wrung a wet rag out, kneeled beside him, and began to bathe his friend's face. "You baited him, didn't you?" The rag came away soaked in bright red. "Gabe, bring the pail closer, please."

"Dude, you're even more of a mess if that's possible." Gabe exchanged the blood-soaked rag for a clean one. "Your face looks like someone did a fancy tap dance on it with spiked heels."

"That bad, huh?" Jean Pierre winced as Xavier dabbed at the cut that ran through his eyebrow.

"Sorry, my friend. Once I get all the blood cleaned off, I'll be able to see the full extent of the damage." He continued working; wipe, rinse, wring, and wipe again. Jean Pierre's right eye was already almost swollen shut and now matched the left one. The cut above it wasn't deep and thankfully it hadn't continued down any farther than the top of his eyelid.

"Lucky for you, I think getting your nose broken again may have actually straightened it out, but it's too soon to tell. Did they hit you anywhere else?" Xavier asked.

Jean Pierre snorted. "Not 'they', Gerald did the honors. Muteko just watched. I got tired of pretending it was an un-coerced interview and asked him who he thought he was trying to fool."

"Looks like that didn't go over too well." Gabe chuckled and shook his head.

Xavier pressed a couple of fingers against Jean Pierre's wrist and watched the second hand on his watch. He was no expert, but it seemed slow to him. He looked over at Gabe, hoping his expression conveyed his concern. He didn't want to worry the man on the cot.

Gabe got the message and reaching into the medical bag, he pulled out the blood pressure cuff and stethoscope. "Why don't we play doctor and get your blood pressure. Xavier can show off his new skills."

The cuff in place, Xavier pumped the bulb, then released it, concentrating on the sounds coming through the earpieces. If he calculated correctly, Jean Pierre's blood pressure was one hundred over seventy, low enough to be worrisome, especially in his condition. The man needed a doctor, a real doctor.

"Well, Doc, what's the good news?" Jean Pierre joked.

Xavier pulled the stethoscope from his ears and let it close around his neck. "I hate to ask you this, but do you think you can sit up? I'd like to listen to your lungs." Xavier wrapped an arm around Jean Pierre's shoulders.

"Here, Dude, let me help you." Gabe grabbed his battered hands and pulled.

Jean Pierre moaned and grimaced, his face screwed up in pain. "Easy, boys."

"This will just take a minute, then you can lie back down. Take a deep breath for me." Xavier pressed the instrument on various parts of Jean Pierre's back, trying to be extra gentle where it rested on the black and blue areas. His recent training told him that what he was hearing wasn't normal. His lungs sounded wet, his breathing wheezy.

Jean Pierre started coughing, mixed with cries of pain. Gabe grabbed a clean cloth and held it over Jean Pierre's mouth as Xavier eased him back down. The coughing subsided, Jean Pierre pulled his arm up and rested it across his forehead as he took in short, shallow breaths.

Gabe removed the cloth. Xavier chewed his lip and looked from the red-flecked fabric to Gabe. The blood was a sure sign there was a problem with one or both lungs. Feeling helpless, Xavier began putting the instruments back in the bag.

God, you need to do something here. Please.

If Jean Pierre died, how would he ever tell Betta?

At one time, when they were younger, Xavier thought he was in love with her. They grew up together and their fathers encouraged the fledgling relationship, hoping to join the two families, even though Betta was Hutu and Xavier Tutsi. His lack of self-confidence stopped him from declaring himself, and his jealousy of his brother forced him to leave her behind when he fled the farm. All these years later, he still cared. The fact that they'd both found true love elsewhere confirmed the truth that their love wasn't meant to be. Betta was Jean Pierre's world now, and he was hers.

He squeezed his friend's shoulder. "You've got to hold on, Brother. Betta needs you."

Jean Pierre didn't answer. He had passed out cold.

Gabe and Xavier moved to the far corner near the door. "We've got to do something, or he's not going to make it." Xavier clenched and unclenched his hands.

Gabe nodded his head. "We need a plan." He held the lantern up and looked along the base of the walls. "Think we could dig ourselves out?"

"That would take too long. We need to get him out of here soon. I don't think he's going to last much longer if Muteko keeps having his goon beat him."

The day passed slow and quiet except for the groans and coughs from Jean Pierre. Finally, hours later, Emmanuel carried in their supper.

He motioned toward Jean Pierre. "How is he doing?"

"Not so good. He needs a doctor." Xavier ignored the plate Emmanuel handed to him. He balanced it on his knees and ran his hands over the stubble on his head. "We've got to find a way to get out of here and get help."

Emmanuel crouched down. "Uncle, what if I go for help?"

Gabe guffawed. "You plan on just walking out of here?" He waved a hand. "See ya, I'm going for a hike. I don't think so, kid."

Emmanuel became animated. "No listen. I've been thinking. The trucks pull out at night and make their way down the mountain. The driver told me they go through Goma, then on across the border to Rwanda. If I managed to be one of the bed loaders, I could hide among the sacks instead of getting off, ride down the hill and jump when they go through town. I could bring help back."

"Look at me," Xavier ordered. "If it was that easy, why haven't you run off already?"

Emmanuel dropped his head. "If they catch you, they shoot you, no questions asked. They shot my friend Kelvin when he tried sneaking away." He looked up and jutted his chin out. "I'm smarter than Kelvin. I won't get caught. Besides, I'm the only one who stands a chance."

He stood up. Gabe and Xavier followed. "I'm all you've got. You have to trust me, Uncle. I can do this." He nodded toward the bed. "I'm his only option."

CHAPTER 11

Tanzania

For two more days, Cyrus watched and waited, a plan forming in his brain. He found out besides working and living at the Lodge, Pretty Thing seemed to spend her mornings at a small bakery in town. The smells emanating from the place brought back memories of the sweet, warm chapatti bread he had her make for him every day.

He grabbed the arm of a man walking by and asked in Swahili, "You know who owns that bakery?" He gestured to the building across the street.

"Sure, that Betta's Bakery. Can't you read the sign? For a couple of shillings you can get the best pasties in town, and if you're lucky, Madame Fontaine herself will wait on you." The man started to pull away. Cyrus tightened his grip on the stranger's arm.

"What does she look like?"

The man's friendly demeanor changed to nervousness. "Go look for yourself. She's the pretty one behind the counter." He jerked his arm free and hurried off down the road.

"Betta Fontaine. So that's Pretty Thing's real name." He smiled at the new bit of information. What had she called the two kids? Cyrus searched his memory. "Freedom and Mercy."

He sauntered off down the street, his plan taking shape.

In a few hours, I'll turn her world upside down. By tomorrow, she'll be mine again.

***

The next day, Cyrus again took up his surveillance from the shadows. He knew the children would start their Christmas holiday the next day. If he was going to make this happen, it had to be today. Each day, their routine was to walk home from school together. They always seemed to lag behind the other children. It didn't appear Pretty Thing joined them unless she had been shopping at the market. He needed the children alone to make this work.

It had been five minutes since the last child walked by. He peeked around the corner and spied his prey in the distance, a half block up. He looked down at his new white button-down shirt, black pants, and shiny, pointy-toed loafers. He lifted each foot and rubbed it against the back of his pant leg to wipe off the dust, pleased at the gleam of newness. The shirt and pants he had stolen from a vendor's table in the open market. The shoes he paid for. The sweat-stained slouch hat he wore constantly was gone, revealing a freshly shaved head. He had trimmed his beard to a respectable length and had worked at cleaning his teeth as best he could. He thought he looked every bit the preacher man, right down to the Bible he carried in his right hand.

With a cleansing breath, he stepped out onto the dirt shoulder and started walking toward the children. As he drew closer, he allowed a wide grin to stretch across his face.

"Excuse me, young man. Could you help me? It seems I've lost my way. I'm the new pastor at Free Will Evangelical Gospel Church. I'm to meet the deacons there this afternoon and I've gotten myself all turned around. I arrived this morning from Mwanza."

The boy stopped. He stepped in front of his sister and shouldered the backpack he'd been carrying. "Mheshimiwa nzuri, mchana *(Good afternoon, sir)*." He extended his right hand, his arm supported by his left hand, and gave a slight bow, with his eyes downcast.

Cyrus shook the boy's hand, impressed by his show of respect and manners. Pretty Thing had taught him well. "Would you be so kind as to show me the way? I'm afraid I will be late if I keep stumbling around on my own."

The children exchanged a look. The girl shook her head. Purple and green beads swung back and forth. She stood on tiptoe to whisper something in her brother's ear. Cyrus heard him reply, "It's okay. Mama won't mind."

The boy looked up at Cyrus. "My mama expects us home in a few minutes, but I'm sure she would want us to help you. The church is just a few blocks from here if we take a shortcut through the alley."

The smile that crossed Cyrus' face was genuine. They had played right into his hands. He had scouted the alley earlier and found the remnants of a few broken down, burned out huts jumbled together in a weed-infested cluster. The area deserted. Beyond them, and to the southeast, was the church in question. To the west was a meandering pathway flanked by tall elephant grass, scrubby brush, and a few thirsty eucalyptuses. He had his Toyota Hilux Surf parked out of sight under one of the trees.

During Cyrus' reconnaissance of the area, he discovered an abandoned cane distillery about fifteen miles past the edge of town. He had used a set of bolt cutters to gain access to one of the empty buildings and set himself up with blankets, a bamboo mat, and a table.

"Asante *(thank you)*." He gestured for the boy to lead the way.

The girl clung to her brother and kept stealing glances back over her shoulder. Cyrus winked at her and continued to smile. "You're a pretty little thing. I'll bet you look just like your mama."

She refused to speak, turning her face into her brother's arm. The boy grinned back at him. "She's Mercy Grace and I'm Andre Freedom, but everybody just calls me Free."

They had worked their way to the path. Cyrus scanned the area. No one was in sight. With the shield of high grass, Cyrus pushed the Bible into the back of his waistband and pulled a plastic bag of chloroform soaked rags from his back pocket. He stepped up behind the boy. In one quick motion, he wrapped one arm around the girl, covering her nose, and with the other, he stuffed the smelly cloth against Freedom's face. Instinctively, the boy reached up and clawed at the hand covering his mouth and nose. Cyrus held them tight until their struggling eased and they collapsed at his feet.

From experience, Cyrus knew he needed to move fast. He gathered the limp bodies, one under each arm, and moved down the path toward his SUV. The boy was heavier, straining his biceps. He hurried the short distance to his vehicle. The back was already open, the gate down. He placed his burden down on the cargo floor and ran back to grab up the backpack. Once in the SUV, he covered them with a blanket, closed up the back, and jumped in the driver's seat.

So far, everything had gone according to plan. He glanced at his watch. The minute hand had barely moved. The note to

Pretty Thing was already written and ready to be delivered. He pulled back onto the road that would take him to the lodge. A half block away, he donned the floppy hat, sunglasses, and hunters vest he'd been wearing for the past few days. Pulling to the side of the road, he got out and checked the children. Satisfied they weren't visible through the deeply tinted windows, he moved down the road toward the well-manicured entrance to Lake Victoria Lodge.

A pull on the bell cord brought the gatekeeper. Cyrus had figured out the old man replaced the security guard at this time of day for about a half hour. The white-haired senior didn't appear to see well, squinting through black horn-rimmed glasses that perched on the end of his broad nose.

"Jambo *(Hello)*." He greeted Cyrus through the bars of the gate. "What can I do for you, sir?"

"Can you read?" Cyrus asked.

"No sir, but I can write my name and I know my numbers."

Cyrus pulled the folded paper out of his shirt pocket and handed it through the bars. "Give this to Madam Fontaine immediately. No one else, understand? It's very important."

The old man snatched the paper and nodded his head. "I can do that. She's in the kitchen preparing the evening meal. I'll take it to her right away." He waved a hand and closed the gate.

Cyrus wasted no time getting back to his car and heading out of town. The drive to his hideout at the plant went quick and uneventful. In less than twenty minutes, he was securing the two kids in a makeshift cell.

The old storage room had only one tiny, barred window high up. A single door held shut by a heavy-duty hasp and padlock he had installed the previous day ensured they would stay put. He laid them side by side on a blanket in the empty room and stopped to study their faces.

They both possessed Betta's general features, although the girl's were more delicate. The shape of their faces and eyes confirmed they were related. The girl's held the promise of great beauty as she grew into a woman. "You will bring a nice sum of money once I get my business with your mama taken care of."

He would normally gag them and tie their hands and feet, but the secluded location meant no one would hear them should they call out, and there was no way to escape the room. After they woke up, he could gauge how easily they would be to manipulate.

"Now we wait for you to come find us, Pretty Thing."

CHAPTER 12

Hands deep in kneading and rolling out dough, Betta hummed to herself. The kitchen was all hers at this time of day. Claudette and the other helpers wouldn't arrive for another hour. She glanced up at the clock above the door, happy to see it was almost time for the children to be home.

A knock surprised her. "Come in."

Moses stepped in, head down and bobbing, hands palm to palm. "Excuse me, Madam Betta. I have a letter for you."

Hands covered in dough, she nodded at the counter behind her. "Just put it down there, please. I'll look at it later."

"He said it was important."

"Okay. Thank you, Moses."

The man smiled and waved goodbye. The screen door slammed behind him.

A half hour later, the dough balls covered and set aside to rise, Betta wiped down the counters. She dried her hands and picked up the paper. Her nose wrinkled at the smell of cigarette smoke wafting from the folds. She couldn't abide the smell. It reminded her of Cyrus.

Holding the note up to catch the light filtering through the window, she read the scratchy, uneven writing.

> Pretty Thing, I said I would find you.
> Now you must come back to me on
> your own. You belong to me. So
> does my son. He looks just like me,
> don't you think? Do not tell anyone
> where you are going. Pack a small
> bag, bring your ID and his. Take a
> bus to Magu Kahangara. I will pick
> you up just outside the station. If you
> talk to anyone, I will know and you
> will never see Freedom and Mercy
> again.
> CM

Betta's knees buckled. In a daze, she slid to the floor. How could he have found her after all these years? Her hand shook so that she couldn't reread the message. A dull ache marched up from her gut to engulf her heart in a deadly squeeze. Her mind worked to processed her most dreaded nightmare.

"Mercy. Freedom. Oh, God, my babies!" She pushed a fisted hand to her mouth to stifle her cry. She began to shake. Uncontrollable tremors took over her body as her mind raced. Half thoughts, words, images, whirled in no coherent pattern.

After the few minutes it took to absorb the threat, she pulled herself off the floor. With trembling fingers, she folded the paper and stuffed it in the rolled edge of her work kanga. "You will not hurt my children," she vowed. Her chin came up. Her hands fisted at her sides.

The clock told her she had only fifteen minutes before everyone would start arriving to help prepare the evening meal. She needed to be gone quickly. Otherwise, they would interfere—try to talk her into going to the police. The police, she huffed, were more interested in lining their pockets than fighting real crime. Their involvement would likely put the twins in even more danger.

"No." She squared her shoulders and pulled her lips into a solid, hard line. "I will get my children back myself." The flutter of movement across her belly served to remind her of her condition and brought Jean Pierre to mind. Would he approve of her going after Cyrus alone? Most definitely not, but what choice did she have? He wasn't due back for a few more days, and if she waited, Cyrus would be long gone, her children with him. The idea of that man anywhere near her precious children made her stomach turn. She shuddered at the thought.

With determined strides, she left the kitchen and ran down the pathway to her little bungalow nestled in the trees. She loved the cream walls, turquoise shutters, and red tiled roof. Now, she didn't even notice the new blooms on the hibiscus near the door as she hurried inside.

What do I take? How long will we be gone? She smoothed her hands across her protruding stomach and took a deep breath. With eyes closed, she offered up a plea. "Please, Abba Father, help me now. Protect my babies from that monster and show me what to do."

Betta's eyes flew to the magnetic strip about her kitchen counter where three knives in various sizes hung. She grabbed the middle one. With a five-inch blade and short wood handle, it was small enough to conceal and big enough to be lethal. Along with the knife, she grabbed a box of matches, a small bag of mealie meal, some dried cassava, chapatti leftover from the morning, honey, salt, and a cooking pot. A couple of bananas and fresh mangos completed her food supply. No matter what happened, they wouldn't starve. That she could make sure of. She pulled an empty meal bag from under the sink and stuffed the articles, except for the knife, in the bag.

Next, she stepped into the room the twins shared. A drape of heavy fabric hung down, separating the two beds. Of late, the twins had been arguing about privacy and whose side was whose. The curtain was the only idea Betta came up with in the little house.

Now she pushed it aside and opened the small wardrobe. Would they need clothes? No, this would be over tomorrow, she determined. They had worn sweaters to school and their uniforms were clean and sturdy. She grabbed them each clean underwear and moved across the hall, where she changed into a loose-fitting blouse. She covered this with a light sweater to conceal her pregnancy as much as possible. Instinct told her Cyrus wouldn't appreciate the fact that she was carrying another man's baby. She loosened the flour-covered apron from around her waist and let it drop to the chair beside the bed. From a drawer, she pulled a clean, floral kanga to cover her stretchy, black pants. Betta kicked off her everyday flip-flops and worked her feet into the pair of flat leather slippers she wore to church. She reached up to grab an extra kanga from a hook on the wall. It would work as a covering, a shelter, and a suitcase of sorts. She looked around her own bedroom, the one she shared with Jean Pierre when he was home.

Betta hesitated when her eyes landed on the wedding picture that sat in a place of honor on their dresser. She couldn't help the smile that came instantly to her face or stop her feet from carrying her across the room. She picked up the elegant silver-framed photo and ran a finger over Jean Pierre's smiling face. A fist squeezed her heart. Her smile changed to a worried scowl. She had a sudden uneasy feeling about her husband. Was he okay?

Please, God, let him be okay. She had enough to worry about with Cyrus' return. God would have to look after Jean Pierre. Not sure what drove her, she pulled the picture from the frame and laid the empty frame face down.

The troubled feeling lingered as Betta rolled the photo into a tight tube, secured it with a scrap of Mercy's hair ribbon from the dresser and edged it in among the clothes. She gathered the ends of the kanga together and knotted it. She jammed both the cloth bundle and the meal bag into the large plastic plaid tote bag she used for shopping and tested the weight. It was heavy, but doable.

As she was about to leave the room she hesitated, twisting the gold band that encircled her ring finger. Would Jean Pierre understand her message if she left it behind? He knew it meant everything to her. It was becoming tight, and he had suggested putting it on a ribbon around her neck as her fingers swelled in the latter months of her pregnancy. She refused, saying she would never take it off, no matter what. She reached for the pen laying atop her Bible on the stand next to the bed. On the cardboard backing of the picture frame, she wrote, "I'll always love only you. Keep this until we meet again." Working the ring off, she kissed it and placed it on top of the message.

Betta moved back into the living room and lifted the curtain on the window. Her house was close to the front gate and the only people she could see were lounging on the sandy beach. Moses was gathering dead palm fronds near the lodge, his back to her. She eased out the door and quick-stepped to the smaller pedestrian gate set inside the framework of the larger vehicle gate. Good maintenance meant there was no creaking or groaning of iron when she opened it and slipped through.

Since it was getting close to "knock off time" for workers, the buses were running to full capacity. This meant a ten-passenger minibus was likely carrying fourteen or fifteen people smashed together. Betta couldn't abide the dala-dalas *(minivans)* at this time of day. The close quarters and mix of body odor more than she could handle in her present condition. She headed down the side road toward the busier paved crossroad. It was getting late. Oncoming foot traffic made walking against the flow back toward town difficult.

Betta took a worried look at the sky. She'd miss the last travel bus if she didn't hurry. A bajaji *(motorized trike)* swung around the corner. The tiny three-wheeled cycles were well known to be dangerous. The drivers zoomed in and out of traffic, ignoring traffic robots *(stop lights)*, but they would get her to the city center in minutes. She flagged him down and climbed aboard. The four-block ride was heart stopping. Betta closed her eyes and held on tight.

"We're here, madam," the driver announced.

Betta opened her eyes. A sigh of relief seeped from between her lips. They made it to the depot in record time and without injury. She paid the man and searched the waiting buses until she found a larger one traveling through Magu Kahangara on its way to the city of Mwanza.

She clutched her bag to her and tried to avoid eye contact with anyone as she settled into the brightly patterned upholstered seat next to the window. A few minutes later, the bus pulled away to begin its daily route from the small outlying towns to its main hub in Mwanza. Betta was glad for the breeze from the open window as she and her seat partner adjusted to the sway of the bus as it bounced down the road.

Other than a polite smile, Betta didn't speak to the older woman beside her. She didn't initiate a conversation and hoped the other woman wouldn't try to talk to her. She needed the ride to give her time to think about a plan. She ran a hand over the knife tied to her leg under her pants. If she had to, she would kill Cyrus. The thought turned her stomach. She'd never intentionally hurt another human being in her life, but if she had to choose between her children and the man who murdered her father and raped her, there would be no hesitation.

Soon enough, Betta stepped down from the bus, relieved to be out in the open. Tight spaces like the overcrowded transports that traveled Tanzania's roads left her with a queasy stomach and sweating palms. The driver spent a good amount of his energy swerving to avoid potholes, pedestrians, and broken down lorries *(big trucks)*. She pulled in a lungful of air and looked around her. Magu Kahangara was smaller than Chumwe, but the bus depot was still crowded. A few taxis, bajaji, and dala-dalas were parked haphazardly around with drivers vying for fares. Her bag pressed to her stomach, Betta pushed her way to the perimeter where she could stand in the shade of a vendor's stall. Her eyes scanned the throng, looking for a face she had prayed she would never see again.

Minutes passed. Betta hesitated while mothers secured babies on their backs, positioned bags on their heads and began the long walk to their destinations. Men moved off in the direction of town. The bus, loaded with new passengers, pulled out in a cloud of exhaust. As the black noxious fumes cleared, Betta saw him.

He leaned against a dull green Toyota Hilux Surf. His arm rested against the snorkel that rode up the driver's side of the windshield and protruded like a black cobra, head raised to strike. He had gained a good fourteen kilos *(thirty pounds)*. Rather than a pouch around the middle, the added weight was dispersed across his chest, shoulders, and thighs. The muscles pushed against the tight fabric of the white dress shirt and black slacks. It was disconcerting to see him in street clothes instead of the bloodstained uniform she'd been forced to wash on so many occasions. He now sported a short beard and a shaved head, shiny with sweat. Aviator sunglasses hid his eyes. Betta didn't need to see them to know they would be black pools of evil, devoid of human warmth. An involuntary shudder quaked through her body.

He didn't move except to give a slight jerk of his head. He expected her to come to him. She suppressed the bile that threatened to choke her and bowed her head. "God, help me please. Help me save my babies." She pulled her shoulders back and lifted her chin. He would not see her cower. Outward defiance hid the cold fear that screamed for her to turn and run. Knowing the only way she could get her children back was through him, she walked across the dirt packed parking lot.

I'm coming, Freedom. Hold on, Mercy, Mama's coming.

CHAPTER 13

Cyrus watched her from across the dirt lot. She hadn't seen him yet and stood scanning the crowd. He knew he looked different. Better, he thought. Clean civilian clothes replaced the drab green blood-stained uniform she had known. The shaved head and beard were new. He had learned to recreate himself over the years. Being a wanted man and working on the other side of the law required the ability to change and disguise himself in plain sight, and he was good at it. Except for the four-inch scar that dissected his lip and cheek, he had no distinguishing features. He knew he could pass for any ordinary, average male.

The four by four behind him was his, paid for when he delivered his first kids to Nguvu ya Giza. Would she be impressed? Somehow, it mattered to him. He couldn't figure out the hold this woman had over him, as strong now as it was thirteen years ago. She was beautiful, with high cheekbones, smooth warm mocha skin, and the most amazing gold eyes. It rankled him that even with all the other beautiful women he'd met and bedded before, she still had the power to get under his skin. So much so that he'd spent over a decade searching for her?

She spotted him. Cyrus started to push off the Surf then decided to let her come to him. He leaned down and crossed his arms. He had the upper hand and she knew it. This time, she wasn't his prisoner and forced to do his bidding. It felt good. To see her walking toward him after all these years sent his whole body into a state of excited agitation.

He played it cool—in control. When she stopped short, it took everything in him not to reach out and crush her to him, but people were watching and he couldn't afford to make a scene.

No, I control her, not the other way around.

She stopped three feet in front of him. "I want my children."

He cocked an eyebrow and sneered. He knew lifting the corner of his mouth caused the scar that ran across his lip up into his beard to stand out. It gave him a dangerous look, one he didn't mind using now. "I didn't care what you wanted thirteen years ago.

What makes you think I would be interested in what you want now, Pretty Thing?"

He pulled away from the SUV, spread his feet, and uncrossed his arms. "I told you, you belong to me. I made you mine a long time ago." He opened the door. "Get in."

Betta made a show of stepping around him without taking her eyes off him. He couldn't resist touching her butt as she climbed across the ratty driver's seat. He felt her stiffen.

"Don't touch me!" She glared back at him, then worked her way over the gearshift and settled onto the passenger's seat as close to the door as she could get.

His hand burned from the touch. Or was it his imagination? How could she still have that kind of power over him? A nervous tic worked his jaw. He slid into the seat and turned the key in the ignition. The motor cranked and rattled for a few seconds. Cyrus cussed at it and pumped the gas. The engine came to life like a grouchy lion, angry to be disturbed. In a cloud of dust, he pulled out and headed away from the station, back the way she came.

Betta remained silent, staring straight ahead. He stole glances at her as they barreled down the road. Was she thinking about him or her kids? He harrumphed. The kids would be uppermost in her mind. He could tell she wanted to ask if they were okay, but hated the idea of having a conversation with him. He remained silent and let her stew.

Finally, her concern overrode her aversion. "Are Mercy and Freedom okay? You haven't hurt them, have you?"

Satisfied he'd won their first battle of wills, he answered, "Now, why would I do a thing like that?"

"Whatever you want from me, leave my son and my daughter out of it."

He looked over at her. "You mean *our* son, don't you?"

Her hands began to tremble where they clutched the bag in her lap. She chewed her lip and looked out the window. Would she lie or admit Freedom was his? Before she turned away, he could see the struggle in her eyes.

Without looking at him, she announced, "Freedom is my son and Mercy is my daughter. I gave them life. I am their mother."

"And I am his father."

She started to reply and stopped. Confusion and conflict waged war on her face.

He sensed her dilemma and snorted, "Don't try to lie to me. The boy looks just like me when I was his age. He must be about twelve and a half, right? We were together over a month so... yeah, twelve and a half sounds about right."

She turned toward him in disgust. "We were never together. I was your prisoner. A captive you brutalized and raped." She held up her mangled hand. "For forty-nine days, you put me through hell. Andre Freedom is nothing like you. He's a good boy, decent and loving. And he is *my* son, not yours."

Tears brimmed her lovely eyes and threatened to spill over. Her luscious lips trembled as she tried not to cry. The fact that she'd gained a certain amount of courage since she'd last been under his control only made her more desirable. He couldn't wait to get her alone.

CHAPTER 14

Northeastern DRC

After a long night of worrying, caring for Jean Pierre and trying to figure out an escape, Xavier and Gabe fell into an exhausted sleep on the dirt floor. Hours later, a commotion outside woke Xavier. He lifted his head and rubbed the sleep from his face. The room was dark. Gabe snored and rolled over, mumbling something about someone named Lizette.

The sound of angry voices and running feet seeped around the door. Something was going down. Had Emmanuel's plan failed? Was his long-lost nephew about to be shot? He came fully awake at the thought.

He jostled Gabe's shoulder.

"Oh, ma cherie *(my darling)*." Gabe moaned, patting Xavier's hand. "Morning will be soon enough."

It was Xavier's turn to roll his eyes. He gave a shove that pushed Gabe over onto his face. "Wake up, Lover Boy."

Gabe groaned, rolled over and flipped on his penlight. "This better be good." He yawned. "I was with the beautiful Lizette."

Xavier put a finger to his lips. "Shhh, listen. Something's going on."

The two lay propped up on their elbows, ears tuned to the noises outside. They clambered to their feet when they heard the sound of the lock being removed. The bar slid, and the door flew open. Expecting Gerald or some other thug, Xavier was surprised when Muteko himself stepped into the dark room. Gabe shined the light in his face.

The commander put a hand up to shield his eyes. "Point that thing somewhere else, you idiot."

Gabe let the beam linger a few seconds longer, then turned it toward the floor. "Sorry, dude."

"Gather your things. You're coming with me." Muteko gestured toward the medical bag in the corner.

"Why? What's going on?" Xavier asked.

"There's been a cave in." Muteko turned to leave without offering any more information.

Xavier looked at Gabe. Even in the dark, he could see his friend's face drain of any color. His eyes took on a panicked look and his usual bravado disappeared. Xavier learned firsthand how paranoid Gabe was about caves when they found themselves forced to spend the night in one full of bats and snakes. Their truck had broken down and rather than be stranded, they made the bad decision to hike toward the nearest town. A sudden violent storm forced them to seek shelter. The little man refused to crawl inside the hole out of the pouring rain. No amount of persuasion would get him to come into the dark confines. Would he be able to hold it together if the persuader was a gun-toting brute?

Gabe gave Xavier a pleading look.

"Our patient needs constant monitoring. Leave my friend here. I'll go with you." Xavier stepped back and picked up the medical duffel. The idea of going alone and under false pretenses twisted his gut in knots. What if they figured out he wasn't a real doctor? Would the basic first aid and emergency assist course he'd just completed be enough?

Muteko's nostrils flared. He pursed his full lips and crossed his arms. Xavier couldn't tell if he was angry at not being obeyed without question or if he was considering his request. He hoped it was the latter.

"No, you will both be needed. I will have someone else watch the reporter." Decision made, he stepped back outside.

Gerald took his place, waved his gun, and jerked his head. "Outside. Now!"

"Sorry, Gabe. I tried." Xavier gave his friend's shoulder a squeeze. He leaned over Jean Pierre and whispered, "Hang on, my friend. God will come through."

Jean Pierre's eyes opened slightly, hampered by the swollen lids. He licked his lips and tried to smile. "Angels, remember?"

"Yeah, I remember."

Xavier knew Jean Pierre was talking about their harrowing experience on the road to Kigali when they were trying to escape Rwanda. They were on their way to the airport in the dead of night when a squad of RPF *(Rwandan Patriotic Front)* soldiers blocked the road.

It was Maria who first noticed the five men on the crest of the hill. A strange glow radiated behind them, illuminating the dark. Gunfire erupted. Tracer flashes showed the trajectory of the bullets aimed directly at the five. None went down. Somehow, the biggest of the five told Xavier to move out around the soldier's vehicle. Logic told him it wasn't possible for him to have heard the stranger—they were too far apart, but Xavier got the message. He told Jean Pierre to keep driving. It was little Gift, one of the children, who announced that the men were angels. Xavier knew in his heart that the boy was right. There was no other explanation.

Xavier shouldered the heavy bag and followed Gabe out the door into the pre-dawn light. A mixed blend of dust and mist swirled around their ankles as Gerald led them to the mine entrance. An eerie sense of foreboding seeped into Xavier's mind, setting every nerve on high alert. He didn't want to go into the mine any more than Gabe did. The chances of coming back out alive did not seem too good.

A couple dozen men milled around in the light emanating from a handful of lanterns. Soldiers stood at attention, rifles at the ready. Even in the gloom cast by a few random lights, Xavier could feel the tension and fear. Everyone directed their attention toward the black hole that scarred the side of the mountain. The remnants of a dust cloud still hung in the air like foggy breath on a cold morning.

"Line up!" Gerald shouted in Kinyarwanda and again in Lingala.

The thin, ragged men fell into single file, picks and shovels hoisted to their bony shoulders. Some placed battered hard hats on their heads and flicked on battery-operated headlamps. Gerald tossed duplicate safety gear to him and Gabe. Xavier tipped the hard plastic helmet onto his head. His trembling fingers found the light switch and twisted it on.

He didn't need the light to see the stark terror on Gabe's face. His eyes were so round and bulging they looked like they'd fall right out of his head at any second. Nervous sweat ran in rivulets down his face. The man was beyond afraid. Xavier bent to look his friend in the eye.

He pushed his glasses up his nose. "Gabe, look at me."

Gabe's eyes moved in transit from the mine entrance to Xavier's face. "I don't think I can do this, Boss." He swallowed hard and passed a shaky hand over his moist face.

"Listen to me. We don't have a choice. Besides, there are men in there who need our help. That's our job. Remember the FARC motto: Lend Aid, Give Hope, Show Love. I need you, buddy."

Gabe flashed a weak smile. "Okay, but don't leave me, please, Boss."

Xavier patted the damp face and grinned. "Not a chance. You got my back, I got yours. Oh and don't forget to breathe."

The line moved forward. Xavier and Gabe were pushed in between the last few men, followed by two armed soldiers. Together, they walked into the dark tomb.

Xavier focused on the back of the man in front of him. The weak beam of light radiating down from his headlamp illuminated the sweat-stained and filthy t-shirt. The man's shoulder blades protruded, making sharp ridges against the soft cloth. A line of varying size holes exposed the dark skin underneath. How many times had he march down into the bowels of the earth? Did he go willingly, or was he forced to do the backbreaking labor it required to dig out the gold ore?

Xavier stumbled and fell against him. "Mbabarira *(Sorry)*."

The man looked back but gave no response. Xavier was caught short by the look of terror in his dark eyes. *This man lived in this hole fifteen hours out of every day and he was afraid?* His own belly turned to jelly and clammy sweat broke out on his forehead, causing the hardhat to slip down. With a shaky hand, he adjusted the helmet and chanced a look back at Gabe. The sheen of sweat and the paleness of his face glistened and glowed in the lamplight.

"You doing okay?"

Gabe ran a trembling hand over his face and grunted. "I'm dandy. I feel like a cat thrown into a pit with a pack of wild dogs."

Xavier didn't know quite how to help him, since he felt much the same. "If we stick together, we'll make it." His efforts to sound upbeat and confident didn't ring true.

"Yeah, sure." Gabe scoffed. "How deep do you think we're going?"

Xavier shrugged his shoulders. They'd already been walking for a good ten minutes. The air was dank and stagnant. The blackness was so thick and solid he felt like he could actually grab a handful. He shuddered to think what it was like for the men trapped and injured. Would they find any alive or just be carrying bodies out? What if they needed real medical care beyond what he and Gabe could offer? He swallowed the hard lump lodged in his throat.

To take his mind off the groaning darkness, he replayed the classes he'd just completed on emergency first-aid. Often his team found themselves in situations where there wasn't enough trained staff to handle the injured and suffering. The logistics part was generally completed at the beginning of an assignment, but his team was required to remain on site to see that things ran smoothly. He hated feeling helpless and in the way during these times. He wanted to do more to help the doctors and nurses ease the pain of the hordes of people who came for help during a disaster. Having lived it himself, he knew the importance of immediate care. When the opportunity came to learn some basic triage skills, he signed his whole team up. Now he was glad he did.

Gabe must have decided to focus on the lessons as well. Xavier could hear him mumbling to himself about the proper way to clean and wrap a wound.

Their descent into the mine came to an abrupt stop when they came to a wall of rock that shouldn't have been there. Men were already in place, chipping and digging at the formidable jumble of giant boulders. The fresh team stepped in and took their place. Exhaustion etched the faces of the men as they staggered past Xavier. The swing of his headlamp cast weird shadows on the walls and ceiling as he looked around him. Focused back on the pile of rocks, he lifted his head until the light caught the small opening near the top of the pile. A bloodied hand appeared and gave a limp wave.

"Someone's alive!" he shouted.

Efforts doubled. Groans of exertion and strain echoed off the walls as the men passed chunks of heavy rock down off the pile. Everyone, including Xavier and Gabe, formed a line to pass the debris along. He looked back to see one soldier lean his rifle against a support beam and fall into line, stacking the rock along the wall. The other armed man stood there stone-faced, his gun balanced on his shoulder.

Within minutes, the hole was widened enough to pull a body through. A second hand appeared, followed by a head covered in dust, blood matted into the tight curls. The men near the top eased him through and passed him down to the floor.

Xavier dropped to one knee. "It's okay. You're safe now."

Clutching at his sleeve, the man's face contorted with relief and he began to cry.

"What of the others? How many are still in there?" Gabe asked as he wiped the grime from the man's face. Xavier repeated the question in Kinyarwanda.

His crying eased. He looked from Gabe to Xavier and back again. "Five alive, eight dead, three missing." The horror of what he'd been through etched itself on his face. "There was a rumble overhead, then the beams started cracking. I called out a warning, but it was too late." He sobbed. His thin shoulders shook in his grief.

Xavier started feeling along his legs. "Where are you hurt?"

The man gingerly touched the top of his head. "Only here."

Gabe, his fear put aside, dabbed an alcohol swab at the wound. "It's not deep, no stitches anyway. Here, hold this pad while I wrap it."

Xavier held the gauze pad in place until Gabe had it secured. "Done like a pro."

Before Gabe could reply, a commotion drew their attention to the gap in the rocks. One of the rescue crew had crawled through and was now back at the opening, talking rapidly and gesturing to Xavier and Gabe.

"What's he saying?" Gabe asked.

Xavier listened carefully. "I think it's Luba-Kasai, a vernacular of Tshiluba, but I can't make out more than a couple of words. I think he's saying something about broken and lots of blood." He shook his head. "We're going to have to go in there."

Gabe made a face. His shoulders slumped. "Aw, come on, Boss. I did good to get this far. Can't I stay out here and you send them to me?"

He looked past Gabe at the soldier who stepped into the small circle of light. The man jerked his head and used his gun to point from Xavier to the top of the pile. When Gabe didn't move, the rebel poked the barrel at Gabe's shoulder. "Move, both of you."

"Sorry, friend. I don't think it's up to me." Xavier stood and shouldered the bag.

Gabe repacked his duffel and grumbled under his breath. The soldier poked him again. "I'm going. I'm going."

They climbed to the top. Xavier pushed the bag through the hole ahead of him. The opening was now big enough to crawl through with ease. He wasn't prepared for the slope on the other side and went tumbling to the bottom, landing on top of the medical bag. His hardhat fell off on the way down and landed some feet away, its light shining up at the dark ceiling. He swung his legs around to get his feet under him but was bowled over when Gabe and his bag slammed into him, sending them both sprawling across the rock-studded floor.

"Ouch! Get your foot out of my face."

Gabe scrambled up. "Sorry, Boss. Sorry." He grabbed the fallen helmet and handed it back just as the light flickered and went out. "Aw, man. Like it ain't dark enough down here already."

Xavier stood, brushing his head on the low rock ceiling. He stooped enough to slide the helmet back into place. "For once I'm glad I'm not any taller."

Groans pulled their attention forward into the darkness. Within a few steps, they found thirteen men sprawled out across the dirt floor. A handful lay motionless, some with injuries so severe Xavier knew without checking that they were beyond anyone's help. The carnage made his stomach roll. He took in a deep, slow breath and let it out. He'd seen worse in Somalia and more recently, after fighting between Israel and Hezbollah left Lebanon's bombed-out streets scattered with rotting body parts.

"Help me," pleaded one man, clutching his stomach.

Realizing help had arrived, the others cried out. Xavier directed his attention toward the living and whispered a prayer for the dead.

CHAPTER 15

Hands lifted Jean Pierre's head and water dribbled onto his lips. His tongue darted out and lapped at the liquid. The automatic response brought him to the surface. His eyes fluttered and opened into slits. He reached up and pushed the tin cup closer to his lips, allowing the contents to spill out over his face. He coughed and sputtered. The action pulled talons of pain across his chest and left him breathless.

"Easy, friend." A voice whispered near his ear.

Jean Pierre turned his head to see a blurry face looking down at him. "Who are you?" he croaked.

"Emmanuel, Xavier's nephew. Remember?" He tipped the cup up again. "Here, have another sip, but go slow. That's it."

The tepid water tasted like fine champagne to Jean Pierre. His thirst sated, he looked back at the young man beside him. He was somewhere between eighteen and twenty-five, all arms and legs on a bony skeleton. His face was angular with dark brown skin stretched over high cheekbones and wide nose. It was his eyes, Jean Pierre recognized. They could have belonged to Xavier, they were so much alike. Their brief encounter earlier slowly came back to him.

The thought of his friend made him struggle to sit up.

"Here let me help you."

Strong hands supported him until he was upright and sitting on the edge of the cot. The exertion washed over him in a black wave. Pain clamped down, its talons again ripping at him.

Emmanuel waited.

The pain eased and Jean Pierre looked out beneath swollen lids. "Where's Xavier and Gabe?" He feared what Muteko might have done to his friends. Were they dead or alive? Had the sadist leader hauled them off to torture them, too?

Emmanuel sat back on his haunches and draped his sinewy arms over his bent knees. "They're in the mine. The Fist brought them here to care for you, but there was a cave in and he ordered them down into the mine to tend to the injured. That was this morning, a couple of hours ago. The Fist won't hurt them as long as he thinks they're useful. The problem is, he thinks Uncle Xavier and Mr. Bourdair are doctors."

It was all coming back to Jean Pierre. The ambush, the beatings, Muteko's demands for a full journalistic exposé about his supposed rise to power over the Northern Kivu area. His last memory was of the four of them plotting a way to escape. Emmanuel was the key.

Jean Pierre looked at the emaciated man before him and wondered how he could possibly save them all. "I'm sorry I was a bit out of it. Could you remind me what the plan was or is?"

Emmanuel shrugged his shoulders. "I've been here a long time, so I know the schedule. I was going to get assigned to loading the trucks, then hide among the bags and ride down to Goma where I could get help. Pretty simple and it would have worked if the cave-in hadn't happened." He rubbed a finger across his chin. "Actually, now is the perfect time to go. With all the confusion no one would notice, except I promised Uncle Xavier I'd take care of you."

"It will take more than a few beatings to take me out. Although I have to admit, Gerald did a pretty good job on me." The more he talked, the clearer his mind became. "I think you getting help is more important than babysitting me right now. We don't know what's happening down in that hole, but we're all still going to need help getting out of here in one piece." Jean Pierre sat back and braced a hand on either side of him. "You do what you can to sneak out. I'll keep playing unconscious, which won't be too hard." An idea surfaced in his foggy brain. "Xavier said Gerald confiscated his satellite phone. He probably gave it to Muteko. Do you think you could get into the office, grab it, and get it to me? That way I can be calling for help in case the police won't listen to you or if they're in Muteko's pocket."

Emmanuel stood. "I spent many long months learning how to stay out of sight when the Interahamwe *(paramilitary genocideers)* came. It won't be easy. Muteko's goons aren't stupid, but neither am I." His face split into a wide, toothy grin. "The guard searches me every time I bring you food or water. You work at digging a hole under the back wall and when I get the phone, I'll pass it to you under the wall. The trucks don't leave until sundown, so between the trip down the mountain and bringing help back up,

I probably won't be back here until tomorrow night at the earliest. Will you be okay until then?"

Jean Pierre appreciated the genuine concern that showed in Emmanuel's eyes. The young man had a good heart, just like his uncle. "I'll manage."

Emmanuel reached out, clasped Jean Pierre's forearms with both hands, gave a slight bow, then stepped to the door.

"Emmanuel, you be careful. Xavier just found you again. I know he wouldn't forgive himself if something happened to you now."

The grin appeared, a white slash in the gloom. The young man saluted, pulled the door open, and stepped out.

Jean Pierre waited, feigning unconsciousness when someone came in. He couldn't light the lantern, so lay in the darkness wondering what was going on outside. Where was Emmanuel? Throughout the long day, he'd managed to dig a hole under the back wall. He checked it frequently, but no phone had been pushed through yet.

Worry for Xavier and Gabe created desperate pictures in his mind. What could be happening to them down there? "God," he whispered into the darkness, "we're all in a pretty serious situation here. Please be with my friends and Emmanuel. Whatever is happening here, let it be for your glory."

The amen was forgotten as a scraping noise announced the arrival of the phone. At least Jean Pierre hoped it was the satphone and not a large rat. He eased himself off the cot and crawled a few feet to the crate he'd set up to block his handiwork. His hand found the boxy shape of the phone. Relief and excitement coursed through him until he realized the phone was there but no battery pack. Didn't Xavier say it wasn't holding a charge?

His exhilaration tempered, he crawled back to the cot, turned his back to the door to shield the lighted keypad when he turned it on. He maneuvered the antenna into position and pushed the toggle switch, praying it wouldn't make any noise powering up.

At first, the glow was dim, then seemed to brighten or was it Jean Pierre's imagination? The signal indicator showed only half a bar. It might be enough to make a call, but Jean Pierre wasn't sure he wanted to chance it and use up any of the precious battery power that might be left. Xavier said he talked to Marie about two in the afternoon. Jean Pierre held his watch up to the soft light—it was after three pm. Would there be another time when the phone could pick up a signal, or would he have to wait until tomorrow afternoon? He turned the power off, wrapped the phone in a scrap of cloth that passed for a blanket, and tucked it under the corner of the cot against the wall. He'd try again in the evening.

When the door pushed open and Gerald stepped in, Jean Pierre closed his eyes and braced himself. Was the man there to beat him again? He wasn't sure how much more abuse his body could take. At forty-two, he wasn't a youngster who could bounce back from this kind of sadistic treatment. Maybe Betta was right, and it was time to hang it up.

"Up," Gerald ordered.

Jean Pierre continued to pretend he was out and laid perfectly still. He heard the sound of a pistol hammer being drawn back. The soldier apparently saw through his ruse.

"Alright. Give me a minute."

With herculean effort, he pulled himself off the low cot and stood. One hand braced against the wall and the other wrapped around his middle. He took a couple of shallow breaths and waited for the dizziness to subside. He staggered outside, favoring his busted knee. Xavier had splinted and wrapped it, but Jean Pierre could feel the shards of bone rub together. Although his eyes were swollen to mere slits, he still had to shield them against the afternoon sun. Two men came up on either side of him and grabbed an arm. "Easy, boys. I'm damaged goods."

He winced as they escorted him down the path that was growing too familiar. Within minutes, he was back at the open shelter where Muteko again lounged. This time he drank from an orange flavored Fanta. A large fly buzzed and landed on a discarded pile of bones. A half eaten chicken rested on a plastic plate along with the remnants of stiff ugali. Jean Pierre's stomach rumbled.

"So, my friend, we are not quite done. I assume you have had time to reconsider your statement from earlier?" Muteko dipped his fingers into a bowl of water and dried them on a towel.

"You have my laptop and camera, so you know I've written what you've said and taken the photos you demanded. What more do you want?" Jean Pierre was pushed down to a short stool just outside of the shade. He held on to the sides and braced his long legs in front of him to keep from swaying.

"Yes, I have read your words and viewed the pics. You are very good. I can see why you won the Pulitzer for your piece on the kadogos *(child soldiers)*." He smiled. The gesture never made it to his eyes. "You seemed surprised. Didn't you think I'd check you out? After all, if you're going to tell the world about God's Fist and God's United Coalition Army, I needed to make sure you were capable. We will finish today. I have other situations that are demanding my attention."

Muteko snapped his fingers and Jean Pierre's computer was produced and placed in his lap. He looked from the machine back to the commander. "It would go faster if I could sit at the table."

The commander ignored the request. "Read me the last paragraph."

Jean Pierre drew up his legs as much as the splint would allow and balanced the small PC on his thighs. He brought up the Word document and read the last bit of drivel Muteko had dictated. The man was an egomaniac, like so many dictators and warlords across Africa. Could he really believe no one would recognize his self-appointed importance?

An hour later, Muteko's dictation was interrupted when one of his soldiers came running up. He whispered something to Gerald, who in turned, leaned in and whispered into Muteko's ear. The commander grumbled and slammed his fist against the table. He climbed out of the lounge chair and stomped off.

Jean Pierre arched his aching back and looked up at Gerald. "What's going on?"

The man looked down at him, sucked in on the stub of cigarette between his lips, and blew out a ring of smoke. "Another cave-in."

An instant chill swept over Jean Pierre. Were Xavier and Gabe still in the mine? Emmanuel said they were taken in this morning. Jean Pierre guessed it was now close to five pm.

"Did they get everyone out before the second cave-in?"

Gerald ignored him. He flicked his butt away and jerked his chin, indicating he was to get up and follow.

Jean Pierre needed more time with the computer. "Your commander wants this piece ready today. I need time to proofread and edit if it's going to be accepted by my boss."

Gerald's eyes narrowed as he considered what Jean Pierre said. "You two stay with him." He commanded the soldiers waiting for their next orders. He walked away. Over his shoulder, he said, "If he tries to escape, shoot him."

Jean Pierre breathed a sigh of relief. He was counting on the soldiers being ignorant of the workings of the computer and the internet. For all he knew, the men were illiterate. Still, he needed to be quick in case Gerald or Muteko returned.

With a grimace of pain, he labored to his feet and shuffled to the table. The cool of the shade brought some reprieve and Jean Pierre was able to sit more comfortably in the full size plastic chair. Dizziness still swept over him. Black dots danced before his eyes and nausea threatened. He hadn't eaten or drunk anything for hours. The morphine had long worn off, leaving him fighting to block out the tentacles of pain that wrapped around his body.

Please, God, I can't blackout now.

With his forearm, he wiped the sweat from his brow and blinked the malady away. The soldiers went to sit in the shade. Unsupervised, he typed up an email that could be set up to send as soon as his laptop was in range of an internet signal. It was short and to the point.

> Held hostage by Bonaface Muteko &
> God's United Coalition Army north
> of Goma in mountains. Hurt. Need
> help. Be careful. Armed and
> dangerous.
> J.P. Fontaine

That done, he worked on the piece about Muteko. Throughout the piece, he changed and added select words and phrases that he hoped his editor would recognize as a code explaining he was writing under duress. If the email was intercepted and he didn't make it out of this alive, at least he hoped the world would learn the truth about Muteko and GUCA.

***

Back in his prison room, Jean Pierre unrolled the blanket holding the phone. It was later than he'd hoped to be back. Muteko had kept him at his laptop for several hours. Had he missed his window of opportunity? He said a silent prayer as he powered it up and watched the screen brighten. The anticipation made his hands shake, or was it his weakened condition? Two bars slid up to indicate signal strength.

"Thank you, Jesus," he whispered to the empty room. Two bars wasn't full range, but it was better than the meager half bar earlier. Now if the power would just hold out, he thought.

He punched in the number he'd memorized decades ago. Through the static, he could hear it ringing. "Come on… come on, Marti. Pick up the phone." Martine Colbert, Jean Pierre's editor, never left the office before six in the evening. Jean Pierre calculated the time difference and hoped he caught him before he left for the night. Twelve hours on, twelve hours off. That was Marti's work-life balance. Very seldom did the man vary from his routine unless there was a huge breaking story in the works.

"Hello, you've reached the desk of Martine Colbert…"

Jean Pierre groaned. His hopes deflated, he left a short, concise message and hung up. Would his boss get it in time? Would they be able to track his location? Looking down at the screen, he noticed the last number called before his. It was a French country number. Marie!

Excited, he hit the redial and waited through the rings.

"Bonjour," came a tiny voice through the static.

"Annie! Annie, it's Uncle J.P.! Sweetheart, is mommy home? It's important I speak to her right away."

Jean Pierre could hear four-year-old Ann Marie set the phone down and holler "mommy". He waited, praying the connection wouldn't fail before she reached the phone.

"Salut *(hello)*. Jean Pierre, is that you?"

"Marie," Jean Pierre croaked, his voice suddenly choked with emotion. "Listen carefully. I'm in Northern Kivu Province, DRC. Xavier is here too, as well as Gabriel Bourdair. We're being held captive by Bonaface Muteko at a mine site in the mountains north of Goma. You need to contact authorities immediately. Have them track the GPS from the satellite phone. And, Marie, I need a doctor." He hated to frighten her, but she needed to understand how dire their situation was.

"Jean Pierre, I can hear only parts of what you're saying. Could you repeat, please?" Her voice faded in and out.

"Marie, Marie can you hear me?" He couldn't speak any louder for fear the guard would hear and investigate. The buzz grew weaker and disappeared. The screen went dark.

Jean Pierre pressed his forehead against the dead phone. He couldn't stop the sob that welled up and broke loose. The lock at the door rattled. He stuffed the phone down alongside the cot frame against the wall and fell back on the bed. The quick motion cost him as a sharp stab of pain swept across his belly and chest. When the guard opened the door, Jean Pierre was clutching his stomach, his face contorted in pain. "I need help. Please!" he begged from between clenched teeth.

Without saying a word, the guard closed and locked the door. Jean Pierre writhed in pain. Had the sudden movement broken something loose? He felt like someone was twisting a long-bladed knife in his gut and enjoying it. He curled into a ball on his side and moaned. A black fog spread behind his eyes. He could feel himself slipping into unconsciousness. He knew he needed to fight it, but the comfort of oblivion beckoned.

CHAPTER 16

Tanzania

Cyrus stopped the car and got out to push the gate open. Betta searched the area, trying to memorize as much as possible. The buildings looked abandoned, rusty, and dilapidated. A tall, narrow smoke stack pushed up against the azure sky. Metal roofing glinted as the sun caught it on its western path to the distant horizon. The few windows she could see were broken out. Would they offer a way of escape? Before she could take in much more, Cyrus was back in the vehicle and pulling around between two of the buildings, out of sight of any passersby.

"Get out," he ordered.

Betta complied without argument, anxious to see her children. Unsure of Cyrus' reaction, she continued to hold her bag in front of her to hide the swell of her stomach. He unlocked another padlock and pulled the heavy steel door open. It screamed in protest at being disturbed.

As if reading her thoughts, he turned to her. "Don't get any ideas. This door is the only way out and if it's opened even a crack, I'll hear it."

She chose not to acknowledge his statement. Instead, she followed him inside. "Where are they?"

Now it was Cyrus' turn to ignore her.

Their footsteps echoed off the walls. Birds fluttered from their perches in the rafters, disturbed by the intruders. Cyrus lit a lantern. Its feeble light did little to dispel the shadows. It took a full minute for Betta's eyes to adjust to the gloom. The large, cavernous room was empty except for a few pieces of broken down machinery. In one corner, large wired bins were stacked. She imagined they were used to haul and load the sugar cane onto trucks or conveyor belts. Movement in one caught her eye.

"Mama?" a small voice whispered, then cried in anguish, "Mama! Mommee!"

Betta dropped her bag and ran to the wire cage. Mercy's fingers weaved through the steel mesh, reaching for her. The top was open, but the little girl was too short to climb out. Her big eyes, so much like her mother's, filled with tears.

"Oh, baby girl, Mama's here."

She turned to Cyrus, fury putting steel in her voice. "I want her out of there, now!" she demanded.

Cyrus stood, feet spread, and arms crossed. "You're in no position to make demands, Pretty Thing."

She needed a bargaining chip, something he wanted. Her mind immediately went to her captivity and Cyrus' obsession. He brought her here to take possession of her again. The children were the bait. Would he let them go if she agreed to stay? Trading herself seemed her only option.

Betta clinched her jaw and pulled her loose sweater across her, using it to cover her pregnancy. She stayed close to the side of the cage, away from him.

"Please. Let her out," she asked, without it sounding like she was pleading.

"If I do something for you, what will you do for me?"

"You'll get nothing from me unless my children are safe."

Cyrus sauntered over to rest an arm against the cage wall. "Still think you're better than me, don't ya'?"

She wanted to step back out of his reach. Instead, she lifted her chin and crossed her arms. "It doesn't take much to be better than a murderer of old men and babies."

Cyrus' face hardened, and the smirk disappeared. "That was another life, another war. I was a soldier just following orders."

Betta sensed regret in his voice. Or was it guilt? Either way, it was something she could use to free her children. "Mercy and Freedom are innocent. They've never hurt you or anyone else. If you want me to see you as something besides a murderous brute, let them go."

Betta held her breath as he seemed to consider her statement. Without comment, he moved around the opposite side and manhandled a large wheel rim over to the side of the cage.

"Lift your arms up," he directed Mercy. Standing on the lip of the steel rim, he reached over the side and pulled the girl up and over by her arms.

Betta reached out and gathered her daughter to her in a tight hug. "Oh, Mercy Grace, my baby girl. I'm so sorry, sweetheart." She pushed the girl back and bent to look into her eyes. "Are you okay? Did he hurt you?" She ran her hands over Mercy's arms and legs, looking for injuries.

The thought that he could have molested her daughter caused Betta to catch her breath. The unthinkable made her hands tremble and her chest tighten. "Look at me, Mercy." When the child looked up, Betta asked in a firm whisper, "Remember when we talked about bad touching?" Her eyes threatened to fill with tears. "Did he touch you where he shouldn't?" She held her breath and steeled herself for the answer.

"No, Mama, but he lied to us and said he was a preacher." She stole a glance at Cyrus, her eyes narrow and challenging. "I don't like him. He's mean. He made us sleep and when we woke up, we were in a dark room. Free's still in there. Then I had to use the toilet, so he took me outside, but I didn't want to go out there with him watching."

"She's sassy like her mother," Cyrus interjected.

"Then when we came back in, he dropped me in that wire box." Mercy shot daggers of contempt in Cyrus' direction.

Relief flooded Betta's senses, and she released the breath she'd been holding. She looked up at Cyrus and mouthed 'thank you', then hugged Mercy to her again. "You're safe now. Mama's here."

With her daughter's arms wrapped around her, Betta struggled to her feet and challenged the man in front of her. "That's one. Now you need to let my son go, too."

"*Our* son is fine. He's over there." He nodded toward a door in the far wall.

Betta grabbed up her bag and hurried as best she could, with Mercy latched to her side. She stopped at the locked door and turned to watch Cyrus pull a single key from his pocket. He unlocked the door and swung it open. The room was more like a closet, probably meant for supplies. There was one small window high up on the back wall. In the light that filtered through the grimy panes and bars, she saw her son.

Freedom was sitting on a bamboo mat, his knees drawn up to his chest and his head tipped back against the wall. When he realized it was his mother standing there, he jumped to his feet. "Mama, is that you?" His bottom lip began to quiver as he fought back the tears.

Betta stepped into the tiny room and held her arms out. "Yes, sweetheart."

In two quick steps, Freedom fell into her arms. "I'm sorry, Mama. I thought he was a preacher. He had a Bible and said he was trying to find the church."

Cyrus leaned against the doorframe. "Sorry, kid. Guess you learned not to trust a stranger, huh?" He stepped back. "Enjoy your reunion. I have some business to take care of." With that, he slammed the door shut.

"No, wait!" Betta ran to grab the handle. She could hear the key turn on the other side. Frustrated, she gave the door a kick, then turned to lean against it.

The twins watched her. They're taking their cues from me, she thought as she looked back at their scared faces. "Okay. It looks like we might be in here a little while. Are you two hungry?"

Knowing the answer even before they replied, she squatted next to the vinyl tote and started lifting things out. "We don't have any way of making a fire, but I have some chapatti and a couple of mangos."

"Who is he? What does he want with us?" Free asked around a mouthful of bread.

Betta needed time to think about how much she wanted them to know and she needed to know Cyrus' plan before she said anything. "Honestly, I don't know what he wants, but Mercy, you're right. He's not a nice man. For now, we need to just do what he says." She hoped her answer would suffice.

Mercy crossed her arms, jutted out a hip, and gave her brother a 'told you so' look. "See, I was right. You should have listened to me."

"Mercy, enough," Betta warned her daughter.

"But, Mama…"

"No. Freedom was just trying to be helpful to someone he thought was a man of God." She could see the guilt well up in her son's face. She settled herself down next to him and wrapped an arm around his shoulders. "It's okay, Freedom. He's apparently gifted at deceiving people. It's not your fault."

The boy handed the mango back to his mother. "Here, you eat it, Mama. I'm not hungry. I think I'll just lay down."

Betta put the fruit back in the bag and leaned her head against the wall. Her mind worked on the dilemma they were in. *I've got to find a way out of this, but how?*

CHAPTER 17

This side trip across the border to Tanzania was the result of a conversation Cyrus had while drinking changaa *(cheap, alcoholic drink)* at a bar in the Kibera slums of Nairobi. The man beside him was complaining about the poor quality fare available at the local shops.

"Last month I was in Chumwe—that's across the border in Tanzania. Anyway, I had the great fortune to stumble across a bakery that served pasties that were out of this world and chapatti bread that melted in your mouth." He smacked his lips for emphasis. "But the best part was the view."

Cyrus raised an eyebrow. "The view was better than the food?"

The man waved his hand, fingers down, and blew out a low whistle. "Yeah, and I ain't talking about the landscape. The lady that runs the place is by far the most beautiful woman I've ever laid eyes on. She had a smile that could melt stone and amazing eyes the color of gold. I went back every day for a week just to get another look at her."

The mention of mouth-watering chapatti conjured up pictures of Pretty Thing forming the flat bread and dropping it into a sizzling pan to fry.

"She was probably short, fat, and missing her front teeth." Cyrus chuckled.

Wanting to be believed, the man grabbed Cyrus' sleeve. "She wasn't fat at all. She was slender with just the right amount of curves to keep a man happy." A frown crossed his face. "But she did have one flaw. Two of her fingers were missing. Not like she was born that way, but like someone chopped them off."

The man continued talking, but Cyrus didn't hear him. The hand holding the glass trembled. His mind went back to the day he pulled his machete and hacked off Pretty Thing's fingers as punishment for trying to run away. Could she be the golden-eyed beauty the man was spouting off about?

"Chumwe, you say? How far across the border is that?"

"Nice little town about seven hours southwest along the shores of Lake Victoria." The man nodded his head. "Not worth the long drive on bad roads unless you have business there." The man chuckled and added, "or you plan on doing more than having a look see."

Cyrus pushed his glass away, stood, and dropped a few shillings on the table. "Have a drink on me, old man, and thanks for the info."

The man's description was accurate about the road and the view, and now Pretty Thing was his again. Cyrus grinned in satisfaction. Everything had gone according to plan so far, but he still had an order to fill for Nguvu ya Giza and only a few days left to do it in.

He toyed with the idea of just grabbing a kid from Chumwe or some out of the way village close by, but he didn't want to take a chance of alerting the police anywhere nearby. Time wasn't on his side. He couldn't afford to drive all the way back across the border to the Kibera slums, where he knew stealing two kids would be easy. With hundreds of thousands living in abject poverty, a couple of missing orphans wouldn't concern anyone enough to call the police or make a fuss.

No. I'll head to Mwanza. It's only a couple of hours away. His mind made up and a plan in place, Cyrus called his contact. The man on the other end used few words and never told Cyrus his name.

"Speak," came the deep baritone voice.

"Munianeza here. Change of plans. Delivery will be made to Dar instead of Mombasa in five days' time." Cyrus didn't offer further information.

"Fine, but make it four. We have a ship leaving on the eleventh."

The call disconnected.

Cyrus dropped the phone back in his shirt pocket and wiped his hand on his pant leg. Four days would be pushing it. He couldn't afford to renege on his assignment or there would be a price to pay. One he didn't want to think about.

The ruthless leader of Africa's largest child trafficking ring wouldn't think twice about culling Cyrus from his team of procurers, even though he'd worked for the mysterious and powerful slave trader for over nine years. Those who didn't produce disappeared. Witnesses were never left behind to someday testify against The Dark Force.

With Pretty Thing and the children secure at the deserted plant, he drove to Tanzania's second largest city, arriving at dusk. He slowed and pulled off on one of the rutted tracks that climbed the hillsides. A conglomeration of shanties spewed down the rocky expanse. Cyrus didn't think it looked as bad as the Kibera slums. There, the tin roofs were all you could see for miles and the stench was so powerful you had to fight the need to vomit. This squatter settlement appeared more prosperous. He needed to find the worst section of town. A place where street kids lived and no one would notice him.

Twenty minutes later, as day seeped into night, he found what he was looking for. He could see it in the faces of the people as they hurried to their rusty tin and mud shanties. They were afraid to be caught in the dark, where gangs controlled the night. Here, violence churned, malicious and powerful like a vicious storm destroying anything in its path.

Cyrus smiled. A sense of familiarity boosted his confidence in his ability to find his prey in this unknown place. This forgotten section of the city was the twin to Kibera's dangerous alleys and backstreets. In Kibera, the people had little else but their life's blood, and they often found it seeping into the rancid open sewers that ran like putrid veins down every street. Like Kibera, life here wasn't worth much.

Cyrus wasn't concerned about the thugs who sauntered past. They wouldn't mess with him, and if they did, they would feel the deathly end of his Beretta. There was no police presence. Hunting here would prove easy. They wouldn't miss a couple of dirty, fat-bellied orphans.

Cyrus drove slow, barely crawling, so he could spy out the perfect prey.

In the graying dusk, Cyrus watched two rag-a-muffin children nimbly hop the open sewer ditches that meander between the tightly packed hovels. Holding hands, they climbed halfway up a tall pile of refuse, then separated. The girl and younger boy, dressed in ragged, filthy clothes, scrounged through the debris, looking for something to eat. They looked hungry, but healthy enough. They'd do nicely.

He smiled and reached for a small sack of store bought candy. The December heat hadn't dissipated much. Cyrus pulled his shirt away from his body as he stepped out and locked the SUV. He worked his way down a narrow, rocky path through the rubbish piles and stopped behind the children.

"Jambo *(hello),*" he greeted them.

The children, startled and wary, clung to each other and backed up onto the pile behind them. The girl wrapped a protective arm around the boy and stared defiantly up at Cyrus.

He pulled a sucky *(hard candy)* out of the sack, made a show of unwrapping it, and popped it in his mouth. The children watched his every move, mimicking the movements of his mouth as he moved the candy from one cheek to the other.

He held the bag out. "Want one?"

The little boy reached out only to have his hand slapped down by the girl. She muttered something to him and looked around for an escape route.

She's a wary one, smart too.

He widened his smile and kneeled down to her eye level. "You don't have to be afraid. I won't hurt you. My name is Jomo, but my friends call me John. What's your name?"

He could see the indecision in her face and, reaching into the bag, he pulled out two brightly wrapped fruit drops. "Orange and banana are my favorites. What's yours?"

"Banana," the boy said as he snatched the sweet from Cyrus' palm.

"I told you no, Taji!" she scolded.

"Taji, huh? That means lion, doesn't it?" Cyrus played dumb.

"No, sir. It means crown. Muruthi means lion." She scoffed at his mistake.

Cyrus shrugged his shoulders. "My Swahili isn't that great. I'm new here. What does your name mean?"

"Sikudhani means the surprise. My mama wasn't expecting me." She announced as she reached for the remaining candy.

"Well, Sikudhani, I was about to go get something to eat. Could you tell me where I can get a good plate of karanga *(beef stew)* and a cold bottle of orange Fanta?"

"You don't want to eat at a mkahawa *(cafe)* here, even if one was open this late." She pushed the candy to one side of her mouth. "If you're rich enough, you can find a good hoteli *(hotel)* in the city." She pointed with her chin toward the north.

He laughed. "I'm already lost. That's why I came to ask you for directions." He snapped his fingers like an idea had just come to him. "Tell you what, if you two would help me out and show me the way back into the city, I'll buy you both a big bowl of karanga. When you're done eating, I'll give you money for bus fare back."

Cyrus could see the battle going on in Sikudhani's head. Taji was pulling on her arm. "Please, Sikudhani," he begged.

The girl narrowed her eyes and crossed her arms. "I have a knife. If you're a bad man, I'll stab you. I've done it before when one of the big boys tried to get at me."

Cyrus stood and raised his hands in surrender. "Hey, I'm one of the good guys. In fact, I'm with an NGO *(Non Government Organization)* that's starting a school here for orphans."

Sikudhani dropped her arms and a look of hopeful wonder came over her face. "A school for kids without parents? Do they get to read books and wear uniforms?"

She was hooked.

It was Cyrus' turn to cross his arms and look skeptical. "At Apex School, we only take in kids without parents, but you have to be well-behaved, and smart. We don't want to waste our time feeding, clothing, and educating kids that don't appreciate it."

A wishful look came over her face. "I went to school once, before my mama and baba *(father)* died. The teacher was so nice and she helped me learn my letters and numbers."

Cyrus rubbed his chin between his thumb and finger. "Hm, you might fit, but that's not up to me. What about Taji? Have you ever been to school?"

The little boy hung his head and mumbled a dejected "no".

He needed to move this along. He chuckled and patted his stomach. "I'm hungry. How about we talk about this over some food?"

Sikudhani and Taji looked at each other, Taji nodding his head and clapping his hands. Sikudhani sighed and seemed to come to a decision. She looked up at Cyrus. "Okay, we'll show you the way, if you promise you'll think about getting us into your school."

Cyrus handed each of them another candy and turned back up the path. "My car's up there."

The children didn't notice Cyrus look around to see if anyone was watching or see the look of triumph he couldn't keep off his face.

CHAPTER 18

The bang of a steel door woke Betta. Freedom stirred beside her, rubbed his eyes, and sat up. "Mama, do you think he'll let us go today?"

Betta ran a hand over the tight curls on her son's head. There was no mistaking who his father was. The boy had grown into a younger replica of Cyrus. Still, she loved him beyond measure. Should she tell him about Cyrus?

So far, the man only thought Free was his. Mercy was so much smaller and fairer, that he assumed she was younger and fathered by someone else. Betta couldn't decide if keeping the fact that they were twins a secret was an advantage or not. For now, she wouldn't say anything.

They could hear muffled crying on the other side of the wall. Cyrus cursed at whomever it was to shut up. The weeping stopped.

Before he came for them, she needed to warn the twins of her decision. She shook Mercy awake. "Listen, both of you. Don't say anything about you being twins, understand? Don't talk to the man. I'll do all the talking, okay?"

"But, Mama, what if he asks me something?" Free asked.

"I won't say anything, Mama. He's scary. He put me in that cage-thing." Mercy patted Betta's hand. "Could you please tell him we want to go home?"

Betta pulled the children to her and hugged them tight. "I'm so sorry this is happening. I know you're afraid. Honestly, I am too. Just remember, we're not alone. God's angels are right here with us. We have to be strong for each other, okay?"

The children nodded, solemn looks on both their faces. Freedom pushed away, stood up, pulled himself to his full height, and crossed his arms. "I won't let him hurt either one of you."

Betta and Mercy stood as well. "Thank you, son, but promise me you won't try anything without talking to me first. Cyrus can be mean and he doesn't like to be crossed."

She didn't mean to let it slip that she knew him. Neither of the children knew her history to the extent that she was held hostage and raped. Now she could see the wheels turning in her son's mind.

"How do you know what he's like or that his name is Cyrus?" Free asked.

Betta didn't want to lie to them, but she would never tell them the whole horrible story. She held up her maimed hand. "He did this to me because I made him angry."

Mercy wrapped her small hands around her mothers. "Poor, poor Mama. I knew he was a bad man right from the first time we saw him." She gave Freedom an accusatory look.

Freedom's face fell, as did his shoulders. "I said I was sorry. He tricked me."

Betta rested her hands on his narrow shoulders. "It's okay. You were just trying to be helpful."

They turned as a group when the door flew open and banged against the wall. Two small, ragged children were pushed inside. Cyrus' form filled the doorway, his hands on his hips.

"I've brought you company. Keep them quiet." He stepped back and slammed the door.

Betta looked down at the two children. They looked to be about eight and six. The girl had a protective arm around the little boy. Both were filthy, their clothes not much more than rags hanging off their bony shoulders. A wild tangle of bushy hair sprang in all directions from the girl's head. The boy's showed the scars from someone's attempts to shave it with a razor blade. Eyes too big for their small faces, they stared back.

"It's okay. We won't hurt you." She put a hand around the twin's shoulders. "This is Mercy Grace and Andre Freedom. I'm their mother, Mrs. Fontaine. What are your names?"

The boy dipped his head. The girl chewed her lip, distrust and indecision in her brown eyes.

"Would you like a piece of chapatti and a drink of water?" Betta moved to her bag and dug out the remaining food she'd fed the children earlier. "Here, Mercy. Take this to them."

Mercy smiled as she handed the girl the bread and plastic jug of water. "My mama makes the best chapatti you'll ever eat."

Hunger outweighed caution as the girl reached for the food and tore the flat slab in two. In a few swift bites, the bread disappeared into their mouths. Cheeks bulging, the little boy smiled and tried to talk around the contents. "It's good."

Mercy set the jug on the floor at her feet. "Told you. My mama owns a bakery. My daddy says she'll be famous one day."

The girl swallowed and announced, "I'm Sikudhani. This is Taji. That man, John, took us from Mwanza. He said he was taking us to a school." She looked around the small, dreary room. "Is this the school?"

Freedom snorted. "Not likely."

"Freedom, be nice," Betta reprimanded.

Contritely, he tucked his head. "Yes, ma'am."

Betta kneeled down in front of the children. "Where are your parents? Did Cyrus—John, talk to them about taking you to a school?"

"We ain't got no parents. They got sick and died a long time ago." She wrapped her arm back around Taji's shoulders. "I take care of my brother." She tipped her chin back at the door. "He gave us sweets and promised us a bowl of karanga. Then he said he was taking us to a new school where I could learn to read and write and even wear a uniform." She sighed and frowned. "I used to go to school, a long time ago. Taji never did, but I've been teaching him his numbers and letters." She looked back at Betta. "You got more of that chapatti? Taji's still hungry."

Betta's heart broke for the two. What was Cyrus going to do with them? She remembered the children he ordered thrown down a well and how he made her leave baby Fellie behind when he took her with him. He wouldn't have taken these children unless he had a plan for them, but what was it? A chill passed over her heart. What was he up to?

CHAPTER 19

Cyrus ran the pen down the blue line that indicated the secondary road. Satisfied he'd picked a good route that would keep them off the main Pan-African highway, he folded the map and stuffed it back in the glove box. The route to the seaport of Dar es Salaam would be long, skirting the Serengeti National Park and traveling diagonally from the northwest corner of Tanzania to the southeast coastline.

Now that his plans had changed so drastically, it made more sense to deliver the kids in Dar, then head toward their ultimate destination of Zambia. Central Tanzania was part of his hunting grounds, so he was familiar with the delivery point on the docks at Dar. Nguva ya Giza had border guards across central Africa on the payroll, just like the two at the Tanzania and Kenya crossing. They had accepted the bribe Cyrus slipped to them with a smile and a wave. He was confident that the crossing into Zambia with Betta and Free wouldn't pose a problem either, as long as the right amount of money crossed hands.

Before grabbing the two garbage kids, Cyrus made a stop at a local pharmacy in a busy part of the city. The man behind the counter showed little more than bored interest as he prepared the order.

"The small brown bottle contains Chloral hydrate pills. You can dilute them in water but it can take up to twenty minutes for the person to pass out depending on if they've eaten and their size. You say you have used chloroform before so you know about that." He handed Cyrus the paper bag. "That should last you awhile."

Cyrus paid the man and left without comment. He felt better about the long, arduous road trip with five captives now that he had a way of dealing with them. The children he could sedate, but Betta would present a problem if she chose not to cooperate.

She had changed since they'd last been together, more confident and assured. If it weren't for the children, he wasn't sure he could control her as easily as he did all those years ago. Now he had the kids to use as leverage to make her comply with his wishes.

The plan was to drive cross-country to the port at Dar, where he'd deliver the two girls and the younger boy. Then Betta and Freedom would accompany him back to the little place he'd bought himself in northern Zambia. No one knew of the small house he'd purchased in another name. It was his safety net when things got too hot with the authorities and he wanted to settle down. Now he was glad he had the foresight to make the purchase.

Going south to the coast, then west would cover their trail sufficiently. With the payoff from the sale, he'd have plenty of money to live on for a while, even with two more mouths to feed.

The Surf loaded with supplies, Cyrus went to gather the children and Betta. He opened the door to find all but the youngest boy sitting with their backs against the wall. Taji lie draped across Betta's lap, sound asleep. The smell coming from the waste bucket in the far corner caused him to pinch his nose and scowl.

"Get up and gather your things. We're leaving."

Betta struggled to her feet and lifted the boy's slack body in her arms. "Where are you taking us?"

Cyrus stepped back out of the room and took a deep breath. "You'll know soon enough."

The children trailed behind Betta as they stepped out into the afternoon light. They shielded their eyes and looked around. With buildings on three sides, he wasn't too worried they knew where they were.

"Here, have a drink before we go. It's going to be a long trip, and I don't intend to make any stops." He handed Freedom a plastic jug, one he'd already doctored.

The greedy little buggers gulped down the contents. Betta took a couple of small swallows. Would it be enough to sedate her? Hopefully she drank enough of the drugged water to do the trick. Cyrus frowned. He wanted them all out cold for the trip.

"Are we going to the new school?" Sikudhani asked.

Cyrus chuckled. "Yeah, sure, kid. Now get in the back and shut up."

Betta situated the children in the back seat, then settled herself in the front, the oversized tote bag on her lap.

"Here, let me put that in the back." He reached for the bag. Betta wrapped her arms around it and leaned away from him. "No, I'll hold it."

He narrowed his eyes and wondered what the deal was with the bag. What was she trying to hide? He'd already checked its contents, but there was nothing but cooking things, food, and a few pieces of clothing.

"Whatever. I was just trying to make it more comfortable for you. We're in for a long trip." Cyrus climbed in and hit the automatic lock on the doors before starting the engine.

When they pulled out onto the main road and headed south, Betta finally spoke. "You're not taking us back to Chumwe, are you?"

Cyrus grinned. "Hardly. I have some business to take care of and then we're off to start our new life—together. Hopefully, the brats will sleep the whole way. You might as well try and sleep too."

When she didn't reply, he glanced over to see her staring out the window, chewing her bottom lip.

"Don't even think about it. You're not going anywhere this time."

She didn't respond, so he turned on the radio.

Within a half dozen miles, they were all asleep. He looked up in the rearview mirror at Freedom. His head tipped back. He snored softly. *My son. My blood and Betta's.* A strange feeling coursed through his body. Was it pride? Fatherly concern? Whatever it was, Cyrus knew he wanted a better life for the boy. An education, a job he could be proud of, a family. Something more than what he'd had growing up.

His father had been a drunkard, mean and lazy. He watched his mother work herself to an early grave caring for him and his six siblings. When she died, Cyrus tried his best to protect his brothers and sisters from their father's wrath until one day he found his father on top of his seven-year-old sister. The man had passed out, Catherine crying softly beneath his slack body. Cyrus rolled him off, sent his sister outside, and used a machete to gut the man who'd sired him.

He and his brothers buried the body in the bush. They told anyone who asked that he'd gone on a drunk and never came back.

No one questioned their explanation. Soon Cyrus' uncle showed up to claim his brother's property. At only thirteen, he could do nothing to stop the man from selling his two older sisters to a wealthy merchant looking for new, young wives. The remaining five—him included—were sent to a Catholic orphanage outside of Kigali.

Living a structured existence was new to Cyrus. Every part of their day was scheduled. He liked knowing he would be fed every day and learning to read and write at the school. It was the long list of rules he was expected to follow that chafed. Then he got caught cheating. The punishment was a beating in front of the whole class. The priest told him to bend over and drop his pants. Mortified, and full of outrage, Cyrus—as big as the priest—grabbed the slender switch. He struck the man across the face with it, and then ran, never to go back.

He spent the next five years hustling and learning how to survive on his own. Joining the Rwanda military took him off the streets of Kigali and gave him a measure of respect, as did earning the rank of commander. He worked to build up muscle and, with his height at just under six feet, he was pleased with the way he filled out his uniform. The uniform and his size gave him confidence, and he quickly learned he could get what he wanted through intimidation and fear.

It had worked on Betta when he took her captive. He glanced at the boy again and then at the woman beside him. Could he still control her with brute force? What of his son?

She leaned her head against the window, her eyes closed, long lashes resting against smooth mocha skin, and her lips slightly parted. She was still the most beautiful woman he'd ever seen. The years having only accentuated her beauty. Cyrus reached over and ran his finger along her creamy cheek and down her long, elegant neck. She didn't flinch. The drug left her unaware and pliable.

His whole body tightened. He wanted her, and he intended to make her his again. This time, he vowed to wait until she came to him willingly. He longed to feel her full, sensual lips against his again. With a deep exhale, Cyrus pulled his eyes away and back to the road. His grip on the steering wheel intensified until his knuckles whitened. He pressed his lips into a firm line and clenched his jaw. *I'll make her love me—to want to stay.*

And if she didn't he would see that she learned that she couldn't leave.

CHAPTER 20

Northeastern DRC

Xavier eased the injured man's head back down to the dirt and looked at Gabe. With a slight shake of his head, he communicated the man's dire situation. They had done a quick assessment of each of the victims. Three were in critical condition with internal injuries way beyond anything Xavier was capable of dealing with. Two more had broken limbs. The other eight were beyond anyone's help, their bodies mangled by the deadly rock fall.

"Go back and have them send a couple of stretchers with enough men to haul them out," he ordered. The man who had followed them through the hole to the other side of the cave-in. nodded, turned, and scrabbled up the pile of rocks to disappear through the small opening.

Gabe sat cross-legged on the floor, wiping the grime from the face of a boy not much more than fifteen or sixteen. "He's just a kid, Boss. So is that one." He nodded toward another of the seriously injured.

Xavier had heard children were being used as forced labor in many of the mines across Africa, but this was his first time seeing it for himself. "They're younger than Gift." He couldn't imagine his own seventeen-year-old son down here in the bowels of the earth breathing stagnant air and only seeing sunlight a few hours a day. The image sent a mixed wave of despair and rage through him. How could Muteko treat these kids this way? Did the man have no soul, no conscience?

A low rumble began to build. The floor beneath them seemed to come awake like a slumbering giant, stretching and heaving.

"Another cave-in!" he shouted and threw himself across the body of the boy at his side. The roar intensified. Rocks and pebbles rained down, slamming into them with killer force. The darkness instantly filled with a cloud of dust that stole the oxygen and covered them like a suffocating blanket.

The thunder stopped. Xavier coughed and worked to lift himself off the boy under him. He groaned with the movement. Stones rolled from his back and piled on the floor around him. He rubbed the dirt from his eyes. It made no difference. He could not see. The dark was too intense. A quick assessment testified to the battering his arms, legs, and torso took. His back had taken the brunt of the assault and he knew in the light of day he'd have a collection of assorted welts and bruises. His thoughts turned to the others.

"Gabe? Gabe, are you okay?" Completely disoriented in the thick blackness, he shouted into the space at large. A groan emanated from somewhere to Xavier's left. He turned and tried to crawl in that direction. Feeling along the rock-strewn floor, his hand touched skin. There was muscle and hair, the knob of a knee. A leg! "Gabe, is that you? I'm right here, brother." A rough-hewn beam blocked his advance. He worked his way over it.

The disembodied groan turned into a cough. "Boss?"

A lump under Xavier's hand felt foreign, smooth, and man-made. Excited, he ran his fingers over the surface until they felt the cylinder-shape of the headlamp. His thumb found the switch. He held his breath. *Please, work!*

A dim, yellow light sifted through the darkness and shined on Gabe's face. "Boy, am I glad to see you," Gabe coughed and grinned.

Relief washed over Xavier. "Me, too." The two clasped hands.

Gabe grunted and screwed up his face. "I can't move."

Xavier shook debris off the helmet and clamped it down on his head, then looked down Gabe's body. The beam he'd crawled over rested across Gabe's thighs, pinning him to the ground. It was at least ten inches by ten inches of solid wood and six feet long. With a deep breath and gritted teeth, he strained to lift the timber. "Push, Gabe, push!"

With Xavier lifting from the top and Gabe pushing from underneath, they heaved the log-sized beam aside. It landed with a thud and stirred up a new cloud of dust. Waving their hands to clear the air, both coughed and choked.

"There was a lantern above me on the wall sitting in a niche. See if it's still there." Gabe pointed a hand over his head.

Xavier scanned the rough surface until the light picked up the curved glass of the lantern. "It's not broken!" He scrambled forward and pulled the lamp down. "Do you have a lighter or matches?"

"Not on me, but there was a lighter in the med bag."

Xavier felt his way along the wall until the light caught the red duffel. The sight of something familiar gave him a moment of relief. He pulled the zipper and clawed through the contents and pockets until he came up with the slim two-inch long plastic lighter. Holding his breath, he raised the glass and flicked the lighter wheel. The blue and orange flame wavered and grew as he touched it to the wick. Soft light illuminated a sphere around the two men. An audible sigh escaped both of them. Somehow, it didn't seem as bad with the light allowing them to see each other.

Gabe eased up into a sitting position, felt along his legs, from groin to boot-tops, and grinned. "I'm good. Nothing broken, but I don't think I'll be doing any marathons any time soon."

"Like you ever did before," Xavier scoffed. The moment of relief dissipated with the thought of the other men buried in the tunnel with them. "Come on, help me find the rest."

Together, the two moved around the room that had suddenly become much smaller. Of the previous five that were alive, three more had joined the dead. The boy Xavier had thrown himself across was still breathing, and the man with the broken leg now had a busted arm and dislocated shoulder to add to his injuries. Rock rubble littered the floor. At each end, a wall of boulders blocked the way. Disoriented, Xavier wasn't sure which was their way out to the surface. Gabe must have read his thoughts.

"It's that pile. I remember crawling around that sharp, pointy rock."

"Glad one of us was paying attention," Xavier muttered as he made his way to the top of the pile to discover the opening to the other side gone. How thick and deep it now was he couldn't tell, but the surrounding space had definitely grown smaller. Would someone be able to get to them before their supply of oxygen ran out? He began to feel some of Gabe's claustrophobic panic. Taking a deep breath, Xavier closed his eyes and placed a hand on the rock in front of him.

"Father God, your Word says the mountains will move if our faith is even the size of a mustard seed. I've never seen a mustard seed, but I stand on your promises and I say to this mountain, move." He waited, eyes closed. The boulder under his hand trembled, then went still. He harrumphed. So much for his less than mustard seed size faith.

Time passed. Had it been hours or days they'd been trapped here in the belly of the earth? Xavier had lost his capacity to discern time. The crystal on his watch was shattered, the minute hand missing. He mourned the loss of the precious gift, but even more so the ability to track time.

As if reading his mind, Gabe asked, "How long do you think it's been?" His voice floated, detached and vaporous in the dark.

They had agreed to douse the lantern to save the kerosene. Neither one mentioned the oxygen it needed to feed on. Oxygen they would eventually run out of. Xavier knew Gabe meant the length of time since the second cave-in blocked their escape. He answered with a lighthearted mocking tone he didn't feel. "About five minutes later than the last time you asked."

Gabe chuckled and huffed. "Give it up, Boss, you just can't pull off sarcastic. Now me, I'm an expert."

"That you are, my friend."

"Do you think Emmanuel really followed through with the plan and got away? I don't see how we can count on an emaciated, cowed kid who's lived in fear for the past decade to suddenly become a hero. I mean, I know he's your nephew and all, but if he could escape, why didn't he do it a long time ago?"

Xavier had the same doubts. As a boy, Emmanuel had been a typical eleven-year-old, adventurous and inventive. He was a bundle of energy that hated the solitary and dull job of a cow-herder only slightly more than he hated school. As a man, had he changed? Xavier could only imagine what he had gone through, seeing his family murdered, running, and hiding from the Interahamwe, trying to survive on his own. Spending days on end slaving away in this dark hole had surely broken him.

"I don't know, Gabe. All we can do is hope and pray he finds the strength and courage. He knows we're all counting on him."

A sharp, hacking cough and groan ricocheted off the walls. "Turn the lantern back up. I need to check Benga's dressing," he ordered as he turned to kneel beside the young man. His initial injuries were serious, but now Xavier worried about the condition of the kid's right ankle. A large rock had crashed down and smashed it into a bloody mess. The foot was black and swollen. Neither he nor Gabe could tell what was dirt and grime, and what could be the first signs of lost circulation. As bad as the foot looked, it was the internal injuries that could prove deadly.

Benga roused and whispered, "Water. Please."

Without hesitation, Gabe dribbled the last few drops he had into the boy's eager mouth. "Easy, dude. Help is coming. You just rest."

Xavier re-wrapped the dressings on the boy's ankle and the one circling his head. Once he was done, he motioned for Gabe to scoot out of earshot. "He's not good. I think we need to work at getting ourselves out of here instead of waiting for a rescue team."

Gabe nodded his agreement.

"Tambwe." He turned to the other survivor. "We're going to climb up and try moving some of the stones from this side. We'll need to take the lantern with us, but you'll still be able to see a little. Watch Benga. If he seems worse, holler, okay?"

"Sawa *(okay)*," the older man replied.

Xavier and Gabe worked their way over the pile and began lifting and moving the top stones. Gabe stopped with a heavy rock in his arms. "Boss, we're going to run out of space to put these."

Xavier thought for a moment. Always the logistical one, he weighed the situation and went over the solutions in his head. "I don't like it much, but we don't have a choice. We'll use the stones to bury the dead. If Muteko wants to dig them out later, he can."

It was a grueling task. There was little space to work in. Both men were drenched in sweat one minute and shivering the next. Their bloody scrapes and cuts were soon covered over with dust. Their fingers became raw as the wall of stone started to change shape. Gabe, at the top, hoisted one rock at a time from the pile and handed it off to Xavier. With reverence, he gently positioned them, creating a grave covering and marker for the dead.

"Boss, we've been at this forever. There's no telling how deep this fall is. Maybe we're just wasting our time and oxygen."

Xavier could hear the defeat in Gabe's voice. "Do you want to give up?"

"Yes… no… I don't know. Can't you just ask God to get us out of here?" he bellyached as he hunched over in the tight space near the ceiling.

Xavier reached up and patted Gabe's leg. "You know I have. We've just got to be patient so His plan can be worked out. Remember, we're not the only players in this drama." He gave the man's leg a tug. "Come on down and we'll split a power bar. If we share one now, that will still leave one for later. Just do me a favor and don't say anything about that being the last of our food or that we're out of water, okay?"

Gabe took the hand Xavier offered and climbed down the slope. "You got it, Boss."

With the lantern wick trimmed back to a faint glow, the three men huddled around the prostrate body of the injured boy. Each, lost in their own thoughts, ate their quarter piece of bar in silence.

Benga came to long enough for Xavier to feed him tiny bits of the granola. He asked for more water, but passed out again before he could tell him there was none.

In the gloom, Gabe's pale skin took on a ghostly pallor, his eyes shadowed and distant. Xavier hated seeing him look so defeated. So quiet. Trying to take everyone's mind off their circumstances, Xavier turned to Tambwe. "Tell us how you came to be here. Where are you from? Do you have a family?"

The whites of Tambwe's eyes were glowing orbs that shifted from one face to the other. His teeth would have done the same if he had had any left in his mouth. "I's live in these mountains my whole life. Had me a good life. I owned a few hectares *(land measurement)* of hillside. Had a cow even. My wife bore me twelve children, three lived to adulthood. Everything was going fine until the Tutsi and then the Hutus came. There was so many of them. They stripped the land of every stick and banana. The refugee camps ruined the land across this whole north end of Kivu." He paused. "Then the cholera came."

His voice took on a pensive, woeful tone as he continued. "It took my wife, my kids, and even my grandkids, except for one. I took little Jetta all the way down to Kibombo to an orphanage. With my farm gone, I signed on with the mine back about seven years ago. It was okay at first, then Muteko came and took over. It got bad real fast. Now we're nothing more than slaves pulling out the gold, making him rich."

"Why don't you leave?" Gabe asked.

Tambwe snorted. "The only way 'The Fist' lets you leave is if you're not breathing anymore. I've tried, but he says I owe him for food and equipment. I can't ever seem to get the debt paid."

Xavier wondered if the story was the same for everyone else. "How many of the men are indebted to Muteko?"

"Most. I think he bought some of the younger ones. The soldiers don't treat them very good. Not that they treat the rest of us much better." He shrugged his shoulders in resignation. "I'll probably die here, if not today, then tomorrow, or some day after that."

"None of us is going to die here," Xavier pledged. It was a promise he hoped he could keep.

CHAPTER 21

The light sputtered and went out. The darkness complete. Xavier closed his eyes and opened them again. Nothing changed. *Is this what it's like to be blind?* He shuddered at the thought.

"Boss, how long do you think we'll last?" Even though Gabe whispered the question, his disembodied voice sounded loud in the enclosed space.

Xavier didn't want to answer the question. There were so many things against them, no water, no food, and now their air supply was slowly diminishing. He remembered the theory of threes—three weeks without food, three days without water, and three minutes without air. He tried to be upbeat. "Don't worry, you won't starve to death." Should he tell him they would be dead long before starvation could take them?

"It's not food I'm worried about." Gabe muttered his response and fell back into silence.

Xavier felt a hand searching along his arm. He reached out to enclose his fingers around Benga's. "Hang in there. Help is on the way."

Hours passed, or was it days? Moving more rock was out of the question. The effort would use up their oxygen too quickly. The men languished against the rough-cut wall side by side, yet each in his own world.

Xavier thought about his precious family—Marie, Gift, Paul, Margarette, and little Ann Marie. He never thought in his wildest dreams he would be so blessed. Marie was his light and the very air he breathed. He couldn't imagine life without her beautiful smile. Gift, the lost little boy who'd stolen both their hearts all those years ago, was now a young man Xavier was proud to call his son. Paul, at eleven, already possessed the self-confidence of a grown man—something it took Xavier years to find for himself. Then there was Margarette and Anne Marie, his sweet baby girls. He couldn't imagine life without their hugs and giggles and all the wonderful little girl things about them. He often said he felt like Job having lost everything only to gain even more back.

And now, had God answered his prayers about Precious? The thought of his sister alive after all the years of searching was almost more than he could comprehend. Would he live to hold Marie and his children again? Would he actually lay eyes on his sister and tell her how sorry he was that he hadn't been there to protect her?

God, please hear me one more time and let me return to my family. The air was dank and still. He felt nothing. Had God abandoned him? His heart sank. Despair descended to wrap its tentacles in a strangle hold around him and pulled him into the depths.

***

A gasp and burst of weak coughs roused Xavier from nightmare-filled sleep. With no distinction between up and down, light and dark, he was completely disoriented. He sat up and pressed his palms to his temples to calm the whirl that made him sway. A band of pressure wrapped around his chest as he tried to take in a deep breath.

"Boss, it's Benga. I think he's worse," announced Gabe from the dark.

Xavier scooted closer until he could feel the young man's clammy, cold arm. He ran his hand down to his wrist and pressed to find a pulse. "His pulse is weak, but rapid. I think he's going into shock."

With no light, he couldn't check for other signs. The crushed ankle wasn't life threatening unless the boy threw a blood clot. It was the internal injuries that worried Xavier. Wounds he couldn't see, even if he had a light. "Pull everything out of the duffel and my pack. We need to keep him warm and elevate his feet." He could hear Gabe dumping the contents of the medical bag.

"Isn't there one of those thermal Mylar packs in here? We always have at least a couple stowed in here for emergencies." Gabe cussed under his breath.

"Feel in the front pockets. Those packs are small enough to have slipped down to the bottom at the seam."

"Got it!"

Xavier could hear the metallic crunch and rattle of the blanket being unfolded from the tiny, compact square. "Pass me the bag and I'll prop up his legs while you cover him." The canvas duffel pushed against his chest. Xavier grabbed it and gently lifted Benga's injured leg. The boy cried out in pain. "Sorry, son. You'll feel better soon." He squeezed the unconscious man's hand.

"Do you think they'll be here soon?" Tambwe asked.

Xavier didn't know how to answer. He could tell they didn't have much longer. It was getting harder and harder to breathe. "We need to conserve our oxygen as much as possible. Everyone settle in and no talking. Save your energy and pray."

CHAPTER 22

Was that gunfire? Jean Pierre eased himself up on his elbows and listened. There it was again, the unmistakable sporadic pop of automatic weapons. The sound echoed against the mountainside. The block walls surrounding him absorbed the noises beyond his prison. Still, he was sure something was going down. He couldn't tell how far away the firefight was happening, but someone had to be engaging Muteko's men.

His hopes soared. Help was coming!

He edged his legs over the side of the cot and braced himself for the agony of pulling himself up to a sitting position. A stab of hot, angry pain seared across his abdomen like a fiery brand. He wrapped his arms tight across his battered gut, took as deep a breath as he was able, and hoisted himself to his feet.

The room spun. The breath sucked out of him, leaving him gasping. Jean Pierre staggered the few steps needed to reach the door and pressed his good eye to the crack. There didn't seem to be anyone standing guard. Through the sliver, he could see the stool outside the door lying on its side. He searched the section of jungle he could see. Nothing. The tramped dirt yard was empty.

Moving to the other side of the door to change his perspective, he scanned the landscape. Through the trees, along the path they dragged him down daily, he could just make out what looked like men running back and forth. *Something's happening, but what?*

He jiggled the handle. Not surprised to find it still locked, he pressed his full weight against the door. There was no give to the solid wood surface. With a grimace, Jean Pierre moved to the end of the cot and pulled it away from the wall. There on the floor against the wall was the dirty blanket, twisted in a wad around the satphone. He stepped into the gap and reached down to retrieve it.

Blinding white flashes pierced his brain behind his eyes when he bent over, leaving him gasping and fighting unconsciousness. *Oh, no!* He wanted nothing more than to give into the urge to lie back down and wait for the flashes to go away.

"Come on, you can't lose it now," he said to himself and the room at large.

He unwrapped the phone and let the scrap of blanket fall to the floor. "Please, God, let it work," he whispered. He raised the antenna and toggled the power on. The screen brightened up to display a wavering slice of one bar. No service flashed at the top of the screen. Frustrated, Jean Pierre threw the phone down on the bed and ran his hands through his hair. He wanted to curse—to rant and rave about his position. Instead, he gritted his teeth, took a couple of ragged breaths, and tried to clear his mind of the ever-present pain that had come to dominate his world over the past few days. He needed to concentrate on his rescue. Did he dare yell, or should he just wait patiently for someone to find him? His options were limited, and with his injuries, he wouldn't be much help to his rescuers. He moved back to the door and slid down the wall beside the crack so he could keep watch.

The gunfire continued off and on for another twenty minutes, then everything got quiet. Anticipation grew until a new thought entered his head. What if it was a battle between rival groups? There were a half dozen rebel groups in this part of DRC. Could they be fighting for control of the mine? Jean Pierre's hopes sank. For all he knew, he was going from one bad situation to an even deadlier one.

Running footsteps brought him back to the crack beside the door. Men in uniform were running up the path toward the hut! On alert, guns up and poised to fire, the soldiers fanned out around the perimeter of the clearing. Behind the last one, the skinny shape of Xavier's nephew stepped out of the tree-shrouded darkness. Emmanuel pointed toward Jean Pierre's prison.

"He made it! He got help!" Jean Pierre banged a hand against the door. "Help, in here!"

"Stand back," came the order from one of the armed men.

Jean Pierre scooted away from the door along the wall and covered his ears. The staccato blast of gunfire riddled the door around the lock. He could hear the scrape of the crossbar. The door fell open, allowing the soldier and Emmanuel to enter. Xavier's nephew kneeled down next to him. "Sorry, it took so long. I had trouble getting anyone to believe me and do something. It didn't take much to figure out the local police were in Muteko's pocket, so I went to the barracks at Rutshuru. They got a call from some big shot in France, and suddenly people started paying attention."

"Marti came through." Jean Pierre laughed and then sighed in relief. He turned to the young man crouched beside him. "And so did you. You don't know how happy I am to see you. I wasn't sure you got away." He reached out and pulled Emmanuel close. "You saved my life. Thank you," he whispered. The words didn't seem adequate, but they were all he had to offer.

Emmanuel looked up at the soldier. "Help me get him up. He's hurt bad."

"I don't think I can walk."

The soldier stepped to the door and whistled. Two more men joined him, carrying a stretcher. With help, he managed to get himself laid out on the board. Straps secured him in place and he was carried out of the room that had been his prison for the past five days. The sunlight never felt so good, nor the air so fresh. Freedom has a way of changing how a man sees the world, thought Jean Pierre, especially when it's been taken away.

Emmanuel walked beside him, his face grim. "Uncle Xavier and Mr. Gabe are still trapped. Muteko ordered the men to quit digging and just left them to die."

"Where's Muteko now?"

Emmanuel smiled. "Chained up like the animal he is. 'The Fist' won't be able to terrorize anyone ever again."

"They've started digging again, haven't they? There could still be people alive in there waiting for us to get them out." Not just people, but his best friend. Jean Pierre didn't want to think about Xavier being dead—buried under a ton of rock. He fought the need to get up and do something.

At this point, he was beyond helpless and it rankled to know there was nothing he could do to help. Betta would have nodded knowingly and said that was the macho man in him—determined to jump in and save the world. She would remind him of the power of prayer. Chagrined, he began a running monologue with God while keeping his eyes on what was happening around him.

They had reached a group of trucks scattered around the open space in front of the mine entrance. All the vehicles had FADRC *(Armed Forces of the Democratic Republic of Congo)* painted in big white letters down their camouflaged-painted sides. Several sported the DRC flag, a light blue background with a diagonal red slash and gold star in the corner. As they hoisted him into the back of one of the trucks, he grabbed Emmanuel's arm. "You can't let them give up."

"Even if I have to go back in there and dig by myself, I won't come out without them, I promise." Emmanuel put his free hand over his heart. "He's my family."

The truck pulled away. Jean Pierre raised his head and watched Emmanuel grow smaller. His hand still rested over his heart, the other raised in farewell.

"Please God, help him get them out."

The ride down off the mountain was excruciating and long. The stiff backboard he was strapped to jerked and banged with the constant movement of the tires dropping in and out of the ruts and climbing over protruding rocks. At some point—much to Jean Pierre's relief—the truck stopped. Were they finally off the mountain? He could hear words being exchanged, and then two people hopped up into the back.

"You J. P. Fontaine?" asked a huge, barrel-chested man with shaggy, blonde hair and several days' growth of reddish-blonde beard.

Jean Pierre looked from one new face to the other. "Yeah, that's me. Who are you?"

"This here's Natalie Cross and I'm Mike Pearson. We're with DWB, Doctors Without Borders." He began a hands-on exam of Jean Pierre's injuries. "When we arrived at our triage site to help the volcano victims, a couple of guys with the French set up team were in a panic. Said their team leader, and another guy were missing, along with a couple of emergency medical bags. We've had people looking for a few days now. Then we got a call about hostages and a mine collapse."

"Seems there are people out there worried about you." The woman smiled at him. Her short-cropped cap of brown hair fell forward over her face as she prepped his arm for an IV.

"Not me, Xavier and Gabe. Nobody knows I'm here." Jean Pierre corrected her.

"Guess it's your lucky day. We were headed to the mine, but soldiers stopped us here, said they had to secure it first." Mike looked over at Natalie. "Give him two amps of morphine and start a saline drip." Looking back at Jean Pierre, he frowned. "We can take you back to our field hospital and treat you or you can let these men get you to the hospital in Goma. You've got at least three broken ribs, your knee cap is crushed, there's definitely internal bleeding and I'm guessing you've ruptured your spleen. No way to know for sure how much damage there is without surgery."

Jean Pierre closed his eyes. He'd been in enough hospitals across Africa to know most were in a time warp. Facilities and equipment were aged and often pieced together by whatever means possible. Patients were left to fend for themselves when it came to bedding and food because of overcrowding, a lack of staff, and few supplies. But did he have a choice? If he let them take him back to their site, there wouldn't be anyone at the mine to treat the cave-in victims once they were brought out. A new resolve settled over him. He would take his chances so Xavier, Gabe, and the others would have medical care when they get out. *If* they get out. "Go. Let these men take me to Goma."

Mike accepted his decision with a nod. He looked at the soldier waiting at the opening. "Take him to HEAL Africa. See that Dr. Lusi knows he's there."

As if she could read his thoughts, Natalie patted his arm. "Don't worry. HEAL is a wonderful hospital started by Dr. Lusi and his wife. The letters stand for Health, Education, Action, and Leadership. You'll be in good hands."

"Thanks." He looked up at the doctor. "Don't let them give up. Promise me."

The burly doctor gave him a reassuring grin. "They don't call me Bulldog Pearson for nothing." He turned to the waiting soldiers. "See that he gets to HEAL in Goma. We're heading on up." He jumped down off the bed and took the med bag Natalie handed him. "Go easy, but don't waste time. Understand?"

Jean Pierre watched the soldier salute and climb in to take the doctor's place beside him. As the truck pulled away, he shouted, "Look me up if you ever get to Tanzania—Chumwe. Ask anyone for directions to Lake Victoria Lodge."

Natalie and Mike waved as they climbed back into their Jeep.

Jean Pierre stared up at the drab green canvas above him. It was gloomy inside the truck bed, but the rolled up flaps on the back allowed filtered light in. Did Xavier and Gabe have any light? Jean Pierre remembered the blackness of the storage container he was first held in and shuddered.

CHAPTER 23

Serengeti, Tanzania

Betta felt woozy and disoriented. Had he drugged her? Her head swam as she lifted it off the headrest and stared out the windscreen. A blanket of darkness concealed the landscape. Where were they? She could see the road in the beam of the headlights. It was dirt, rutted, and riddled with potholes filled with stagnant water. Several pairs of glowing pinpoints gathered and moved as a herd of zebra swept into the light and out again.

She turned and looked into the back seat. All four children were asleep, collapsed on each other like a pile of discarded rag dolls. Freedom had a protective arm around his sister. Taji was draped across Sikudhani's lap, while her head rested on Mercy's shoulder.

"They'll sleep for at least another few hours. Time enough to get us where we're going." She looked up to see Cyrus looking at her.

"Why are you doing this? If you want me, why bring the children into this? What do you intend to do with Taji and Sikudhani?"

Cyrus chuckled. "Full of questions, aren't you?" He reached over and placed his hand on her thigh. "I'm in a good mood. Everything is going according to my plan, so I guess it won't hurt to share a little information with you. It's not like you can do anything."

It took everything in her to not flinch at his touch or pull away, but if she wanted to learn what he was up to, she needed to play his game. She said nothing, waiting for him to continue.

"Since the last time we were together, I've had to find a different career path." He smirked at her. "My new job has taken me all across central Africa—Angola, DRC, Burundi, Zambia, Malawi, Mozambique, Kenya, and Tanzania. For reasons I'm sure you understand, I can't go back to Rwanda." He shrugged his shoulders. "No great loss there."

She turned to look out the side window into the velvet blackness. "I can imagine there are rebel groups in any number of places that would appreciate your ability to kill without compunction."

He snorted and removed his hand. "You're brave to be so sarcastic. I'm surprised you have the nerve. I remember you being more timid and submissive."

Betta refused to be baited and ignored his comment. He was right, to some extent. She had changed. Being a mother and responsible for two—no, three—other lives, she had gained courage and strength. She laid her hand on her stomach. No one would harm her children. Not while she had breath in her body.

They drove in silence for a ways before Betta was forced to speak. "I need to relieve myself." Now it was Cyrus' turn to ignore her. She turned to him. "Did you hear me? I need you to stop."

Without a word, he braked and killed the engine. "You'll have to unlock the door." He didn't move. Exasperated, she added, "Please."

The lock clicked up, and she climbed out. Except for the twin beams of the headlights, the night was thick and black, a shroud she could wrap around her. "Please turn off the lights."

She wanted the privacy the darkness provided. Instead, Cyrus got out of the SUV and came around to her side of the vehicle. "What are you doing? Do you honestly think I'd try and run away and leave the children behind?"

A high wail pierced the night. Betta gasped and stepped back against the side of the car. A chorus of barks and human-like chuckles joined the first lone howl.

"Fine, you want me to leave, I will." He turned as if to walk away.

"No, no, I didn't realize..." She felt the comfort of the metal under her hands.

"That you could easily be supper for a pack of hyena?" He lit a cigarette and leaned back against the fender. "Just pee so we can go."

Betta slid down to the opposite end. Embarrassed and humiliated, she took care of business and climbed back inside without speaking. Cyrus finished his smoke and ground it under his boot. He grinned at her through the windscreen as he took his time getting back in. She hated that self-satisfied smirk and wanted to slap it off his face. "God, help me," she muttered under her breath.

Underway again, Betta was determined to learn more of his plan. "So if you're not killing people anymore, what are you doing?"

Cyrus laughed. "You don't give up, do you?"

Betta feigned indifference. "You really think I care or believe anything you say?"

Cyrus' hands tensed on the steering wheel. "You'll care, Pretty Thing, *that* you can believe."

"You think you can just take me against my will again, and my children, too. This isn't Rwanda and no one will condone what you're doing now. I have people who'll miss us. They won't give up looking for us. *That* you can count on."

"Africa is Africa. People disappear all the time, especially women and children. A few might try to raise an alarm, but I've learned they give up soon enough. A few shillings to a hungry man can buy a lot of silence," Cyrus scoffed. "You think your value is in the baked goods you sell or anyone cares about a couple of slum orphans? Your value is in what someone is willing to pay for you. And you, Pretty Thing, are worth a lot. Those kids back there will set me up for months."

Betta stilled. Was he talking about—selling people? Selling her and the children? She knew it happened. It was epidemic across Africa. Jean Pierre had told her thousands of vulnerable children were sold into slavery, sex trafficking, and debt bondage across the continent and over a million globally every year. Was that his plan, to sell her and the children to the highest bidder? Fear grabbed her in a strangle hold. What could she do? How could she fight him? The baby must have felt her distress. He or she kicked and rolled. With the bag between them, Betta massaged her belly with trembling hands. She had to remain calm for the baby's sake. She had to find a means of escape for all their sakes.

CHAPTER 24

Cyrus stifled a yawn. He'd been driving for hours. Dawn set on the eastern horizon waiting to burst forth into another hot, dry day on the savannah. They'd been heading south along the western edge of the Masai Steppes. Avoiding the B3 highway as much as possible, he'd been traveling a rutted dirt road for the past ten hours. His body ached from the jostling and tension of watching the beam-lit track. By his calculations, they were a couple of hours outside of Tanzania's capital city, Dodoma. He would avoid the city and circle around to the east, but for now, he needed rest and food.

He slowed the Toyota as they entered the town of Haneti. It was quiet, too early for children to be going to school or the men marching off to the mines that dotted the hills to the west. With a population of less than ten thousand people, the town consisted of a dozen dirt streets meandering off the paved main road that marked the central market area. Cyrus had been here several times over the past five years. He headed down one of the dusty side roads past a dozen mud and cinderblock homes until he came to a gated wall. He gave the horn one long blast, followed by two short bursts.

Betta roused in the seat beside him and stretched. "Where are we?"

"Just a scroungy little town in the middle of nowhere." The gate swung open, and he pulled the car inside. "Stay put until I tell you otherwise, understand?" She nodded and turned to the children in the back. They were waking up, yawning, and stretching like a litter of puppies after a long nap. "And keep them quiet, or else," he warned.

Cyrus stepped down out of the dusty vehicle and reached under the seat. He pulled the Beretta out, released the magazine, and checked the clip. He looked at Betta and smiled as he snapped the clip back in place. "Does it remind you of old times?" She narrowed her eyes and looked away. He laughed and settled the pistol in his waistband.

"I see you, karibo *(welcome)*, Boss."

Cyrus turned to greet the tall, long-faced Masai. "Jambo *(Hello)*, I see you, Nikusubila."

A huge grin split the old man's face. "Habari ya asubuhi *(good morning)*."

Cyrus pulled out his wallet, searched the contents, and handed the man a wad of paper money. "Niku, go to the market and get food, enough for five people for two days. Take the jerry cans and fill them with petrol."

Niku bobbed and grinned. "No problem, Boss, except my cart is broken. I will have to make several trips."

Cyrus turned back to the car. "Free, get over here." The boy stared at him from the side window, but didn't move. Anger rose. Cyrus hated not being obeyed instantly. He had had men beaten for not responding fast enough. He stomped over, flung the door open, and yanked Freedom from the vehicle. The boy landed in the dirt at his feet. "When I tell you to do something, you do it," he hissed.

Betta jumped from the car and raced around the front. She sprang at Cyrus like a wild woman. "Leave him alone, you monster!" She screamed and pummeled his chest.

Cyrus pushed her away, sending her sprawling next to her son. "Woman, you need to be careful," he warned through gritted teeth. "I've been driving a long time and I'm too tired to put up with any crap from you."

He pulled the boy to his feet. "Go with Niku, and help carry back the supplies and fuel." He bent and drew Freedom up on tiptoe so they were eye to eye. "Don't try anything funny or something really bad will happen to your mother and sister. Understand?"

The boy nodded his head and gulped, "Yes, sir."

Cyrus let him go. "And the next time I tell you to do something, you'd better jump."

Free stumbled backwards, then turned to help his mother to her feet. "Are you okay, Mama?"

"I'm fine, Free." Betta stood and hugged her son. "It's best you do as he says."

Freedom gave Cyrus a nasty look. "Don't you hurt them or I'll... I'll..."

Cyrus chuckled. "You'll what, boy? Hurt me?" He looked him up and down. "Someday maybe, but not today." He shoved him toward Niku. "Now go."

As soon as the gate closed behind them, Cyrus turned back to Betta. It was then he noticed the roundness of her belly. Nervous, she pulled the edges of her sweater across the bulge and looked away. She'd always made sure it was covered before. Now he could see she was obviously pregnant. The revelation enraged him. She was his. No other man was going to plant his seed in her. Before he could stop himself, he reached out and backhanded her across the face, sending her sprawling back in the dirt. "You mayala *(whore)*."

"Mama! Mama!" Mercy cried from the backseat, where Sikudhani kept her from jumping out and racing to her mother's side.

Cyrus slammed the car door shut, effectively blocking out the screams. "Get up."

Betta turned to her knees and pushed herself up to stand in front of him. Her chin jutted out in defiance and her arms crossed. "So now you know, but I am not a whore. I'm married."

Cyrus sneered. "You liar, I don't see a ring. Besides, what man would want you." He grabbed her hand. "Maimed and used?"

Betta jerked her hand away. "Why do *you* want me?"

Cyrus had no answer. He didn't understand his obsession any more now than he did thirteen years ago. He pulled the passenger door open again. "Take them over there to pee, then get them into the house and keep them quiet."

Betta eased past him and lifted each of the children down. They were all crying and clutching at her. "Shh, it's okay. Just do as he says." She herded the children to the small mud and stick structure that served as the latrine.

Cyrus opened the back and took inventory, one eye on her. *Pregnant.* He still raged at the idea. He didn't want another man's child, but he wanted Betta and the boy. They were his. He would make the problem go away once they reached Zambia. With new resolve, he slammed the tailgate closed and followed his prisoners into the house.

CHAPTER 25

It had been a long day. Now the daylight had surrendered as the gray of dusk seeped over the wall and quickly took control. Betta stood at the kitchen window and watched Cyrus with Freedom. It was uncanny how much the boy looked like his father. They were far enough away that she couldn't hear the conversation, and that worried her. What was that sadistic madman saying to her son? Was he poisoning his mind, telling him about the things he did to her all those years ago? A shiver of dread goose-fleshed her arms.

They had spent the day locked in a bare room while Cyrus slept. Betta had tried to entertain the children. Keeping them quiet was a chore, especially little Taji. The boy was a bundle of pent-up energy after his long, drugged sleep. The girls chattered and giggled, playing rhythmic games, slapping their hands and knees in unison. Freedom worried her. He was quiet as he sat splay-legged against the wall. She'd asked him if he was okay and tried to get him to talk, but the boy only shrugged his shoulders and remained mute.

Now, Free stood with Cyrus. He seemed animated, almost happy as they loaded supplies and the jerry cans in the back of the Toyota.

I've got to find a way to get us away from him.

From what little he'd told her, it sounded like Cyrus was a profiteer working the countryside looking for children to take and sell. Did he really intend to sell Mercy, Sikudhani, and Taji? Betta's jaw tightened. She clenched her fists and pounded them against the stucco wall. "You will not harm these children, you monster."

"Did you say something, Mama?" Mercy Grace came to stand next to Betta. "Is the ugali and chapatti almost done?" she asked.

Betta looked down at her daughter. Her heart swelled with love she never imagined she'd ever experience. Few knew the twins were a product of rape by Cyrus Munianeza, and she hoped to keep it that way. She looked back out at her son and frowned.

Turning from the window, she smiled down at Mercy. "Yes, Sweet Girl, your supper is ready."

The children had just settled down to eat when Cyrus and Freedom came in. The boy's face went from open and happy to sullen and closed when he saw his mother. Ignoring her, he took the plate. A mound of ugali, a pile of beans, and a slab of bread covered the surface. With a mumbled thank you, he turned away and settled on a low stool to eat.

Cyrus looked from him to her and smirked. "The boy is smart and strong for his age. Must get it from his old man."

Betta wanted to reach out and slap him. Instead, she looked at her son. He was watching her as he used the bread to scoop a mix of ugali and beans into his mouth. "Andre Freedom, this man will tell you all kinds of lies. Don't believe him. He is evil. Remember, we've talked about the bad men who prey on innocent people." She nodded toward Cyrus. "He's one of them."

"Yes, Mama," Free answered around a mouthful of mush, then lowered his head to the task of finishing his meal.

"Seems our boy here is interested in guns." Cyrus pulled the pistol from his waistband and wiped a hand down the barrel. "We get away from town and I thought I'd show him how to shoot. Right, boy?"

Freedom grinned at Cyrus, then caught his mother's expression. His smile evened out to a flat line. "No, sir," he replied in a whisper.

Betta couldn't stop the tears from gathering in the corners of her eyes. She turned away and busied herself cleaning up. "Once you children are done, wash your hands and face and use the latrine. I imagine we have a long ride ahead of us." She stiffened under the hand Cyrus placed on her shoulder.

"He's not stupid, Pretty Thing. He's figured out I'm his father and there's nothing you can do about it so you might as well accept the fact that we're going to be a family."

Her chest tightened at the implications. What must Freedom think? She'd never really revealed the story of her abduction, and she would never tell either of them they were a product of rape.

Without looking at him, she stepped out from under his hand. Making sure the children were out of ear-shot, she whispered, "He may have your blood, but you have never been nor ever will be his father. He has a father who loves him, and would give his life for him, someone who is teaching him right from wrong by example." She gave him a look that bespoke her contempt. "You can only teach him about hate, and greed, and selfishness."

She watched the rage build as his jaw tightened and his nostrils flared. "Go ahead, hit me. Show him what kind of man you really are." She stiffened her posture in preparation to accept the blow that might come. At the moment, she didn't care. It felt good to let him know she despised him.

Through clenched teeth, he spoke with barely controlled fury. "Don't push me, woman. You'll regret it." He took a deep breath and relaxed his fists. His face changed. A nasty grin twisted his mouth, and he raised an eyebrow. "I won't hurt him or you, but there's nothing stopping me from inflicting a little punishment on the other three."

The blood drained from Betta's face as she looked over at the kids as they finished their meal. He would hurt Mercy, knowing it would hurt her. And what about Sikudhani and Taji? What horrible abuse would he exact on them if she didn't comply? Knowledge and experience told her his threats weren't empty. She was beaten.

For now, she would do as she was told in order to keep the children safe. But soon she would have to talk to Freedom, to explain the circumstances of his conception. She would leave Mercy out of it as long as she could to preserve the child's innocence.

Knowing he won, Cyrus snickered and headed out the door. "Have them ready. We head out in five minutes."

As the children filed past her to put their empty bowls on the counter, she put a hand on Free's shoulder. "Freedom, stay with me a minute. I need to talk to you."

The boy stopped but didn't look up. "Yes, ma'am."

Betta pulled him to the small table and pushed him down in a chair. She kneeled on the floor in front of him and took his hands in her own. "Andre Freedom, you know you are named after my father, your grandfather, and you know he was a good man, right?"

The boy nodded.

"You were named 'Andre' for your grandfather and 'Freedom' as a reminder that life is precious and no human being should have their freedom or their life taken away. Cyrus Munianeza doesn't believe that. He has let Satan control him for a very long time. Many years ago, when terrible things were happening in Rwanda, Cyrus found me. He became obsessed with me. Do you know what that means?"

Again, Free nodded his head.

Betta wasn't sure how to continue. Her time alone with him was limited. She needed to hurry. "He held me against my will, and when I tried to leave, he hurt me." She watched her son look down at the hand that held his own. "I did manage to escape eventually, but it wasn't until I met Auntie Royal, Claudette, and Sonia that I realized I was pregnant."

His chin dropped, and he looked away. What was he thinking? Was he ashamed, hurt? Did he understand what she was trying to say? She lifted his chin. "Son, look at me." His eyes raised to hers. "I was so happy when I learned I was going to have a baby. God gave me a wonderful, precious gift. Having you and your sister was worth everything I went through. I love you more than you'll ever know, and I'm not going to let anyone take you away from me. Understand? Ever." She stood up and pulled him to his feet with her. "No matter what Cyrus says, he is only the man who gave you life. He is not your father. Your father…"

The door banged open. Cyrus stepped in. "Didn't you hear me? We're leaving. Get out to the truck, now!" He stepped aside and waited for them to go out ahead of him.

The vehicle was loaded and running. Niku stood at the gate, ready to open it at Cyrus' signal. Betta went around to the passenger side, Freedom in front of her. He opened the back door to climb in.

"You're riding up front with me this time," Cyrus announced. He was looking at Freedom.

Stunned, Betta wasn't sure what to say or do. What did he have planned? She squeezed Free's hand. "Do as he says. Freedom." She looked into his eyes. "Remember what I said, okay?"

"Yes, Mama," he replied as he swung into the front seat.

Cyrus picked up a jug off the driver's side floorboard and filled a cup. "Here, drink this." He handed the plastic mug across the backseat to Betta. "I've already given the kids theirs."

Betta looked at the faces of the children beside her on the bench seat. The effects of the drug hadn't taken hold yet.

Mercy leaned into her mother. "I'm glad you're riding back here with us. I just wish we could drive during the day so I can see all the animals. Do you suppose we'll be able to see some giraffes before it gets too dark?"

Betta hugged the girl close as she took the cup Cyrus handed her. "I don't know, Darling, but you need to be real quiet, just in case, okay?"

She held the cup without drinking and stared at Cyrus. "I want to stay awake."

Cyrus winked at Freedom. "Our boy here is going to keep me company this time. You drink up and get some sleep."

"But...," Betta stammered.

In an instant, Cyrus' face stilled and became rigid. "Drink it."

Betta's hand shook as she brought the cup to her lips. How could she protect the children if she was asleep? She knew it was out of her hands. She had no choice but to comply.

CHAPTER 26

Darkness enveloped the car as they headed toward the sea. Cyrus looked over at the boy beside him. In the soft glow of the dash, he took in the strong jaw, the proud nose, and the eyes so like his mother's. An unfamiliar feeling struggled to the surface, one he wasn't altogether sure how to deal with. Was it fatherly pride or just macho ego at what he had produced? He had to admit Betta had done a good job raising him. The boy was self-assured, polite, and if the questions he'd asked already were any indication, he was smart and inquisitive.

"So what's your favorite subject in school?"

Free shrugged and wagged his head. "I like math and science a lot, but I guess my favorite is English. Jean Pierre says I have the makings of a good writer."

The thought of another man with Betta made him seethe with jealousy. If he wanted to take him out of the picture—which he did—he needed to know more. "Jean Pierre, huh? Must be French. So what does this Frenchman do for a living?" he asked.

Free's face became animated. "He's a world famous journalist. He goes all over Africa and sometimes the Middle East, taking pictures and reporting on what's happening. That's what I want to do someday, except I want to travel to America, then China, and then to Antarctica. Can you imagine seeing all those cool places?" Without taking a breath, the boy continued expounding on the merits of being a photojournalist. "I could take pictures. Jean Pierre is teaching me how. Maybe, I could even win a big prize like he did. Can you imagine getting to take a photograph of a giant panda in the wild or penguins jumping off of icebergs?"

Cyrus continued to fume, his temper rising the more the kid talked. How could he compete with a famous muzungu *(white foreigner)*? The man would have to be dealt with at some point if he wanted Betta all for himself. For now, Cyrus would have to be satisfied with knowing he had her and his son. Would the boy ever look up to him like he did the Frenchman? *I'll show him a real man.*

"We're away from any towns and everyone else is asleep. Want to try out my pistol? We could pull off the road and do a little target practice. I'll show you how a true marksman handles a gun." He could see the hesitation on Freedom's face.

"My mother wouldn't like that." The boy slumped back against the seat.

Cyrus chuckled. "Who's going to tell her? Not me. Look, she's sound asleep, she'll never know. It will be our little secret." He nudged the boy's shoulder. "You want to be a real man, you got to know how to handle a gun 'cause a camera sure ain't gonna save you if a lion decides you look tasty enough to eat."

Free looked up at him, chewing his lip, and then glanced in the back seat. "Okay, but only for a few minutes, just so I can see what it's like."

Cyrus smiled. "That's my boy. I'll make a man out of you yet. Your mama will be proud when she sees you can protect her."

Freedom's chest puffed out. "Yeah. I'm the man of the house when Jean Pierre's away, so it's my job to make sure nothing bad happens."

Cyrus' smile turned to a grimace at the mention of the Frenchman. "You can forget about him. I'm your father and you're with me now. Understand?"

Freedom's eyes got big and his expression sobered. "Yes, sir."

The headlights picked out a track leading off the side of the road into the bush. Cyrus jerked the wheel and guided the Surf off the shoulder and onto the rutted trail. A jog around a tangle of brush and a large termite mound brought them to a clear space and a wadi of stagnant water. The light beam swept across a tusked warthog drinking at the shallow pool. He lifted his ugly head, snorted, and dashed away with his tail raised like a flag.

Cyrus killed the engine but left the lights on. "Come on." He climbed out of the car and stretched, wondering if Free would join him. A small smile crossed his face when the boy came to stand silently beside him, arms folded across his chest.

He pulled the gun from where it rode in his waistband and checked the clip. The Beretta Px4 Storm was a couple of years old, but Cyrus made sure it was always clean, loaded, and in working order. "First rule is, don't point a gun unless you intend to fire it and when you do, shoot to kill. When you're ready to fire, release the safety or nothing's going to happen." He spread his legs and pulled the gun up to shoulder level. "You want a good solid stance and a two-handed grip. Aim down the barrel and ease the trigger back."

He fired off a half dozen rounds in rapid succession. Free jumped back when the spent casings started flying and covered his ears. Satisfied with the damage he'd done to the community of weaver bird nests hanging from the branches of an acacia tree, Cyrus lowered the pistol. "And that's how it's done." He looked down at the boy. "Ready to give it a try?"

Free looked from Cyrus to the gun and shook his head. "No, sir, I might kill something."

Cyrus laughed. "That's the idea, kid. This ain't a toy." He grabbed the boy's arm and pressed the gun into his hand. Standing behind him, he kicked the boy's feet shoulder width apart and placed his hands over Free's. He could feel them tremble. "Relax. Take a deep breath and hold it through the shots." Cyrus pulled Free's arms up and whispered in his ear. "Close one eye and sight down the barrel through the crosshairs. Aim for that group of nests on that lower branch. You got it. The gun will fire each time you pull the trigger. You have about five shots left."

The gun jerked in a series of sharp explosions. The cluster of round teardrop nests swayed, but stayed intact. Free smiled up at Cyrus, his eyes round with excitement. "I almost did it!"

Cyrus took the gun and extracted the dead clip. "You'll be a pro in no time, just like your old man." He slid a full magazine in place and chambered a round. "Ready to try by yourself?"

Free took the pistol in both hands. His tongue worked his lips as he squeezed one eye shut and straighten his arms. Without Cyrus to take the brunt of the recoil, Free flew backwards with the first shot and bounced against his chest.

"Easy, don't forget your feet. Plant them solid. And don't lock your arms."

Free steadied himself and tried again. This time two of the nests disintegrated. "Wow, did you see that? I did it!"

Cyrus took the gun, put the safety back on, and walked back to the car to retrieve the leather holster from under the driver's seat. "You're a natural. Come on. We've got to get to Dar before sunup."

CHAPTER 27

Northeastern DRC

It was Tambwe who heard the first rock tumble down the pile. A pinprick of light as bright as the sun at full day, blinded the four men. A surge of adrenalin and hope sent Xavier scrambling up the heap, Gabe right behind him.

"They've found us, Boss!" Gabe exclaimed.

"Here, help me move these rocks." Xavier handed one down to Gabe who shimmied down and added it to their previous pile. It was a slow process, but gradually the tiny beam of light enlarged and a lantern was passed through followed by Emmanuel's head.

"Uncle Xavier, am I glad to see you," He laughed, then grew serious. "How many are alive?"

"There's only four of us left to take out. Two injured that will need medical care. One is pretty serious."

Emmanuel managed to get an arm through. Xavier clasped his nephew's forearm. "Thank you for not giving up." He almost broke down, his voice cracking with a jumble of emotions.

"Come on, let's get you out."

Xavier stepped back down the slope. "No, the injured go first. Can you get a backboard in? I don't think Gabe and I can get Benga up here without doing more damage."

"Benga's alive?" Emmanuel's face brightened. He backed out, and Xavier could hear more rock being moved. The hole widened substantially, and a canvas stretcher slid through the opening. Gabe helped Xavier work it down to the bottom and unfold it. Nestled inside were four bottles of water and a C collar. Xavier passed a bottle to Tambwe and unscrewed another to take a long drink. Nothing ever tasted so good.

He gently lifted Benga's head and pressed the bottle to his lips. "It's water, Benga. Drink up." The moisture on his dry, cracked lips roused him and he gulped the water with greed.

"Whoa, slow down. We have plenty." Xavier laughed. "I'm going to put this collar around your neck to support it and we're going to strap you on this stretcher and get you out of here. I won't lie, it's going to be rough and will probably hurt, but you're getting out. You're going home."

A single tear escaped and slid down Benga's dirty face. "Thank you," he whispered.

Gabe helped him secure the injured man to the board. With one of them on each side, they lifted him up and handed him off to Emmanuel and another man pressed into the opening. Tambwe was next. Gabe maneuvered another stretcher down and laid it out alongside the older man. They eased him onto the canvas, taking care not to jostle his leg. The compound fracture to his femur was severe. Xavier had packed gauze around the protruding bone and wrapped an Ace bandage around the site of the injury to secure it and reduce the blood loss.

As they prepared to lift him, Xavier at his head, Tambwe reached up and grabbed his wrist with his good arm. "You said we'd get out, and you were right. You kept us from giving up. Now I'm gonna see my granddaughter again." He grinned and gave him a thumbs-up. "You get me out of this here hole, and I ain't never coming back."

Xavier's strength was stretched to the limit. The lack of nourishment and air had taken a toll on his body. He grunted and groaned as he worked up the slide, Gabe pushing from the bottom end. "Almost there, keep pushing."

Finally, he was relieved of his burden. He took a couple of deep breaths and reached a hand down to Gabe. "Come on, my friend, let's get out of here."

Xavier helped the little man through the opening. He looked back at the hellhole that had been their prison and a tomb for those who didn't survive. A chill ran through him at the thought that it could have been his grave as well.

Understanding the miracle God had given him, he bowed his head in gratitude. "Thank you, Lord. The mountain moved." He looked at the newly formed resting place of the victims. "Rest in peace, my friends. Rest in peace."

Cheers and backslaps followed as he was helped through the hole to the other side. Emmanuel threw himself at him, almost knocking him down. Xavier wrapped his arms around his nephew.

Spent with emotion, he cried into the young man's shoulder, "You saved my life. Thank you."

Gabe's voice boomed off the walls. "I hate to break up this happy reunion, but I really want to get out of here. This place isn't safe, and it gives me the creeps. Save the hugs for outside, okay?"

The stretchers were already headed topside, leaving a small contingent of men to help get Xavier and Gabe out safely. Xavier chose to walk out, Emmanuel supporting him. Two men made a sling with their arms, and Gabe settled in for a ride to the surface. "Now this is the way to travel," he joked as he raised a water bottle in salute.

Fifteen long minutes later, they stepped out into the daylight. Xavier flinched and covered his eyes. White flashes exploded behind his eyelids. As they slowly dissolved, he drew his hand away and squinted at the scene around him. There were soldiers everywhere. Red berets and FADRC patches on their uniforms indicated they were regular army and not Muteko's men.

In the back of a green, canvas covered truck, Xavier could see a white man and woman working on Benga and Tambwe. Relief flooded him, knowing the responsibility for their care was now in the hands of qualified physicians. Xavier moved to the back of the truck. "Will they be okay?"

The burly, bearded man grinned down at him. "You did a good job of keeping them alive. We're taking them down to Goma. Both will need surgery, but they'll pull through thanks to you."

The lady came to kneel at the edge of the truck bed. "Are you Xavier? Henri and Peter have been worried sick about you as well as a man named Gabe."

Xavier chuckled. "Glad they missed us." He frowned in concern. "What about the other white man, J.P. Fontaine? How is he?"

"He's down the mountain at HEAL Hospital as we speak." The big doctor jumped from the back to land in front of Xavier. "We've got to get these two out of here. Any message we can give your friend?"

"Tell him we're okay and will see him soon." Xavier shook the man's hand. "And thanks for coming to the rescue."

"That's what DWB *(Doctors Without Borders)* does best." The American hopped up onto the truck bed.

Xavier watched the truck pulled away, the two Americans back attending to their patients. He turned to Emmanuel. "Come on. Let's get something to eat. I'm starving."

Gabe, having made the surface quicker than Xavier and Emmanuel, sat at a table slurping what looked like a huge bowl of stew. An empty bottle of Coke sat in front of him.

The two joined him under the kitchen tent. Xavier pulled out a chair and settled in with a weary sigh. The adrenalin that had kept him going for the past hour had drained away, leaving him completely spent.

Emmanuel pushed a Coke in front of him and put another to his own lips.

"Could I have some water too, please?" Xavier asked the server as an identical bowl of steamy stew was placed before him.

"I think it's monkey," Gabe said between bites, "but it's the best stuff I've ever tasted."

Xavier stabbed a chunk of meat, blew on it, and dropped it in his mouth. Gabe was right. It tasted wonderful. "Mmm, that's good." It didn't take long to finish the whole bowl. His hunger satisfied, Xavier was working on his second bottle of water when he steeled himself to ask the question that had been plaguing him since he crawled out of that hole.

He turned to his nephew. "So how did you do all this?" He waved the water bottle around to take in the controlled chaos that surrounded them. "More importantly, how was Jean Pierre when they took him out of here?"

Emmanuel patted his arm. "Like the doctor said, he's in a hospital in Goma as we speak."

Before Emmanuel could elaborate, an Army Jeep pulled into the clearing. Xavier's face broke into a huge grin as Peter and Henri jumped out and ran over to the shelter.

Gabe jumped up, knocking his chair over. "Dudes, am I glad to see you!" He and Xavier limped over to greet their team.

Henri gave Xavier's hand an enthusiastic shake and planted a kiss on each cheek. "We're so glad you're safe. When we found the office unlocked, and you two gone, we didn't know what to think. And when you didn't come back by nightfall, we knew something was wrong. Peter drove down to Goma to call headquarters, while I tried to figure out where you guys went."

It dawned on Xavier he didn't know what day it was or how long they'd been trapped. "What is today?"

Henri and Peter traded places. Peter pumped Xavier's hand. "Bonjour, Boss. It is Tuesday, December twelfth."

Xavier and Gabe exchanged looks. In a voice filled with raw emotion, Xavier said, "We were in that hole for three days."

"Felt more like a couple of weeks," Gabe added.

From the time they were taken at gunpoint, their ordeal had lasted a total of five days. Xavier had a sudden thought and turned to Henri. "Does Marie know?"

Henri and Peter looked at each other. One rubbed his neck. The other chewed his lip.

"What?"

"Well, Boss, it's like this, we couldn't find the satphone so when I took the truck down to Goma to report you missing to the police, I called headquarters. They said they'd get a hold of Mrs. Mwena and wanted us to stay put in case you were just at one of the devastated villages. So we didn't do anything, just finished getting ready for the medical teams to arrive." Peter hung his head. "Sorry, Boss, we didn't know you'd been taken."

Henri picked up the story. "We've been going crazy waiting, not knowing what had happened. We were at the field hospital when army guys came and asked Dr. Mike and Miss Natalie to come with them because of a cave-in at one of the mines. They sent word from the hospital in Goma about what was happening here. Before that, we didn't know you and Gabe had been kidnapped and were trapped down in the mine."

Xavier could see the two men felt bad about not figuring out what happened sooner, but he was more concerned with what Marie was going through. He shrugged off their regrets. "Don't worry about it. It's over now. Back to my wife—so no one has called her to let her know we're out and safe?"

Peter and Henri looked at each other and shrugged their shoulders. "We don't know."

Xavier gave them each a pat on the back and raced off to find a phone. He headed toward a man shouting orders. "Excuse me, sir. Are you in charge?"

The formidable-looking officer turned toward Xavier with a scowl that looked like it was permanently etched onto his dark face. He braced his hands on his hips. "Who are you?"

Xavier extended his hand. "Mwena Xavier. I was one of the captives and was rescued from the mine. I want to thank you and your men for all your efforts."

The officer's countenance changed dramatically. A grin replaced the scowl. His eyes lost their angry glare behind heavy black-rimmed glasses. He took Xavier's hand in his and pumped it enthusiastically. "Monsieur Mwena, it is a pleasure. I'm Commander Lubuya.

"I just wish we could have been here sooner, but between quashing rebel activities, directing evacuations, and overseeing security, my men are stretched to their limits. It seems you have a troop of people looking out for you. First, a young man came to our barracks telling us this wild story of wazungas *(white people)* being held captive and a cave-in at a gold mine. Then Mr. Fontaine managed to get a message through to his editor in France and also made a call to a lady named Marie. Between the three of them, they were able to alert the proper authorities. The lady was very insistent that the government send troops in immediately. The young man, Emmanuel Kabewe, gave us all the details. We've been monitoring Muteko's movements for a while, but this was the first time we've had legitimate cause to arrest him and his men."

"The lady you spoke of, Marie, is my wife." Xavier chuckled. "She can be very persuasive when she sets her mind to something. Sir, I need to let her know I'm okay. Would it be possible to use your phone?"

"I've set up communications in Muteko's office over there. Tell my man you've got my permission. He'll put you through."

Xavier gave him a quick bow. "Thank you, Commander Lubuya." He hurried to the block building, anxious to hear Marie's voice and tell her he was alive.

CHAPTER 28

Goma, DRC

The room came into focus bit by bit. Jean Pierre could make out fuzzy figures clustered at the end of his bed. He tried to lift his head and shoulders, but fell back as if weighed down by a ton of bricks stacked on his forehead and chest. His movements caught everyone's attention and when he opened his eyes again, they were lined up on either side of his bed. He looked up into the anxious face of Xavier. "So you made it out."

"Yeah, Gabe and I and two others, thanks to you and Emmanuel." He wrapped an arm around Emmanuel's shoulder and gave it a squeeze. "This guy is a hero."

Emmanuel stood a little taller. "I just followed our plan, that's all."

"Dude, you were brilliant."

Jean Pierre carefully swiveled to see Gabe. The little man's head barely cleared the elevated side rail. He was wearing a hat, sporting the FFF rooster, the logo of the French soccer league. "New hat?"

"Yeah, I found it in a shop in town. I lost my other one in the mine."

Jean Pierre looked back at Xavier. "Has anyone contacted Betta?"

"Your editor, Mr. Colbert, has been trying to reach her for several days. She's not answering his calls." Xavier pulled a cell phone from his pocket. "We can try again. Goma's cell service is okay in-country. I'm not sure how good it is going to Tanzania." Xavier hit the contact number and handed the phone to Jean Pierre.

He pressed the phone to his ear and willed it to ring. A computer voice came on to announce that the phone was out of service and to try again later. Frustrated, he handed the phone back. "No answer. That's not like her to have her phone off. Can you try the Lodge? Ask for Tom or Gwen."

"There's no need, J.P."

Jean Pierre turned toward the door. Tom McMillian's frame filled the doorway. "Tom, what are you doing here?"

The lanky Englishman twisted the hat in his hands and stepped into the room. "I flew in and came right to the hospital. J.P., I hate to be the bearer of bad news, especially in the shape you're in and with what you've been through." He hesitated. The hat in his hands was a crumpled mess, his knuckles white to match his pasty face. "Betta's disappeared. The children are gone too."

Without thinking, Jean Pierre pushed himself up on his elbows. Pain tore across his torso and flattened him back against the sheets. Through clenched teeth, he whispered, "How? Tell me everything."

Gabe moved back out of the way and the tall Englishman took his place beside the bed. "Moses delivered a letter to her four days ago. We didn't know who it was from or what the contents were. We wrongly assumed you had summoned her and the children to join you here. Both Gwen and I thought it was odd that she'd leave so suddenly without letting anyone know. Then when we heard from Marie what had happened, we knew you couldn't have sent the letter. Royal and Claudette searched your house and found this under one of the children's beds." He pulled a folded sheet of paper from his pocket and handed it to Jean Pierre. "She must have dropped it and a breeze swept it under the bed where nobody noticed it."

With a thundering heart and shaky hands, he unfolded the message. It was short and written in a manly scrawl across the page. When Jean Pierre reached the bottom and read Cyrus' initials, his hammering heart stopped. He gasped for air and struggled to comprehend this new nightmare. Xavier eased the paper from his hand. Jean Pierre watched his face blanch as he read the letter. They locked eyes. "He's got her. That madman has my wife and kids," Jean Pierre announced in a tight voice.

Xavier was one of the few people who knew the whole story of Betta's captivity. Having grown up with her in Kamena, everyone had assumed the two would marry. Xavier's flight to Kigali to find himself, and the subsequent genocide, changed everything. It wasn't until Jean Pierre asked him to be his best man at his wedding that he learned what had happened to his beautiful neighbor. He found out Cyrus was the one who ordered the killing of his family and many others across the countryside. Like Jean Pierre, he knew what the man was capable of.

Careful to avoid the intravenous needle taped to the back of Jean Pierre's hand, Xavier reached over and wrapped his hand around his friend's in a show of solidarity. In a voice solemn with resolve, he made a promise. "We'll get them back. No matter how long it takes or how far we have to go. You saved my wife, now it's my turn to help save yours."

Tom interrupted. "The police traced her to a bus depot in Magu Kahangara. A man there said he saw a beautiful, pregnant woman meet a bald, bearded man. They got in a green Toyota Hilux Surf with a black snorkel. After that, nothing."

Jean Pierre's brow creased. "What about the kids? Did the man see them?"

Tom shook his head. "I'm afraid not. He must have had them stashed somewhere. J. P. I've come to take you home. The police are searching and as soon as you're well enough, I know you'll want to join them."

Jean Pierre steeled himself against the pain and sat up. He pulled the needle from his skin. "Get me my pants and get me out of here. I'm going after them."

It took some convincing to get Jean Pierre to rest in bed while arrangements were made. Tom needed to get the plane ready for their return flight to Tanzania. After a call to FARC headquarters, it was decided that Gabe would head back to the refugee hospital site with Peter and Henri. He would oversee the operation there while Xavier dealt with the authorities about allowing Emmanuel to leave the country. The biggest hurdle was telling Marie that he wasn't coming directly home.

"Marie, honey, I'm fine really. Jean Pierre is the one that needs looking after right now. He's frantic, as you can imagine. No one knows where Munianeza may have taken Betta and the kids. I have to help him. If nothing else, I need to be there to see that he doesn't overdo after everything he's been through, plus the surgery." He didn't exactly tell her Jean Pierre was determined to go after Cyrus himself. She wouldn't appreciate the idea of him possibly exposing himself to a known murderer.

"I know he's your best friend and I know you feel like you owe him—that *we* owe him for my life, but please come home as soon as you can. I need you. The kids need you." Marie's voice took on a softer tone. "I need to feel your arms around me so I know you're really safe."

Relieved, Xavier smiled. "I need that, too. I'll be home soon, I promise. In the meantime, keep praying for Betta and the children." Tom tapped him on the shoulder and pointed to his watch. "Marie, honey, I've got to go. I love you."

"Sorry to rush you, but we only have a small window to get in the air before the runways are closed. The army restricts any planes from taking off or landing after 5pm."

Xavier stepped back into the hospital room, where Emmanuel was helping Jean Pierre with his shoes. "Okay, looks like we're all set."

Emmanuel stood, concern etched on his face. "What about me, Uncle?"

Xavier stepped around the bed and gave his nephew's shoulder a reassuring pat. "You don't think I'd leave you here after I just found you again? Jean Pierre's boss and my boss both managed to pull some strings. We'll pick up your travel permit on the way to the airport. The governments involved are granting you temporary amnesty under Article fourteen of the Universal Declaration of Human Rights. Once we get back to France, we'll get a permanent VISA worked out. You're coming home, Emmanuel."

The room remained quiet except for the sobs emanating from the young man in Xavier's arms. "I can't believe I'm finally going home—that I'm safe."

CHAPTER 29

Dar es Salaam, Tanzania

Betta woke to a strange mix of smells and sounds. She rubbed her eyes and looked out the window. They were parked next to a wooden building with a bright red door that didn't match the rest of the gray, weathered siding. The car windows were each down an inch, letting in the sour smell of dead fish and salt water. The screech of sea gulls drew her attention to a flotilla of boats bobbing on choppy water. Men, naked to the waist, were lifting and pulling nets from the boats to shore. In the distance, several huge ships sat like a pod of hippos relaxing after an evening meal.

The children were beginning to stir. Betta sat Mercy up and leaned forward to touch Free's shoulder over the seatback. "Freedom, are you okay? Where's Cyrus?"

"I'm fine." He shrugged her hand away. "He's talking to those men over there."

Betta could hear the confusion and troubled tone in her son's voice. "Did he hurt you while I was sleeping?"

"No."

Betta swallowed the lump that was threatening to cut off her air. "Freedom, what did he say to you?"

"He told me he wanted to be my father, but you ran away from him and he's been looking for me for a long, long time."

Betta sighed and let her hand drop back into her lap. "He lied. He hasn't…"

Before she could say anymore, the driver's door opened and Cyrus slid into the seat. He looked back at Betta. "Awake. Good. I'm going to pull around to the back. Get the kids ready to get out and move quickly. No crying or noise, understand? Everyone goes inside, children first. No one talks. When you get inside, set them down along the wall and don't move until I tell you differently."

Betta knew better than to argue. She shook the children. "Time to wake up. We're getting out here."

The car had stopped next to a set of double metal doors. One side opened and the biggest man Betta had ever seen stepped out. Xavier's brother, Theo, was a giant of a man, hard muscled from working the fields, and as tall and solid as a baobab, but this man was a monster. His small, dark, deeply scarred head sat on a block of muscle and sinew that connected to bulging shoulders. He wore a white t-shirt that strained to cover his powerful chest. His legs, each the size and length of a tree, were encased in faded denim. Cyrus, as big as he was, looked like a child next to the man.

"Don't talk. Don't look at him. Just do as I said," he instructed.

The door locks clicked up and Betta used a shaky hand to pull the handle and push it out. "Children, do as he says and come with me." She waited as the three children scooted across the seat and climbed out to stand around her.

"Mama, I have to go to the bathroom," Mercy announced.

"Me, too." Taji and Sikudhani both added.

Freedom got out and turned to face the group. "Shut up. Didn't you hear what he said?"

Betta reached out and grabbed Free's chin in her hand. "That wasn't necessary. You may be angry with me and scared, but you don't talk to others that way. Now hold Mercy's hand and go inside."

They trouped past the giant at the door, all eyes to the ground. Taji stopped, craned his head back, and stared at the man, openmouthed. A puddle appeared on the ground between his feet. He wrapped an arm around Betta's leg and whimpered. She hustled them inside and settled them along the wall as instructed. Taji buried his face against the roundness of Betta's lap. She stroked the boy's course curls and watched Cyrus follow two men into a lighted half-glass windowed room. The giant remained at the door, arms crossed, and feet spread.

The men spoke in low voices Betta couldn't hear. At one point, Cyrus turned and pointed toward her. There was some backslapping and laughter, then a pile of bills was pulled from a drawer. One of the men methodically counted out the money into Cyrus' hands. Their deal concluded, he came out and walked toward the prisoners along the wall as he stuffed the money into a pouch concealed under his shirt.

"Time to go. Freedom, help your mama to her feet and get back out to the car."

The boy jumped up. "Yes, sir."

Betta came to her feet with Taji still clinging to her side.

"Only you and Free. The others stay here." Cyrus pulled the little boy away from her.

He whimpered and stretched out his arms to her. The look on his little face bespoke his terror. Betta froze. Could he really expect her to leave without all the children? Her heart sank and fear flooded her body in trembling waves. Yes, he would. He'd done it to her before when he forced her to leave baby Fellie behind the day he took her captive all those years ago.

She had to think fast. What could she say to stop him? To get him to change his mind? The image of the money being counted out flickered across her mind like a scene on the TV in the lounge at the lodge. Hope surged. He wanted money. She would convince him she could get him more than the men had counted out.

"Cyrus, I need to talk to you." She looked at the other three men in the room. "Alone."

Cyrus huffed, pulled at his waistband, and grabbed her hand. Pulling her along behind him, he headed back to the glass room. "Seems the little lady needs some private time. Wouldn't want to disappoint, now would I?"

The men laughed and joined the giant at the double door. In single file, they stepped outside. The last one made a crude gesture and reached for a cigarette pack as the door banged shut.

Once inside the room, Betta closed the door and leaned against it. She would have to be convincing if she wanted Cyrus to believe her. She looked out through the glass at Freedom. The boy stared back, his mouth a firm line. His face guarded. She couldn't do this with him watching. What would he think? *I'm doing this for you and your sister.*

She felt for the light switch behind her and turned it off. The room plunged into semi-darkness with only enough light to make out Cyrus' features. She checked to make sure it was dark enough that the children couldn't see into the office. It was time to put her plan into motion. She prayed he would not dismiss it out of hand. If she could make it enticing enough, maybe she could convince him it was a better way to go. She pasted a smile on her face and looked up at him. "I know how we can get our hands on a lot of money. That way Freedom and Mercy can both stay with us. I know someone who would take Sikudhani and Taji, so they wouldn't be a problem."

Cyrus pinched her chin between his thumb and finger. "More money would be a good thing. I'm tired of moving around so much. But the kids are no concern of mine, and I've already got a pocket load of money for them, so why would I change my plan now?"

This was it. She had to tell him the truth and pray he would believe her. She pulled her chin from his grasp and chewed her lip. With an audible sigh, she began to explain. "Mercy is more than Freedom's sister. She's his twin. I didn't know I was pregnant with twins until I delivered them. Freedom is your son and Mercy Grace is your daughter."

She dared to look up and watch for his reaction. His jaw clenched and unclenched. His eyes narrowed and his nostrils flared. "Why didn't you tell me?" He backhanded her before she saw it coming. The force of the blow knocked her to the floor. A flood of expletives rained down on her.

His reaction brought back all the memories of the beatings she had endured as his captive. She knew from experience to grovel and apologize was the only way to placate him. She stayed on the floor. "I'm sorry. It was a while before I realized you thought she was younger and someone else was her father. By then I thought I was protecting her." She rose to her knees in front of him. "Don't you see now, you can't sell her?

"You saw the bakery in Chumwe. It belongs to me, a wedding present from my husband. I could sell it. It's worth a lot of money. And Jean Pierre would pay a lot of money to get me back. It's his child I'm carrying." She wrapped an arm around her belly.

Cyrus was still. Then he surprised her by wiping a hand across his face and dropping into the lone chair in the room. Betta could see he was thinking about everything she said. *Please God, let him agree.* He stood and turned his back on her. The quiet was unnerving and uncharacteristic for him. Betta's hands began to shake. Her palms grew moist. If he didn't go along with her, she didn't know what she'd do.

Abruptly, he turned around and pulled her to her feet. "You stupid whore. You should have told me about Mercy sooner. These men don't play games, and they won't like losing out on the profit she would bring. I'm not giving up my money. I earned it. The other two will have to stay, but the girl goes with us." He gripped her arms and drew her up to eye level. "And you, Mrs. Betta Fontaine, aren't going anywhere but with me, understand?"

"But... but Taji and Sikudhani are just babies. How can you discard them like that? Please let me find them a home," she pleaded. "I know a couple who would take them." An idea sprang to life in her head. "I'm sure they'd be willing to cover your expenses. They're the English couple who own the lodge where I work."

That got Cyrus' attention. Talk of money always did. Betta plowed ahead, improvising as she went. "We could take them with us and I could make a few calls to make the arrangements for selling the bakery and making the exchange with the McMillians." She didn't bring up Jean Pierre again. That seemed to agitate him and was probably useless, anyway. She placed her hand on his arm. "We could go away with enough money to start over. To be a family." The thought turned her stomach, but she would do whatever was necessary to protect her children, even if it meant sacrificing herself for them.

CHAPTER 30

The muscled giant made Cyrus nervous every time he was around him. He reminded him of the man he'd battled and killed at the church that day in Kamena. He ran a finger along the jagged scar that dissected his lip and cheek. That man had been strong, but not as strong as an eight millimeter round in the back.

This man, Mwamba, was an enforcer for Nguvu ya Giza. The Dark Force had men like this stretched across central Africa making sure merchandise didn't escape, money wasn't stolen, and to mete out punishment to those stupid enough to cross them.

He just wanted to make his delivery, get his money, and be on his way. Having three less in the car and a pocket full of cash would make the next part of their journey easier.

"So you want some alone time, huh?" Cyrus reached for Betta. She pushed against his chest but remained in the circle of his arms.

"How much did they pay you?" she asked.

"Enough to keep us in style for a few months. Why?"

"I want my daughter with me. I'm not leaving here without her. Taji and Sikudhani, either."

Cyrus looked at her and snickered. "Sorry Pretty Thing. It's a done deal. Besides, we'll need the cash to live on."

The next words out of her mouth sent his mind whirling. The little girl that looked so much like her mother was his daughter, Freedom's twin. Could he believe her? Somehow, he knew she wasn't lying. The fact that she'd kept the information from him sent him into an instant rage. He hated not having control. His reaction was immediate.

Blood trickled from the corner of Betta's mouth. He turned away from her and collapsed on a chair.

The realization that he had just sold his own daughter to sex traffickers caused his stomach to churn. He'd lost count of the numbers of children he'd rounded up and handed over. It had been a lucrative business for the past nine years. Would his reputation among the traffickers gain him any leverage in keeping Mercy? He thought not. She was a beautiful child and would likely go for a high price—more than he had in his pocket right now, anyway.

He needed to think, and Betta was yammering on about the bakery and the Frenchman. Who did she think she was, telling him what they should do? He jumped to his feet, pulling her up with him. He was the boss here. She would do what he said or else.

As angry as he was, he paid attention when she mentioned more money from the English couple. He'd seen how beautiful the lodge was. Only affluent wazungas *(white people)* or rich Africans could afford to stay in an upscale place like that. They had money, no doubt about that, and the bakery looked prosperous and well maintained. Maybe she was on to something.

The biggest problem was the deal he'd already made. These guys didn't mess around. They wouldn't take kindly to him reneging on their deal. In fact, they were more likely to kill him, take the money back, and sell off the whole lot including Betta and Freedom. He opened the door and pushed her out. "Go sit with the kids. I need to think."

"We could do it, Cyrus. Think about it. Enough money to go away and start over."

He shut the door in her face. He didn't have much time. The big brute and the other two would be getting restless. He needed a plan that would guarantee The Dark Force wouldn't come after them. What good would all that money do if he was dead?

He left the inner office and headed to the outside door. Betta and the children were huddled together along the wall. "Follow my lead and don't mention anything we talked about. If you want this to work, keep your mouth shut." He pulled the metal door open and stepped out. Twilight had settled in. The wharf and shoreline were quiet and virtually deserted. He took out his cell phone and dialed a number from memory. It was answered on the first ring.

"Report," commanded the person on the other end.

Cyrus walked up to the group smoking and leaning against the wall. He wanted them to overhear his side of the conversation. "The shipment you requested has been delivered. Yes, I understand. I'll be leaving right away. Next delivery to Mombasa." He paused. "Yes, sir, always a pleasure." He closed the phone and pulled a crushed cigarette pack from his shirt pocket.

"Seems I'm headed back to Kenya tonight." He leaned in to catch a light from one of the men. Cyrus didn't know this one. He was new since the last time he was there. The man looked like a child next to Mwamba. Abdul, the other man, was about the same size as Cyrus and just as powerfully muscled. He hoped he wouldn't have to take either of them on, especially Mwamba.

His cigarette finished, he crushed it under his boot. "Guess I'll get my wife and son and head out. You keeping the others here or taking them out to the ship tonight?" He opened the back of the Toyota and pulled out a plastic bottle of water and took a long pull, then wiped his mouth. Behind his back, he fumbled with the bottle of pills and managed to slip it in his pants pocket.

Abdul took a long drag from his cigarette. "Got another load coming in, due in a few hours. Faheem drew the short stick, so he's standing guard duty while Mwamba and I get something to eat. Once this last batch arrives, we'll take 'em out."

This was good news for Cyrus. Faheem was short and skinny. With a scruffy beard and a thatch of wild, kinky hair, he looked more Ethiopian than Tanzanian. Cyrus could slit his throat before the man felt the knife against his skin.

"Well, if I want to make it back to Kenya by tomorrow afternoon, I'd better get a move on." He tucked the water jug under his arm, moved to the door, and stepped inside.

"Let's go." He motioned to Betta.

All five stood and started toward him, Freedom first, then Betta carrying Taji. As she walked past, Cyrus reached for the boy. "I'll take him. Go get in the car. Remember, no talking. Don't say or do anything, just get in. Don't look at those men. Keep your eyes down like a good, obedient wife."

He pulled her face up to look into her eyes. "If you don't do exactly like I say, you'll all die right here, right now and it won't be me that does the killing." He could see the fear in her eyes, along with something else. Was it defiance? He hoped for her sake it wasn't.

She stepped through the door. Cyrus put his foot up against the jamb, effectively stopping Mercy and Sikudhani. He sat the boy down next to them. "You girls take Taji and go back and sit down." He pulled a few loose sweets from his pocket and flipped them to Sikudhani, and handed the jug to Mercy. "Here's something to drink. Try to sleep and we'll be back for you soon." Mercy looked up at him. She tried to look defiant, but her lip trembled and tears welled up in her eyes.

"I want to go with my mother."

He gave her a pat on the shoulder. "Your mama's coming back in a little while. Remember, no crying. Everything will be okay." It surprised him how much her tears affected him now that he knew she was his daughter. He gave her a smile and closed the door behind him.

CHAPTER 31

The door shut behind Betta. Startled, she turned around and tried the handle. It was locked with her children and Cyrus inside. "Freedom, help me!" she called to her son.

Freedom raced back to her side. "Mama, he said to get in the car." He tried to pull her away from the door.

"But your sister's inside."

"Please, Mama, do as he says. Those men are watching."

Betta looked back at the curious stares of the three men leaning against the wall at the end of the building. The big one pulled up and looked like he was about to head their way. Was she making things worse? Her whole being was in turmoil. She couldn't trust Cyrus, but these men were an unknown quantity. Would they even flinch when they drew their guns and shot them all?

"Come on. We'll wait in the car," Free pleaded.

She didn't want to move. A moan welled up within her. She pressed it down and took a step away from the door. With slow reluctance, she allowed Free to lead her toward the car. After only a dozen steps, the door swung open and Cyrus stepped out. His lips tightened and a muscle in his jaw worked when his eyes met Betta's. In a few long strides, he was at her side and gripped her arm.

"I told you to wait in the car," he hissed as he marched her along. He opened the passenger door and pushed her in. "Free, get in the back."

"I suppose I'll be seeing you in a month or so with another order," he shouted to the men. He climbed in, started the engine, and backed out of the alleyway without looking back.

Betta's lip trembled. Tears threatened as the door her daughter was behind grew smaller. "She's your daughter and you're just going to leave her to those monsters? You'd let them put their filthy hands on your own child and do God knows what to her?"

Cyrus didn't answer as he turned out into the narrow street. Several blocks away, he pulled over and swung sideways in his seat. "This is all your fault. If you had told me the truth to begin with, Mercy would be with us. Now I have to risk everything to get her out of there." He saw the look on her face and knew what she was thinking. "They won't touch her. It's against the rules. Dark Force doesn't like his property damaged or used, before it gets to its new owner. If you want your daughter back, you'd better do everything I say, without argument." He didn't wait for her reply as he swung back out onto the roadway.

"What are you going to do?" Betta asked, her voice subdued.

"First, we're going to get some more supplies and something to eat. By that time, Abdul and Mwamba will be off feeding their faces. If we can time this just right, they'll be busy with another shipment coming in and I can sneak in and get Mercy out."

"What about Taji and Sikudhani?" Free asked from the back seat.

"Them too, if I think I can get away clean." He looked at Betta. "You better hope those rich friends of yours want those kids 'cause if they don't pay, they're gone."

Twenty minutes later, they finished loading the car with enough supplies to last at least a month in the bush. Cyrus looked at his watch. "It's time for you to make a call, Pretty Thing. What's the number to the lodge?"

Betta recited the phone number. Cyrus handed her the phone as it rang. "I put it on speaker, so no funny business. Tell them you're fine but you needed some time away, and that you found two kids who are in desperate need of a home. Make sure they understand that unless they are willing to pay twenty-two million shillings, the children will be sold."

The phone clicked. "Jambo. This is Lake Victoria Lodge. How may I help you?"

"Gwenny, I'm so glad you answered the phone. It's me, Betta."

"Betta! Oh my goodness, we've been so worried about you and the children. Are you okay? Where are you?" came the distant voice Betta had come to love like a sister.

"We're all fine. Andre and Gracie are with me on a little holiday. I'm sorry I didn't let you know beforehand, but you know how spur of the moment and spontaneous I can be. Listen, Gwenny, I've found two children, a brother and sister, six and eight. They're going to be sold by traffickers if I don't find them a home. Gwenny, you'd love them. They're so sweet, and I know how much you and Thomas want children. You can take them to the coast and go boating like you've always dreamed of. If you can raise twenty-two million shillings, they're yours, no questions asked. Please, you're their only hope." Betta held her breath. Would her dear friend read between the lines? She'd peppered her speech with hints that all was not right.

"Betta." The voice on the other end sounded confused and concerned. "Honey, there's something I have to tell you. Jean Pierre is in a hospital in Congo. He's going to be okay, but he was held prisoner by rebels. We've been trying to find you and when we couldn't, Tom flew there himself. Oh, Betta, you need to come home."

Betta's heart dropped at the news. Jean Pierre, hurt? She wanted desperately to be by his side, but her children's safety came first—not that she had a choice. She looked at Cyrus' hard expression and forced the next words out of her mouth. "I'm sorry to hear about J.P. and I'm glad that Thomas can be with him, but you should know it's over between us. I just can't handle his long absences and the dangers he always seems to find himself in. I want to sell the bakery. I'm taking the children and moving to South Africa."

Cyrus pulled his gun from its holster and laid it in his lap. With the other hand, he covered the phone. "Good. Tell her you'll call her tomorrow with where to send the money. Once it arrives, you'll arrange to send the children to her."

Betta nodded her head and cleared the lump in her throat. "If you and Thomas will buy the bakery from me for another twenty-two million, you can resell it at a great profit. Please, Gwenny, I need your help here. I want to start a new life, and I want to help these kids out." There was silence on the other end. Betta waited, afraid to breathe. Would she go along with the ruse?

Finally, Gwen spoke. "We'll miss you, but if this is what you want then yes, we'll buy the bakery and take the children."

Cyrus' face broke out into a relieved smile.

"I'll call you again once I know where to have you send the money. And, Gwenny, thank you. The past five years working for you have been great."

Cyrus motioned for her to end the call.

"I've got to go now. I'll call you soon. Goodbye." Betta folded the phone and handed it back to Cyrus. "You heard. She agreed to everything. Now can we go get the children?"

CHAPTER 32

Tom guided the Cessna 182 down onto the dirt runway at Musoma, on the northeastern shores of Lake Victoria. Xavier could see a grimace cross Jean Pierre's face as the wheels made contact with the ground. He was putting on a good show, but Xavier could see his friend was barely hanging on, physically and emotionally. A late model Range Rover with the Lake Victoria Lodge logo on its side waited near the low building that passed for the terminal. The four men climbed in and set off.

There was little conversation in the hour and a half drive south to Chumwe. Xavier assumed they each were thinking of the search to come. How would they find Betta and the children after so many days in a country the size and breadth of Tanzania? The task seemed daunting, if not impossible.

Rather than heading to the lodge, Tom had the driver take them to the Chumwe police station. Like most small-town police departments, the building was unimpressive. Only one vehicle, an aged Toyota Corolla with Polisi *(police)* stenciled on the side, sat in the dirt car park.

Xavier climbed out and stretched, glad to be standing after almost two hours in a plane and then crammed in the backseat of the Rover. He retrieved a pair of crutches from the back. Jean Pierre hadn't moved. Concerned, he came around and opened the front passenger door. "You doing okay?"

Jean Pierre took a deep breath and reached for the doorframe. "Yeah, just a little slow. Give me a hand, will ya?"

Inside the sweltering building, the men were directed to the chief of police, the esteemed Mr. Frederick Kajembe. The stout officer's uniform stretched across his bulk, the buttons pulling on the buttonholes. The remnants of his supper covered the surface of his cluttered desk and the corners of his mouth. "Aw, gentlemen, I was not expecting you." He swallowed the food in his mouth and quickly cleared away the debris. Familiar with Tom, the man directed a smile at him. "Mr. McMillian, it's good to see you, sir. I assume you are here concerning your missing employee and her children."

Before Tom could answer, Jean Pierre leaned forward in his chair. "She's my wife, Betta Fontaine, and my children, Andre Freedom and Mercy Grace. The man who took her is Cyrus Munianeza, a criminal wanted in multiple countries and jurisdictions for war crimes against humanity."

Mr. Kajembe waved a pudgy hand. "Yes, we are aware of all that. My best men are on the case. They've tracked your wife to a bus stop in Magu Kahangara. Mr. Fontaine, your wife was seen getting into a vehicle voluntarily and no children were seen on the bus with her or in the vehicle. I'm sorry, sir, but we have no evidence she or the children were kidnapped. There's been no ransom." He turned to Tom. "In fact, your wife, Mrs. McMillian, got a call from Mrs. Fontaine just this morning." He pulled on a pair of glasses and picked up a sheet of paper. "She said your wife stated your marriage wasn't working, and she was moving to South Africa to start a new life."

Jean Pierre struggled to his feet, his face set in a mask of grim determination. "That, sir, is a lie. She must have been saying whatever he told her too." He pulled the note out of his shirt pocket and tossed it on the desk. "Her kidnapper wrote that. He made his demands pretty plain."

The chief picked up the single sheet of paper, read it through, and handed it back to Jean Pierre. "It seems Mr. Munianeza had a prior claim on your wife. Were you aware he was the father of her son?"

Xavier watched Jean Pierre strain to push the words out he was so tired and angry. "He raped her. He didn't even know about the children,"

Kajembe folded his arms across his ample chest and leaned back in his chair. "It appears this is a domestic issue best handled by the courts, Mr. Fontaine."

"Frederick, exactly what does that mean to this case?" Tom asked.

The chief gave an elaborate shrug of his fat shoulders. "There doesn't appear to be enough evidence that a crime has been committed. My police department, as you know, is stretched to its limits. We don't have the funds to pursue a case that looks more like a family squabble than a kidnapping." He leaned back in his chair and placed his hands flat on his desk, his sausage-like fingers splayed. "Now if we were to receive assistance of say, fifty thousand shillings, I could probably pull a couple of men off other duties and concentrate on your missing wife."

Xavier, anticipating Jean Pierre's reaction to the barely concealed request for a bribe, grabbed his arm and put his other around his friend's shoulder. "Come on, Jean Pierre. I don't think we're going to get any more help here."

"Yes, I think we need to talk to Gwen and learn exactly what Betta said," added Tom.

The four men turned as one and marched from the room.

"If you change your minds, I'm always at your disposal."

"Thanks for nothing," mumbled Xavier in reply.

The short ride to the lodge was silent, each man lost in his own thoughts. Xavier knew there had to be more to what Betta said and why she left like she did. Hopefully, Tom's wife could give them a clearer picture.

Fifteen minutes later, they were all seated around one of the large metal tables on the spacious patio. A floral-patterned umbrella provided shade from the afternoon sun. Claudette, Betta's dearest friend, wrung her hands in the background and whispered prayers directed toward heaven.

Xavier observed Gwen McMillian with an appreciative eye. She was tall and blonde. A deep tan accentuated her long, straight, sun-colored hair and made her athletic-looking legs stand out against her white skirt. She wasn't as beautiful as Marie or Betta, but by European standards, he supposed she would be considered attractive. Right now, she had a very agitated look on her face.

"Tom, I'm telling you, she didn't sound right. She changed everyone's name. Like you were Thomas and Free was Andre, and she called Mercy, Gracie. Jean Pierre was J.P. and you know how annoyed I get when anyone calls me Gwenny. Then there was the thing about only having lived and worked here the past five years when it's been almost twelve. She was trying to tell me something."

"Did she say anything else?" Jean Pierre asked.

"She did say something quite queer." Gwen put a finger to her lips and screwed up her face in concentration. "She said if we took the children, we could take them to the sea and go boating like I've always dreamed about. Betta knows I get seasick. And why would we go clear across the country to go boating when we have a boat and the lake right here? Do you suppose she was trying to tell us something?"

The gears in Xavier's mind whirled and fell into sync. "She's telling us they're on the coast! Gwen, did you hear any sounds? Horns, bells, waves, anything like that?"

Gwen's face brightened. "Yes, there was the blast of a ship's horn in the background. It sounded big, like maybe a cargo ship or something."

"Tom, what ports are big enough to handle a large ship?" Jean Pierre's voice raised in urgency and hope.

"I'm not sure—Dar es Salaam is the biggest and probably Tanga. Then there's Mombasa and a dozen others up and down the coast."

Xavier had an idea. "Tom, can I use your computer?"

Everyone trouped into the office and stood behind Xavier as he positioned himself in front of the computer screen.

In the seven years since he first laid eyes on a computer, he had become proficient at searching out information, setting up logistical strategies for out of country assignments, and managing field inventory. With a couple of keystrokes he had the names of all the ports along the east African coast from as far north as Somalia to the south end of Mozambique.

Xavier stared at the map. "Now we need to narrow them down. I don't think he'd take them across two borders clear up to Mogadishu or down to Maputo or even Nacala."

"And unless he has connections at the border crossings, he's not going to get them out of Tanzania. Neither Betta nor the kids have passports." Jean Pierre dragged a hand through his hair, making it stand on end. "What does that leave us?"

Tom jabbed a finger at the screen. "In country, I'd say Tanga is our best bet. It's the closest. I've flown into their airport. It's just west of the city. Let me call them and arrange for a car. We can be in the air in less than an hour."

"Tom, Jean Pierre needs to rest. Having his spleen removed and broken ribs are nothing to mess with," Gwen admonished her husband. "And he shouldn't be on that leg, either."

Jean Pierre stood—a bit wobbly, but determined. "I'm fine. I can rest on the plane."

Xavier looked up at his friend. The pasty pallor of his face under the mottled black, blue, and yellow testified to the trauma his body had endured. The swelling around his eyes was down enough to see the hard glint in their blue depths. The set of his beard-stubbled jaw spoke to his resolve to find his family. *He's not going to stay put. Who could blame him?*

"I'll keep a close eye on him. Betta would give me an earful if I didn't."

"*Will*, not would. And thanks." Jean Pierre squeezed his shoulder.

The next forty-five minutes were spent outfitting Emmanuel, making calls, and reassuring Gwen and Claudette they'd do everything they could to bring Betta and the children home.

CHAPTER 33

Jean Pierre's eyes swept the room he'd been sharing with Betta since they returned from their honeymoon. Her handprint was on every surface, from the serene watercolors hanging on the walls to the colorful kanga laying across the chair next to her side of the bed. He fingered the soft floral print and pulled it to his face as he gently settled himself in the wicker chair.

Honey, fresh bread, and hibiscus mingled as her unique scent filled his nostrils. The thought of her back in that madman's hands made him want to yell and break something. Instead, he vented his rage and frustration by howling into the cloth. The pain that racked his body wasn't from his injuries, but from the helplessness he felt. "Betta, my bella amour *(beautiful love)*. Where are you?"

He slipped from the chair to the floor, his head bowed and resting against the side of the bed. "Father God, you've given me the most wonderful wife a man could ask for and allowed me to become a father to two beautiful children. That alone is more than I could ever have dreamed of, but you chose to bless me even more with the new life Betta carries inside her. God, please don't take them all away from me." He sobbed into the bedspread. "Show me where they are, lead us in the right direction, and help me bring them home. I beg you, please send your angels of protection to surround them and keep them safe from harm."

There was a knock on the door and Xavier stepped in. "We're ready."

Jean Pierre looked up at his friend and wiped a shaky hand across his eyes. "God will keep them safe until we get there. Won't he?"

Xavier crossed the room and helped him to his feet. "You know he will."

"Betta didn't go willingly."

"I know she didn't. None of us believes that."

Jean Pierre started across the room and paused at the dresser. A shaft of sunlight danced on the gold band laying on top of an empty picture frame. He picked up the ring and brought it up to where he could read the inscription. 'Always and forever J.P.F.' was engraved around the inside of the circle. He smiled. Betta had insisted on a plain band, one she wouldn't have to take off while baking.

Writing on the cardboard easel caught his eye. He picked up the pretty filigree metal frame and read the message. "She didn't leave me." His heart quickened as any doubt vanished. New resolve flowed through his soul. His body responded with renewed energy as he limped away, the ring buttoned into his shirt pocket. "I'm coming, Betta, my love."

The minute Tom swung the Rover through the gates onto the roadway, Jean Pierre pulled his phone out and put a call into Marti Colbert. If anyone could get them info on Munianeza, it was Marti and his network of connections.

"Marti, J.P." Before Jean Pierre could get two words in, Marti was asking him how he was, why he wasn't still in the hospital in DRC, and when would he be ready to file his story. Jean Pierre cut him off midsentence. "Marti, shut up a minute and listen. This is important. I need all the information you can dig up on Cyrus Munianeza. He's a Rwandan national wanted for war crimes, so he probably hasn't been in Rwanda since the '94 genocide. He could have hired himself out as a mercenary anywhere across Africa. My guess is he's been making a living illegally.

"He was last seen driving a newer model Toyota Hilux Surf, green with a black snorkel up the driver's side. Could be his or stolen. Check it out. Send me any pictures. It looks like he's worked at changing his appearance. Marti, he has Betta and the kids." The lump in his throat threatened to cut off his words. "I'm going after them, but I need your help."

His boss assured him he'd do the impossible and uncover the whereabouts of a man who had worked hard at becoming invisible. The call ended with Marti's pledge to call him back within the hour. That done, Jean Pierre turned in his seat and looked at Emmanuel and Xavier. "Did I miss anything?"

Xavier gave him a reassuring smile. "You've done everything you can. It's in God's hands now."

CHAPTER 34

Dar es Salaam, Tanzania

Cyrus eased up to the back of the building and peeked into the dirty window. In the glow of a single bulb, he could see Faheem lounging in the glass windowed office, his feet up on the desk, a cigarette in one hand and a bottle in the other. He moved to the other side so he could see the children. All three were asleep, piled on top of each other like a litter of pups. There was no sign of Abdul or Mwamba. They were probably still eating. Apparently, the other delivery hadn't been made yet. In anticipation, he edged around the end of the warehouse to the front. He would have to time this just right. As soon as the other delivery truck backed into the space they had occupied earlier, he would jump into action. Until then, it was a waiting game.

He thought of Betta and Freedom, back at the room he'd rented for the balance of the night. Another dose of his "magic juice" and they were out cold and would stay that way for at least a few hours. Long enough for him to take care of business here and get away from Dar. He wondered if Betta had been truthful when she told that woman it was over between her and the Frenchman. He wanted to believe she was ready to make a life with him. Could he trust her? Only time would tell.

The rumble of a diesel engine drew his attention. He watched as twin taillights appeared in the darkness. Abdul's voice could be heard speaking to someone. This was it. He moved back around the building to the door he'd wedged open just enough so that the lock wouldn't engage. Years of training as a soldier kicked in and he slid through the opening and moved across the empty space without making a sound. He couldn't get to Faheem from behind, so he pitched a small stone against a barrel ten feet away. The noise brought the man to his feet. Cautiously, he moved toward the back corner where the noise came from and where Cyrus waited in the shadows.

Faheem struck a match and held it up. He hissed when the light found the whites of Cyrus' eyes, but it was too late to sound an alarm. Without a sound—other than the sucking of the knife as Cyrus pulled it out of the dead man's gut—he dragged the body to a pile of metal drums. Less than a minute later, he was securing the lid down on Faheem's resting place. He grabbed a stiff, fish-smelling oilcloth, tossed it over the small pool of blood on the floor, and rolled another barrel onto it.

Now it was time to get the kids out before Abdul and Mwamba came back. He unfolded a new square of tarp, laid each child inside, rolled and secured the ends, and heaved the bundle onto his shoulder like a sack of meal. The three together weren't light. Cyrus' muscles bulged and his back strained against the weight. He moved back through the door and was gone. In less than five minutes, he had the kids stowed on the back seat and was cruising back through the empty streets to Betta and Freedom.

With any luck, Abdul would think Faheem had double crossed them, taken the kids, and was making his own deal with one of the outgoing ships. Cyrus chuckled, pleased with his success. Things were going his way. Soon he'd have a stash of money big enough so that he could become a man of leisure. The little house in northern Zambia would be a perfect place to hide.

Within the hour, he was turning off Nelson Mandela Rd. and heading west away from Dar es Salaam. Betta's head lulled and swayed with the rhythm of the road as she sagged on the seat beside him. Freedom's sleeping form had joined the other three, now free of their shroud, on the backseat. In a good mood, Cyrus hummed a tune as he headed west into the night.

Six hours later, just as the sun was coming up at their backs, Cyrus drove through the bustling city of Iringa. They would spend the day here. He pulled up to a high steel gate and honked the horn. A lanky teen, all arms and legs, stepped through the pedestrian door and came to Cyrus' window.

"Habari ya asubuhi, bwana *(Good morning, sir)*." The boy grinned and bowed.

"My family and I need a room with a bathroom and cooking area. We've been traveling and, as you can see, they're all done in. Do you have something secluded, away from all the noise?"

"Yes, sir. Please, let me open the gate and you can pull into the courtyard."

The gate rolled back and Cyrus pulled in, glad to see only two other cars in the car park. They were shown a room with two double beds at the back of a long u-shaped building. When the boy offered to help with their luggage, Cyrus flipped a shilling coin to him and sent him on his way. He roused Betta. "Pretty Thing, wake up."

Betta's eyes fluttered. She sat up and looked around her. "Where are we?" Cyrus watched her come fully awake. She jerked around and looked in the back seat. Relief flooded her face, and she turned back to Cyrus.

"Thank you."

"Help me get them inside." He sensed he had moved up a notch in Betta's esteem. It felt good.

Freedom yawned and stretched. "I'm hungry."

"Carry that box inside. There's cooking supplies and some fruit. I'm starving, too. Betta, make some of your chapatti."

Betta gathered Mercy, carried her inside, and laid her on one of the beds. Cyrus followed her in, a child in each arm. "How did you get them back?" she asked.

"That's not something you need to know. Just be glad they're here and not in Abdul's hands." Cyrus laid the two alongside Mercy.

"Did you kill him?" She whispered.

"No. Enough with the questions. Get me something to eat."

She busied herself in the tiny kitchen. Soon wonderful smells wafted through the room, causing Cyrus' mouth to water. Yes, he thought as he watched her back, this could work out very well. When she turned sideways, Cyrus frowned. The baby she carried would have to be taken care of. He wasn't about to raise another man's child.

CHAPTER 35

Tanga, Tanzania

The plane touched down in Tanga at sunset. A Nissan van and driver waited on the edge of the tarmac to take them the three kilometers into the city. The humidity coming in off the Indian Ocean hit Xavier in the face as soon as they stepped onto the wharf at the harbor.

Emmanuel's eyes were huge, his head craning every which way to take it all in. Even though Xavier was an old hand at travel now, seeing the big ships lining the docks and the monster cranes loading and unloading them still filled him with awe. "They're something, aren't they?" He stood next to the young man and took in the view.

Emmanuel looked over at him. "How will we ever find them? This place is huge, they could be anywhere."

Xavier glanced over to see if Jean Pierre heard. He and Tom were talking to the Harbor Master. He had to agree with his nephew. Their odds of even finding a clue weren't great, but he didn't want to discourage his friend so early in their search.

A few minutes passed, and Tom and Jean Pierre joined them. "The Harbor Master says they haven't had any passenger ships come in or leave in the past seven days. Pretty much everything is cargo ships, tankers, and a multitude of fishing dhows *(large sailed boat)*. He may not have tried to get passage, but I can't think why else he'd bring them to a port unless he was planning on leaving the country." Jean Pierre scratched his head in frustration.

"Maybe he had a contact in Tanga that could get him forged papers."

Jean Pierre's cell phone rang. "Salut *(Hello)*."

Xavier watched his friend's face grow more animated, although he said little. He waited until Jean Pierre disconnected the call. "Whoever that was must have had good news. You look like a kid on Christmas morning."

Instead of answering Xavier, Jean Pierre turned to Tom. "How long will it take us to get to Dar?"

Tom pursed his lips and tapped a finger against his watch. "It's about two hundred kilometers so, if we catch a good tailwind, I'd say we could be there in just about an hour. Why, what's up?"

Jean Pierre's face broke into a wide grin. "Marti came through. He tracked down the Toyota. It belongs to a Charles Sharanga."

"I don't get it. Who's Charles Sharanga?" Xavier asked.

"None other than Cyrus Munianeza. Seems he's been using several aliases over the years. Charles is the most recent. He's been a suspect in a rash of child abductions, but the authorities have never been able to catch him. He's part of a trafficking network called Dark Force."

"Nguvu ya Giza, I've heard of them. I got a report awhile back that they're believed to be responsible for over ten thousand abductions across central Africa in the past three years." Xavier sighed in disgust. "They steal kids and sell them into slavery for sex or forced labor. If I remember right, Dar es Salaam has been targeted as one of the transit export centers for the Middle East. Big oil money can buy a lot of kids. It's horrible."

Tom snapped his fingers. "That must be what he was doing with the two children Betta told Gwen about. Maybe he thought he could get more money from them without going through Dark Force." He started to walk away. "Come on, I need to fuel up before the airstrip closes down for the night."

Their driver made it back to the small airport in record time, but not before everything was locked down for the night. No one was around. The guard at the gate tried making a few phone calls to no avail. "Sorry, Bwana *(Sir)*. You'll have to come back in the morning. Operations start up again at o-six hundred hours."

Back in the car, Jean Pierre asked, "If we can get to the plane, can you take off?" Xavier could hear the desperation in his voice.

Tom shook his head. "No way. They've turned off the runway lights. I haven't filed a flight plan. And we need fuel. Best thing we can do is to be here first thing in the morning. Sorry, my friend, that's our only option. Besides, the men we need to see in Dar have probably gone home for the night, too."

Xavier reached over and gave Jean Pierre's shoulder a squeeze. "We'll get some sleep and be back here at daylight. We'll catch them, don't worry."

***

Dar es Salaam, Tanzania

The dawn sky was steel gray with a splash of pink. Clouds, heavy with rain, rolled in off the ocean and settled over the seaport like a wet, dreary blanket. After all the necessary prep was completed, they were finally in the air. The small plane lunged and swayed as Tom maneuvered it through the turbulence.

In the light from the control panel, Xavier could see Emmanuel was turning greener by the minute. He held an open paper bag out to him. "Here, I'll share with you. Believe me, I've filled many of these over the years. Never have liked flying in rough weather, especially in small planes."

Emmanuel looked at him, his eyes watery and his lips pulled in a grim line. "Are we going to die?"

Tom piped up from the pilot's seat. "Not on my watch. We should be approaching the airfield at Julius Nyerere International in about fifty minutes. Hang on a little longer and I'll have you safe on the ground."

The crew of four staggered off the plane, exhausted from the tense ride. Each was quiet with their own thoughts as they took a rental car east into the city of over a million souls. The ride into the seaport was uneventful and quiet. Tom drove while Jean Pierre poured over a worn map of the city he'd found in the glove compartment. Emmanuel and Xavier sat in back, each lost in thought.

Jean Pierre pointed to a spot along a creased line. "There's the location that Marti said Interpol suspects is a collection point for traffickers. Interpol's headquarters are in Lyon, France. It's not far from the paper and Marti knows some of the big dogs there." He smiled back at Xavier. "Guess it helps to have a real 'French Connection'. Tom, you'll need to turn on Chuba Road. That will take us to the Mikocheni Police Station. We're supposed to meet an Inspector Chenge."

A half hour later, they pulled up in front of the station. Its exterior appeared freshly painted and quite busy, if the number of

169

people entering and exiting were any indication. The four men stepped through the main doors and were immediately greeted by a muscular, barrel-chested man with a bushy mustache and a bald head that reminded him of dried monkey fruit—dark brown and perfectly round.

"Aw, you must be our friends from up north." He bowed and shook hands with each man. "I am Inspector Paschal Chenge." He gestured to another man entering the building. "And this is Rajab Gemji with the Tanzanian Ports Authority."

The newcomer wore the traditional Islamic white kanzu under a black sports coat. A beautifully embroidered gold kofia rested on his small skeletal head. Even with the bulk of the flowing robe and jacket, Xavier could see the man was extremely thin, but the sharp intelligence in his eyes spoke volumes. *He started assessing each of us the minute he walked in the door.*

Introductions were made, and Inspector Chenge led them to a small conference room. "Now gentlemen, from what I gather, you are private citizens and none of you are Tanzanian. Interpol has been in contact with both myself and Mr. Gemji regarding a certain wanted criminal—one Cyrus Munianeza, alias Charles Sharanga. It seems Mr. Munianeza/Sharanga has been seen doing business with certain suspicious lowlifes here in Dar es Salaam. Mr. Gemji oversees the security of this section of the waterfront. Munianeza's vehicle was spotted among the warehouses along the wharf yesterday evening." He turned to the Muslim. "Mr. Gemji, could you elaborate, please?"

The slight man cleared his throat, his voice startlingly deep. "Mr. Munianeza was seen in the company of two men known to us as traffickers in a variety of illegal commodities such as drugs, weapons, minerals, and children. The body of a third man was found this morning stuffed in a barrel, in an empty warehouse.

"I tell you this only as a courtesy. As I'm sure you are aware, the police force as well as the Ports Authority is not well funded or endowed with a large staff. As Inspector Chenge stated, you are foreigners and we are not necessarily required to extend resources to you…"

Xavier could see where this was going. He looked at Jean Pierre, who stiffened and started to interrupt.

Mr. Gemji held up a hand to stop him. "Please, let me finish. We do not have to assist you. However, the sharing of information is free. I myself will take you to the warehouse where the body was found, and the suspect was last seen. What you do from there will be of your own volition. As long as it is not illegal and does not interfere with legitimate business, you are free to conduct your own investigation. Perhaps you may have information you would like to share with us as well?"

Jean Pierre grunted and shifted his weight on the cane he had replaced the crutches with. "I've told you who the killer is, and that he has my wife and children. That's all I've got. Betta hinted that the children were in danger if Tom here, didn't take them. No matter how it looks, my wife didn't go willingly with that man and she'll do everything in her power to protect those kids."

Gemji gave a slight nod. "Of course. Come, let's check out the warehouse. Maybe you'll notice something my men didn't." Inspector Chenge led them out the door.

After a short ride along the waterfront, the two vehicles pulled up to an old, weathered building along a busy section of shoreline made up of a dozen wharfs and commercial enterprises. Xavier took in his surroundings. This port made Tanga's look puny. Cranes loaded heavy containers on dockside cargo ships. A stream of sweating black men carried crates and bulky sacks up gangplanks. A sheen of oil floated on the water's surface along with rubbish and dead fish. It was ugly, dank, and smelled of rotting fish. They moved down the enclosed alley behind the Inspector and Mr. Gemji. When he stepped through the big metal door at the end, a new sensation assaulted him. It was fear. The place reeked of it. It clung to the walls and settled on the floor like a rug. A chill spread through Xavier's body. He stopped inside the door, Jean Pierre beside him. He put a hand on his friend's arm. "Do you feel it?"

"Yeah, not good, not good at all." Jean Pierre gave a shudder and swiped a hand down his face. "Keep your eyes open. Betta or one of the kids may have left something behind."

For the next twenty minutes, they scoured the bare, open room. Except for the black powder left from gathering fingerprints in the office and the clutter of steel drums along the back wall, there was nothing. Gemji told them the drum with the body discovered inside, was now back at the morgue being examined further. The empty room held no clues to tell them Betta and the children had been there. Could they already be on one of the huge cargo ships? Dar was one of the busiest ports in Eastern Africa, with dozens of ships sailing in and out every day. Xavier worried Jean Pierre might never see his family again. Hope dimmed in his heart. Were they too late?

CHAPTER 36

Iringa, Tanzania

The children quickly became antsy in the small, confining room. It was a beautiful sunny day outside and they whined about going out to play. Betta wanted to get them out in the fresh air as much as they did. She needed time alone to work out an escape.

In the little washroom, she climbed onto the toilet. If she stood on tiptoe, she could see out the tiny window. Her eyes searched the landscape. Trees and bushes blocked most of her limited view, but she could tell there wasn't much there. Their room sat at the very end of the long row of adjoining rooms. In frustration, she grabbed a bar in each hand and jerked hard. The iron framework was solid. The burglar bars meant to keep thieves out were effectively keeping them in.

She came back into the single main room. The one big window along the front was also covered by the same iron grid work. After filling his belly, Cyrus had pulled one of the beds forward to block the door then sprawled on top of it. For a while, he just watched her clean up, not saying anything. She ignored him as she tidied the room. Seated on the other bed, the children made up a game to occupy themselves. An hour later, she ventured a glance in his direction. He had one arm draped over his eyes and the other across the gun in his waistband. His soft snore confirmed he was asleep.

Betta pressed a hand against the knife strapped to the inside of her leg. Could she really do it? Could she stab him while he slept? She had forgiven the man a long time ago—at least she thought she had. She looked at his sleeping face, at the scar that ran across one side. Old feelings of hate and anger boiled up. A battle of conscience waged in her head. She closed her eyes. *God, please give me back my peace. Help me find the forgiveness I had. Save us.*

She looked up to see the children watching her. Their innocent stares confirming what her heart already knew. She could not take his life. If he was about to kill of one them... maybe, but not now, not here. God would have to step in—she'd just have to be ready when he did.

She tiptoed to the window above his head. Through the thin curtains, she could see a woman sweeping the walkway across from their room. If only she could get a message to her. She put a finger to her lips and motioned for the children to follow her into the bathroom. It was a tight squeeze, but they managed to all get in and close the door. "Is everyone okay?" She looked at each face as they nodded. "Good, now I need to figure out how to get a message to someone. Free do you have anything left to write with? I know Cyrus dumped your book bag, but I need you to go check it and see if anything got left behind. A stub of pencil and maybe a scrap of paper would be perfect."

"Mama, I don't understand. If he's my father, why do you want to get away from him so bad?" Freedom crossed his arms and waited for an answer.

Mercy pushed at her brother. "If he's your papa, then he's my papa, too." She turned to Betta. "He's scary. Am I supposed to love him, Mama, 'cause I don't know if I can do that? I like Papa Jean P. better."

Betta pulled both children to her. She expected Freedom to lay his head on her shoulder. He resisted and instead, looked up into her eyes. "Maybe he was mean to you a long time ago, but, Mama, he's my father." His soft brown eyes pleaded with her to understand.

Betta put a hand against Free's cheek and gave him a reassuring smile. She could see the confusion in his eyes. "Son, you need to trust me. Cyrus isn't someone you want for a father. Yes, his blood flows through your veins, but that doesn't automatically make him someone you can call Papa. A true parent loves unconditionally and sacrificially. They'll do anything and everything to protect you and keep you safe. I'm sorry, Free, but no matter how much you might want that from him, it's not going to happen. Cyrus Munianeza lives for Cyrus Munianeza. He always has and he always will." Betta gave him a reassuring smile. "Now, quietly go back in there, and get your book bag."

She sent Freedom back out, bent to Sikudhani and Taji's level, and gave them the same reassuring smile. "I want you two to know that I'm doing everything I possibly can to keep you safe.

Hopefully, when this is all over, you'll have a new home. But for now, I need you to be really good for me and as quiet as a bush baby sleeping in a tree. Can you do that?"

Both heads gave a solemn nod.

Free returned and rummaged through his bag. His face brightened, and he pulled out a small stub of pencil. "It was stuck in the lining!"

Betta pulled out the five by seven photo she'd taken from her bedroom. She hated to leave it behind, but it was the best clue she could give the authorities. She wrote out a quick message on the back, rolled the photo in a tight tube, and wedged it between the toilet and the wall, out of sight. If the cleaning woman did a thorough job, she'd find it after they left. Betta could only hope and pray it would make it into the hands of the police. She sent the children back out and closed the bathroom door. Out of Cyrus' sight, she pulled the knife from the cloth band tied to her leg. With the tip, she scratched 'help! BF' on the wall behind the door. The knife secured back against her leg, she pulled the door open and stepped into the room.

Cyrus was sitting up. He stretched and yawned. "I'm hungry."

"I have some ugali I can warm up and there's two pieces of chapatti left." Betta moved to the short counter against the back wall.

"That will do."

The children huddled together on the other bed, remaining silent and watchful. Cyrus stood and headed for the bathroom. He stomped and shouted, "Boo!" All four kids jumped. Taji hid his face in his sister's chest. Cyrus chuckled.

Betta held her breath as he stepped into the small space. He had never closed the door before, wanting to keep an eye on them. Would he this time? He grinned at her. She looked away.

"What about Sikudhani and Taji? When are you going to have me call the McMillian's and set up the exchange?" That would give her another opportunity to secret them some kind of message.

"Soon. You think they'll have all the money for the kids and the bakery?"

Betta knew Tom and Gwen had most of their funds tied up in the lodge and the plane Tom had recently purchased. Whether they could come up with the money for the bakery didn't matter because she didn't intend to sell it. She didn't intend to stay with Cyrus a minute longer than she had to, but she wasn't about to tell him that. "Yes, they won't let me down." She prayed that what she was saying was true.

CHAPTER 37

Cyrus' plan was moving along better than he had hoped. There would be more money in his pocket with the sale of the two children and the bakery. Along with the payoff he already had, he felt pretty good. The next step could prove the trickiest. If the McMillians decided not to pay and called the police instead, he could be walking into a trap. He looked up the address to the local Western Union. There were several, but the closest one was at the CRDB Bank on Uhuru Ave. in downtown Iringa. *Perfect!* Being the A104 was the main thoroughfare, he could get in and out quickly. He wrote out his demands.

"Pretty Thing, come here. It's time to make a call." He motioned Betta to join him at the small motel room table. "I've written out a few key things you are to say. Don't elaborate, but make it clear that the kids will be sold if they don't want them. Play on their guilt." He brought up the redial on his phone. As soon as he heard it ring, he hit the speaker and handed the phone to her. Two rings and the phone was answered.

"Hello Gwenny, it's Betta. I hope you and Thomas made the right decision. I'm counting on you to help me out here and so are these children."

Gwen McMillian sounded stressed. "Betta, please come home. Bring the children and we'll work something out. Everyone is worried sick about you."

Betta looked at Cyrus. "How's Jean Pierre?" Cyrus didn't like her wasting time on the Frenchman and motioned for her to cut the chatter.

"He got out of the hospital and when he heard you'd left, he went on another assignment to South America. He said you can do what you want. A year of marriage was enough. He's through." Gwen's voice quivered.

Cyrus watched Betta. She looked shocked. He smiled. The Frenchman wasn't such a great guy after all, if he wasn't willing to fight for her. He tapped the paper. "Get the money."

Betta cleared her throat. "Gwennie, you need to send the money to Western Union, the CRDB Branch on Uhuru Avenue in

Iringa. It needs to be here by 3pm. As soon as I get it, I'll put the kids on a bus. Their names are Taji—he's six, and Sikudhani is eight. Taji's like Freedom, he's allergic to groundnuts. Remember how much he swells up and can't breathe? And Gwennie, thank you for doing this. Sonia should make you a good cook."

Cyrus pulled the phone from her hand and covered the face. "I said no extra talking. Say goodbye." He uncovered the phone.

"Gwennie, I have to go now. Please do as I've asked. I'll miss you. 'Bye."

Cyrus disconnected the call. "You'd better hope she gets that money here real fast. If she doesn't..." He nodded toward the kids. "They're gone."

Betta crossed her arms and tilted her head. "So are we staying here then? I need to wash clothes and we're about out of food supplies."

Cyrus stepped closer and ran a finger down the inside edge of Betta's blouse. He could feel her quiver. She dropped her arms and stilled under his touch. "How'd you like some new clothes? You treat me right and I might buy you a whole new wardrobe." He licked his lips at the thought of her naked. His hand jerked as it reached the swell of her belly. The thought of her carrying another man's child squelched any lust he might be feeling. That would have to be taken care of immediately. He wasn't willing to wait much longer to satisfy his growing need.

He stepped to the door and unlocked the deadbolt. "I'll be right outside, so no funny business, understand?" Betta nodded and sat down at the table.

Cyrus stepped outside and pulled a cigarette from the pack in his pocket. Lighting it, he looked around. The motel appeared pretty much deserted at this time of day, most travelers having moved on earlier. A young woman backed out of the room next door, a loaded bucket in one hand and a broom in the other.

"Hey, sweet thing, you want to make some extra money?" He flicked ash off into the shrubbery.

The woman turned and looked at him shyly. "I ain't that kind of girl, mister. I's just a maid."

Cyrus looked her up and down. She was probably nineteen or twenty, on the short side, but well proportioned. A cheap, brassy-colored wig framed a pretty face with pouty lips and big brown eyes. He took a long drag and smiled at her through the smoke as he exhaled. "I didn't think so, and that wasn't what I had in mind, although you're awfully pretty." He smiled and moved up to her. She set the pail down, but held the broom in front of her. Cyrus laughed. "No need to be afraid, I just need some help."

"I'm Shateka." She leaned the broom against the wall and gave a slight curtsey.

"My wife isn't feeling well and I need someone to wash up our clothes and do some shopping for me." He pulled a wad of bills out and held them up. "I'll make it worth your while if you take the rest of the day, and take care of those things for me."

Shateka's eyes rounded along with her full lips. "I's will have to ask my boss, but he's my uncle, so he'll let me off if I's tell him I'm helping out a guest. 'Sides you're the only ones we have left, so once I's clean the last couple of rooms, including yours, I'll be done for the day."

Cyrus folded a handful of bills and stuck them down the front of the girl's low cut tank top. "Go check with your uncle and come back to get the list."

Shateka pushed the money farther down into her bra. "I's always liked a man not afraid to spend his money." She smiled and sashayed away, picking up the broom and pail as she went.

Cyrus stepped back inside. "Okay, the laundry, and food will be taken care of." He looked at his watch. "Your friend has two-and-a-half hours to get the money here."

Betta looked up at him. "You do realize they'll have to drive to Mwanza? That's the closest city with a Western Union and it takes two hours. You're not giving them much time. What if there's an accident or roadwork?"

Cyrus shrugged his shoulders. "Not my problem. I don't want to give them extra time to get the police involved, just in case."

"Just in case, what? Gwen believed me, and I know they'll do anything to get the children."

Cyrus tapped a finger on his lip. "Hm, maybe I didn't ask for enough." He looked down at her with suspicion. "Maybe they're richer than you let on."

Betta stood up and stepped away from him. "They're good people, but no, they're not rich. They've worked and sacrificed for everything they have. Years ago they lost both of their children, a boy and girl, so saving these two would be worth the money they've worked so hard for."

Cyrus wasn't sure he believed her. The McMillians might prove to be a good source of income in the future. A little blackmail and extortion down the line could be lucrative. Cyrus smiled at the thought.

CHAPTER 38

Dar es Salaam, Tanzania

Exhausted and disheartened, Jean Pierre leaned back against the warehouse wall and slid to the floor. Where could they be? *God, please show me.* He sat there for a minute, ignoring the others. His eyes closed, he tried sending Betta a message. Most people would think it was nonsense, but Betta seemed to have an uncanny ability to sense what he was thinking or about to say. Gwen said it was just the close connection some husbands and wives shared.

"It's time to go, my friend."

Jean Pierre opened his eyes to see Xavier standing over him, his hand extended to help him up. He pressed his hand down on the floor beside him to push himself to his feet. Something bit into his palm. As Xavier pulled him to his feet, he looked down to see a small, round plastic bead stuck to his hand. The rich glittery purple stood out against the light flesh color of his palm.

"What's that?" Xavier asked.

Jean Pierre pulled the trinket from his skin and held it up. A grin spread across his face and a surge of hope and joy welled up within him. "That, my friend, is one of Mercy's hair beads. She won't leave the house without having Betta put at least a dozen in her hair, all purple and green so they'll match her school uniform." He gave Xavier an impulsive hug. "They were here. Less than twenty-four hours ago they were in this room."

Excited, the two men joined the others. "Where was the last place Munianeza's Toyota was seen?" Xavier asked the Inspector.

"He went through a checkpoint on Julius Nyerere Road. out by the airport. We have a camera recording all vehicles going through that one because it's our busiest. He was heading southwest. There was a woman with him but no children we could see."

"The TamZam highway is the main road to the border. He could be headed to Mozambique, Malawi, or Zambia," Mr. Gemji interjected.

Jean Pierre limped to the door. "Then that's where we're headed. Thank you for your help." He ignored the nagging thought that the children might be gone—shipped out of the country. Betta would do everything in her power to stop that. *Hold on, I'm coming.*

Re-energized with the new information, the four men piled back into the rental car and headed back toward the airport. In the small office on the far end of the terminal, they stared at the large map hanging on the wall. The continent of Africa spread from one edge to the other, criss-crossed with red lines marking roadways, green lines indicating borders, and push pins to designate airports. Seeing it laid out like this filled Jean Pierre with a growing sense of dread. There was such a huge amount of land to cover, and much of it was wild and uncivilized. How would they ever find them?

As if reading his mind, Tom draped an arm across his shoulders. "It's not as bad as it looks. We just have to be smart and think like Munianeza."

Next to him, Xavier studied the map. "He'd head across the border to put distance between him and the authorities. Maybe down along the coast of Mozambique or into South Africa. He won't stay in Tanzania, that's for sure."

"Uncle, how would he get across the borders?" Emmanuel asked.

"It's not that hard. Just head cross-country and avoid the major crossings."

"Or pay off the border guards," Jean Pierre added in disdain.

He ran a finger down the coastline. "If he's headed south to Mozambique on the B-5 highway, he'd cross at Negomane, but no matter which road he takes, he's got to cross the Rovuma River. That would mean a ferry or bridge, so he's limited which way he can go. It's over fourteen-hundred kilometers from Dar to Nampula. With a twenty-four-hour head start, he could be well past that." He turned to Tom. "If we fly into Beira that should put us ahead of him."

"Then we'd better get going. The plane's fueled up and ready." Tom headed to the door.

***

Beira, Mozambique

Hours later, Tom's radio disrupted the silence that filled the plane's interior as it taxied across the runway at Beira Airport. "Cessna bravo alfa six four nine. This is Mozambique Beira tower. I have received an emergency call. Turn to 123.575 MHz and I'll patch it through. Over."

"Cessna bravo alfa six four nine. Roger, tower. Thank you. Over." Tom adjusted the radio dial until the static cleared and Gwen's voice seeped through the transceiver. "It's Gwen," he announced to the others and held the receiver up so everyone could hear.

"Hey, sweetheart, any news?" He guided the plane to a stop in front of a small hanger.

The four leaned in to hear the tinny voice coming through the radio.

"Tom, I've been trying to reach you since this morning. Betta called. She said to send the money to Western Union in Iringa, and she'd put the two children on the bus headed to Mwanza. I calling from Mwanza. I've already sent the money—all of it."

Jean Pierre pulled the transmitter out of Tom's hand and keyed the mike. "Gwen, how did she sound? Was Munianeza there? What about the children?"

"J.P., she sounded okay. She mentioned Free's allergy to nuts."

"He doesn't have any. That kid loves nuts."

Gwen laughed. "I know, that's why I think she was telling us they're okay. She called me Gwenny again and said the strangest thing about Sonia making a good replacement for her. We all know how bad a cook Sonia is." She hesitated. "Jean Pierre, I did like you said and told her you moved on and she was free to do whatever she wanted. I hope she knows it was all a bluff."

Jean Pierre exhaled. "I do too. I'm sure Cyrus was listening, and I wanted him to think he didn't have to worry about me coming after them. Maybe he'll relax and let his guard down."

Tom held his hand out. "May I?"

Jean Pierre handed the mike back to him.

"Gwen, we've just landed at Beira, Mozambique. We thought he was headed to South Africa. I'm glad you called, or we'd have been on a wild goose chase in the wrong direction. I'll need to refuel, and then we're headed back to Iringa. Call the police in Dar es Salaam. Ask for an Inspector Chenge at the Mikocheni Police Station. Tell him what you told us. Munianeza is a suspect in a killing there. We'll call you as soon as we get to Iringa. What Western Union was she picking the money up at?" Gwen gave him the details and pleaded with them to be careful, but find them. She signed off with the assurance that she'd keep praying.

"The flight to Nduli Airport in Iringa will take approximately seven hours. We're going to still have to go through customs, and I'll need to file a new flight plan. That could take an hour or four hours, you never know."

Jean Pierre wanted to be in the air immediately. Wading through red tape and trying to convince custom agents the importance of their mission would take time he didn't want to waste. They moved into the small terminal where they were ordered to have a seat and wait until a custom agent could speak to them. Jean Pierre collapsed onto a plastic chair. His body had been protesting since he left the hospital in DRC, his mind fatigued beyond measure, but his heart wanted to keep moving toward Betta.

Xavier settled beside him, leaned forward, and rubbed the back of his neck. "Man, I'm stiff. What about you? You doing okay?" he asked.

Jean Pierre knew the rest were as tired as he was after zigzagging across the country. He sighed and closed his eyes. "Yeah, I'm good, just frustrated, and worried. It's hard to stop now. What if he disappears and we lose the trail?"

Xavier squeezed his shoulder. "Remember when Marie was attacked and Dr. James was trying to save her life?" Jean Pierre nodded his head, but didn't look up. "You told me to have faith. That God is in control even when it looks like he's not. Now I'm giving you the same advice."

Jean Pierre raised his head and tried to smile. "Thanks, mon ami *(my friend)*." He turned to Tom whose long legs were stretched out in front of him, his head back and eyes closed. "You good to head back up as soon as we're cleared?"

Tom straightened and pulled his legs in. "As soon as they let us go, we'll get back in the air." The Englishman couldn't hide the fatigue that showed around his eyes.

I've asked so much from these men and yet they don't hesitate. Jean Pierre looked from one man to the next. *Thank you, God, for true friends.*

CHAPTER 39

Iringa, Tanzania

Cyrus watched from outside the bank as Betta made her way to the Western Union counter. He tensed as the man in front of her left and she stepped up and spoke to the clerk. What he wouldn't give to hear what she was saying. With the gun laying across his lap, he'd warned her before she got out of the car not to do anything stupid. Now he watched the clerk's expression closely for any sign of distress or concern. The man looked over some papers and frowned. Had she slipped him something? Cyrus' shoulders tightened, then relaxed as the man started counting out the money.

Two minutes later, Betta walked out under the green and white CRDB Bank logo, a cloth bag clutched to her chest. Cyrus grabbed her arm and led her to the car parked at the curb. "You had me worried there for a minute. Was there a problem?"

Betta handed him the bag. "He was warning me about carrying so much money around. Seems there are a lot of thieves here in Iringa. You probably know some of them." She glared at him and wrenched the passenger door open. "Now to the bus station."

Cyrus chuckled. She had spunk. He liked this newer version of the timid girl he knew so long ago. He hustled around to the driver's side and got in.

"I expect you to keep your word and send the children to the McMillians." Betta worked the seatbelt across her lap and looked straight ahead. "The clerk said the through bus north leaves from Ipogoro, three kilometers south off Uhuru Road on the 104A highway."

"Hey." He shrugged his shoulders. "I'm all for two less to deal with as long as they sent all the money."

"You can count it for yourself, but it's all there—for the children and the bakery—forty-four million shillings."

They made their way to the bus depot but found the northbound bus left at six am. Cyrus cursed at the delay. He didn't like the idea of hanging around, but he wanted to get rid of the kids. It crossed his mind just to abandon them in the city, then he thought better of it. He needed and wanted Betta's cooperation, and getting the kids on a bus north would be one step closer to getting her to trust him.

Cyrus found them a place to stay the night right across the street from the busy depot. While the children stayed locked in the car, he and Betta gathered fruit and dried meat at a roadside market. "One thing I've never forgotten in all these years is what a good cook you were. I mean, even though we were out in the bush, you managed to make everything taste good." He smiled at Betta and tossed her a mango.

"No sense in making bad food, even for you." She raised a winged-shaped eyebrow. "You know, I could have poisoned you a dozen times if I'd wanted to… but I'm not a murderer like some people." She turned her back on him and walked away.

Cyrus smirked. "I'll keep that in mind," he said under his breath.

***

Betta shook Sikudhani's shoulder. "Siku, sweetheart, it's time to wake up."

The little girl sat up and stretched. "What time is it?"

"Early, but we have to get you and Taji to the bus."

Siku looked up at her, pleading in her eyes. "Do we have to go? We like it here with you and Free, and Mercy. Not so much with him." She pointed her chin at Cyrus, where he lounged on the other bed.

"Don't give her any lip, girl. What she has in mind for you is a whole lot better than where I was sending you." Cyrus pointed his cigarette at her. "Now get up."

Siku pouted, but slid off the bed and headed to the bathroom. At the door, she turned, stuck her tongue out at him, and wagged her head.

"That kid has too much sass. I hope your friends can smack some manners into her."

Betta helped Taji up. "Beating a child isn't the only way to get them to do what you want, you know. My children have wonderful manners, and I've never been violent with them." She gathered a sleepy Taji and carried him to the bathroom. "Tom and Gwen will love them. That's what counts."

"I wouldn't know about love," Cyrus mumbled.

Betta had closed the door, so she didn't hear him. He ground out the stub of cigarette and got up off the bed to pace the room. How did that woman manage to aggravate and fascinate him at the same time? He'd spent the past twelve, almost thirteen years, trying to figure out the hold she had over him.

Maybe once they settled down in their own place, they could learn to love each other and the kids would look at him as their father. Wasn't that what he'd been after all his life—a home, family, and someone who loved him?

CHAPTER 40

Betta handed a small bundle to Sikudhani and kneeled down in front of her and Taji. "You've ridden a bus before, but this will be a long ride. When it stops, you can get off and use the washroom, but get right back on so they don't leave you behind. I've put some food in the bundle for you when you get hungry. Some really nice people, the McMillians, will be there to meet you in Mwanza."

"But, Auntie, why can't we stay with you?" Taji wrapped his arms around her neck.

Betta's heart wrenched at his plea. The little boy had already known such loss she hated causing him any more pain, even if it was for the best. She kissed his forehead and ran a finger down his nose. "You're going to love the lodge. You'll have all the food you can eat and toys to play with. Tom and Gwen will be the best mommy and daddy in the world."

"Will we get to wear uniforms and go to school?" Siku asked, hope and wonder in her voice.

"Yes. You'll go to the same school Free and Mercy go to."

Mercy put an arm around the younger girls' shoulder. "You'll like it. The teachers are real nice as long as you listen and do your work."

Free bent to Taji's level. "I'll bet the boys in your class will teach you how to play football."

"Really? Do they have a real soccer ball? I've only played with one we made from plastic bags and twine."

Free laughed. "Yeah, a *real* one, just like the pros use." He gave each of them a solemn look. "I need both of you to do me a big favor. Could you play with Mowge and Cinder for us? They're our cats, and I'm sure they're lonely."

The brother and sister looked at each other. They replied in unison. "You bet!"

Their faces transformed, Betta felt reassured about sending them away. She pushed off her knees and stood. She turned to Cyrus. "Give them some money."

He made a face. "What for?"

Hands on her hips, she held her palm out. "They'll need a few shillings to buy something to drink and pay the toilet attendant."

Cyrus rolled his eyes, but pulled a handful of change out of his pocket and dumped it into her hand. "That better be enough 'cause that's all they're getting."

The conductor shouted from the bus door.

Betta stood and took each of their small hands in hers. "It's time." She walked the children over under Cyrus' watchful eye. Once she was sure he was out of earshot, she pulled the children to a stop. "Siku, tell Gwen and Tom as much about what's been happening as you can remember. Tell them not to give up looking for us, okay?"

Siku nodded her head solemnly. Her chin quivered. "Will I ever see you again?"

Betta smiled, her eyes awash in tears. "I hope so. I'll be working real hard to get Free, Mercy, and myself back home. One other thing, when you meet a tall Frenchman named J.P. Fontaine, tell him I'll always love him. Can you do that for me?"

"We have to go, miss. Come along, children." The conductor herded them onto the bus.

Betta watched for them in the windows. As the bus pulled away, two little faces pressed against the glass. The children waved. "Goodbye, safe journey!" she called and waved back.

An hour later, they were on the road again. Not more than ten kilometers out of the city, they came upon a terrible accident. A semi and minibus had collided, partially blocking the road. Police, rescue, media, and onlookers were crowded around the scene.

Cyrus inched forward. "You kids get down."

As they came abreast of the mangled scene, Betta closed her eyes to the carnage only to open them to a police officer directing them to keep moving. They passed so close she could have reached out her window and touched the man's uniform. She didn't.

"Smart move, Pretty Thing. I wouldn't want to add to the death toll."

"How much farther are we going? It seems like weeks since I've had a good shower and a change of clothes."

"It won't be long now and we'll be home."

Betta watched his face soften the tiniest bit.

"I think you'll like it. Chila is like an oasis with plenty of privacy, trees, and the house is ready for a woman's touch. Hey, how would you kids like a dog?" he asked over his shoulder. "Something big and loud to keep strangers out?"

Free leaned forward. "That would be great. I've always wanted a dog. We have a couple of cats at the lodge, but they're just cats."

Betta needed as much information as she could gather, and Cyrus seemed in a mood to talk. "So is there a town or village close by where I'll be able to do the shopping? And a school for the kids?"

"Yeah, but that's not going to happen for a while. Once you prove I can trust you, then we'll see."

"I haven't tried to get away so far."

He huffed. "Only because you couldn't take the kids with you. Once we get settled and you become Mrs. Charles Sharanga and we change the kids' names, then we'll work on the trust thing."

Betta hadn't realized he'd planned so far ahead. Changing their identities? Would Jean Pierre be able to find her if she was someone else? The baby kicked. Without a thought, she rubbed her stomach.

The motion caught Cyrus' eye, and he looked over at her. "I don't intend to raise another man's kid, you know."

Betta looked at him. "What do you mean?"

"That baby you're carrying isn't mine. I know a doctor who'll take care of it for the right amount of money."

Shocked and immobile, Betta's hands began to tremble where they rested on the mound of her belly. A new dread chilled her. Did he expect her to consent to an abortion? The realization that that was exactly what he expected caused bile to rise in her throat and her mind to reel. She looked away so he wouldn't see the panic and terror on her face. She pressed her forehead against the cool, smooth surface of the window and closed her eyes. *Father God, please help me!*

CHAPTER 41

Beira, Mozambique

Weary and disheartened, the four men waded through customs. It was all Jean Pierre could do not to punch somebody when they were given a hard time about Emmanuel's permit, since he had no passport. After explaining the situation to several different agents, it was decided they could return to the plane and leave under the condition they didn't reenter the country without proper paperwork. Relief washed over him as they hustled to the plane. He cast a worried look at the steel-gray sky where a billow of dark cloud hung heavy with rain. The cross wind over the ocean promised to make the takeoff memorable.

Strapping in, Tom gave him a look of concern, then smiled for Xavier's and Emmanuel's benefit. With a thickened British accent and a wag of his head, he said, "What say? Only a tad bit of weather. Don't worry, chaps. Piece of cake."

Jean Pierre couldn't help but smile at Tom's attempt to calm their nerves. He looked back at Xavier, who was white-knuckled and tight-lipped. The man clutched the sides of his seat as the small plane lifted into the air. Emmanuel's hand was clamped down over his uncle's. The boy's eyes were squeezed shut and his teeth clenched in a horrified grimace. "Hey, Emmanuel, we're up. It's okay. You can let go now."

Emmanuel opened one eye and peeked at Jean Pierre, then at Xavier. "Are we going to crash?"

"I hope not." Xavier gave a feeble smile. "Marie would kill me if I didn't bring you home to meet her."

"You'll be an old pro by time this is over." Jean Pierre assured him.

"I don't think I like flying." He took a hesitant look out the side window. "It's a long ways down there."

Tom slipped the headphones off of one ear. "Looks like we have to make up some time, boys. The air's going to be a bit bouncy, so keep buckled in. I'm going to take us above the clouds to stay out of it as much as possible. The good news is, once we head inland we should pick up a tailwind."

The winds prevailed and the single-engine plane made the return trip to Tanzania airspace in just under six hours. They landed at the Nduli Airport just after noon. The ordeal with customs was much easier this time due to a courtesy call from Inspector Chenge explaining the circumstances of their journey. While the others took their turns with the agent, Tom arranged for a four-wheel-drive SUV. It stood ready at the door when they left the terminal. They headed into town. Their first stop was the downtown branch office of the CRDB bank that housed Western Union.

Xavier supported Jean Pierre as he limped to the counter and produced a small photo he handed to the clerk. "Pardon, sir. I was hoping you could tell me if this woman was in here yesterday? She received a large amount of money wired in from Mwanza."

The man across the counter took the photo. His eyebrows raised. He gave a slight whistle. "She is certainly too beautiful to forget easily, but I'm afraid I've been out sick. This is my first day back on the job since last week."

Jean Pierre didn't try to hide the despair that registered on his face and gripped his gut. He reached for the snapshot of Betta and the children playing at the water's edge.

"Is the person who was working here that day around? Perhaps, they'd remember her?" Xavier interjected.

The clerk shook his head. "No, I'm afraid he's not here today, but if you come back tomorrow, I'm sure he can help you."

Jean Pierre thanked the man, and the men moved back outside. He turned to Xavier. "We're getting close. I can feel it."

Xavier gave him a reassuring smile. "This will be over soon and we can all go home."

Jean Pierre hoped he spoke the truth, and that Betta and the children would be returned safe and sound. Out of habit, he whispered the same six words he'd been praying for days, "Please God, bring them home safe."

Trumpets from Tom's phone announced an incoming call. "It's Inspector Chenge." The men crowded in to try and catch the conversation on the busy sidewalk. "Inspector, I'm putting you on speaker. I assume my wife reached you."

"Yes, Mr. McMillian. I spoke to her a couple of hours ago. Pleasant sounding woman, I must say. I assume you've landed in Iringa?"

"Yes, we're just outside the Western Union. We can't confirm Betta was here, but this is the one my wife sent the money to. We flew in from Mozambique a little bit ago. Thank you for paving the way. It saved us precious time we lost heading down the coast. Do you have any new news?"

"That's why I'm calling. Can you get your hands on a newspaper?"

All four men looked up and down the busy sidewalk. A half block away, a kid was hawking newspapers on the corner. Xavier handed Emmanuel some change, and he sprinted off.

"We're getting one now. What's happened?" Tom asked.

"Look at the picture on the front page. I believe there's a photograph of Cyrus Munianeza's vehicle with him and Mr. Fontaine's wife inside. It's not real clear, so I need you to confirm that it's them. Seems they were passing a terrible car crash on the TanZam highway just as a reporter snapped a photo. Good luck for us, I'd say."

Tom looked over at Jean Pierre and shouted into the phone. "Whereabouts did it happen?"

"Just past the town of Mufindi. Looks like he's headed to Zambia through Iringa."

Emmanuel skidded to a stop and held out the newspaper. A large black-and-white photo of a horrific accident held the predominant position above the fold just under the headline. Jean Pierre flipped the paper over. There, next to the columns of print, Betta stared back at him. She looked scared, but okay. Hope reignited. He grabbed the phone out of Tom's hand. "It's her."

The Inspector's voice took on a more authoritative tone. "Thank you for confirming that, Mr. Fontaine. I will alert all police forces in the area and the border checkpoints. It appears this man is armed and dangerous. I must strongly advise you to step back and allow the proper authorities to handle this. But, I believe that advice will fall on deaf ears, so I will wish you good luck instead."

"Luck isn't necessary, Inspector. We have God on our side."

Tom reached for the phone. "Inspector Chenge, we're going back to the airport now. Where do you suggest we head?"

There was the sound of papers rattling, then the Inspector cleared his throat. "My best guess is that he's headed into the heart of Zambia. You should be able to get in front of him if you fly into Kasama. I'll call ahead so you'll be expected."

"Thank you, sir. You've been a tremendous help." Tom grinned at Jean Pierre, "And given us new hope. Keep us informed if you hear anything new. We'll do the same." Tom folded the phone and dropped it back into his pocket.

Rejuvenated, Jean Pierre hobbled toward the car. "Come on. Let's get back to the plane. It looks like we have a chance to get ahead of them."

They grabbed some food at a Hasty Tasty and headed back to the airport.

CHAPTER 42

Nakonde, Zambia

Betta stared at the back of the border guard talking to Cyrus, willing him to reject the bribe Cyrus was pushing on him. The guard stole a furtive glance around. Apparently satisfied no one was looking, he shoved the wad of cash into his pocket and handed Cyrus back his passport and Betta's ID card. She let out a disappointed sigh. Weren't there any government officials out there who weren't corrupt? She'd just witnessed the same exchange on the Tanzanian side of the border, although Cyrus seemed more agitated and had to pass the guard more cash.

Smiling, he strode back to the car and got in. "We're all set. By this evening we'll be home." He turned in the seat. "Bet you kids will be glad to get settled into your new home and get out of this car."

Free mumbled something about playing soccer and a dog, but Betta didn't catch it all. Mercy sat silently, staring out the window, refusing to speak to Cyrus or acknowledge his comment.

Good for you, sweet girl, thought Betta.

Cyrus pulled into a petrol station just south of town and ordered the attendant to fill the tank, check the tires and oil, and wash the windows. He leaned against the side of the car and watched the two uniformed men dash around doing his bidding.

Betta hadn't been able to leave any kind of clue since leaving Iringa. She couldn't count on the bribed border guard to provide Jean Pierre any information. *I have to get word to him.* She spied a small, open market and bottle shop across the road under a thatched awning and had an idea.

She leaned across the driver's seat and spoke through the open window. "We need to replenish our supplies with some fresh fruit, and the children are thirsty. Could I go across the road there and get a few things?"

Cyrus turned and ducked down to eye level. He didn't say anything for a minute, then nodded. "Okay, but you go by yourself.

The kids stay here with me." He pulled a few shilling notes out of his pocket. "Get me a packet of cigarettes, if they have any."

Betta took the money and turned to the kids. "I'll be right back. Stay in the car."

She climbed out and hurried across the black tarmac, where she smiled at a couple of ladies fanning themselves in the shade. In Swahili, she greeted them. "Hamjambo *(Hello, how are you all)*?"

Sensing a sale, they both stood and began showing Betta their produce.

"Do you speak Swahili?" she asked. They continued to smile and shove fruit at her. "How about French or English?" She asked in each of those languages. Still smiles, but no reply. Disheartened that they didn't understand her, she picked a few bananas that didn't look overly ripe and four mangos. She glanced back across the road to see Cyrus watching her every move. Her purchase made, she smiled, held up the bag where he could see it, and gestured to the bottle shop. He nodded. Relieved, she hurried to the entrance before he could change his mind.

Now that I'll be out of sight, I might have a chance.

Her hopes soared as she stepped into the cool, dark interior and let the door close behind her. Quickly, she stepped to the counter and asked for a pen and paper in English.

The young lady looked up from her school books. "We don't sell that stuff. This is a bottle shop." She smacked her gum and returned to the page she was reading.

Aware of every second ticking by, Betta reached across and touched her shoulder. "Please, I just need a small piece of paper and to borrow a pen. My name is Betta Fontaine. My children and I have been kidnapped. I need to get a message to my husband."

Brought out of her boredom by the pleading tone of Betta's voice, the girl looked around and back at Betta. "So where's your kidnapper?"

"He's across the street with my children. Please, I don't have much time."

The girl ripped a page from her notebook and handed a pencil to Betta. "Why don't you run away?"

Betta frantically scribbled out her message. "I can't leave my kids." She looked up. "Could you get me a packet of cigarettes and four bottles of Fanta Orange?" She laid the shilling notes on the counter.

"We don't take shillings. You're in Zambia now. You'll need Kwacha."

Betta stepped back so she could see out the door. Cyrus was paying the attendant. Her time was running out. She pushed the note and pencil back at the girl. "Please, this is a matter of life and death. I need you to get this to the police. My husband, Jean Pierre Fontaine, is looking for us. You're my last chance... please, help me." She looked out again to see Cyrus heading across the road toward her. "Here, take all of this." She pushed the whole pile of shilling notes toward the girl. "I'm sure you can exchange it." She jammed the bottles into the bag and was just about to snatch up the cigarettes when the door opened.

Cyrus looked from her to the girl. "What's taking so long?"

The girl looked from Cyrus to Betta. For just a second, Betta saw a knowing glint come into the girl's eyes. She held her breath, waiting to see what the teen would do.

She pushed the pile of money back across the counter toward him. "I was telling your wife here that we don't take Tanzanian shillings. You need to go to the bank and exchange them for Kwacha."

Head down, Betta watched from the corner of her eye as the girl secreted the folded paper into her schoolbook. Her head jerked up when Cyrus stepped up and slammed a hand down on the counter.

"I don't have time. Just take the money the little lady gave you." He grabbed the cigarette packet in one hand and Betta's arm in the other. "Come on. We're wasting time."

Betta stole a glance back as he pushed her out the door. The girl had her fingertips against her lips. Her eyes wide with fright, she gave Betta a slight nod. Betta wanted to mouth a 'thank you' but didn't dare. She smiled instead.

Cyrus gave her a push toward the roadway. "Let's go."

A short ways outside of Nakonde, Cyrus turned off the TanZam highway and headed west. Before the turn, Betta felt more hopeful than she'd been in days. The chances of Jean Pierre getting her note were good if he followed their trail. With the turn, her spirits sank. A paved road meant people, towns, and opportunity to leave clues. This dirt side road would take them God-knows-where. Maybe Cyrus was thinking the same thing as they plowed along, leaving only a cloud of red dust in their wake.

"How much farther?" she asked.

"It's only about three more hours, but we won't be going to the house right away."

"Is Chila where I'll be shopping and where the kids will go to school?"

Cyrus chuckled and looked over at her. "Chila's not a town, Pretty Thing."

Betta was confused. She remembered he said they'd live in Chila by a lake. That's what she put in the note. Had he lied to her? The last threads of hope seem to unravel and disintegrate. "But you said..."

"I said you'll like Chila. That's the name of the lake where the house is. The town is Mbala. It's not real big, about twenty thousand people, but it's quiet and in the perfect location. We'll be near the borders of DRC and Tanzania. Port Mpulungu on Lake Tanganyika is close if we need to make a quick get-away." He puffed out his chest. "I've had a long time to plan this. Everything is in place. You were the only thing missing." He reached over and squeezed her leg.

Betta tensed. Cyrus' hand was less than an inch away from the knife strapped to her leg. She forced a smile and laid her hand over his. "It seems you've thought of everything. Maybe you're right and this will be a new start for all of us."

The rest of the dusty ride, Betta sat lost in thought. All the information, all the statements he'd made, all the actions he'd taken, led her to believe he was as dangerous as he was thirteen years ago. He was delusional if he thought she'd willingly consent to be his wife and let him raise her children.

Her mind jumped from scenario to scenario as she thought up and eliminated a dozen different escape plans. Whatever she chose to do would have to happen soon. Her gut was telling her they were running out of time.

CHAPTER 43

Exhausted physically and mentally, Jean Pierre jerked awake as the plane made contact with the runway. He couldn't believe he'd actually fallen asleep. He straightened up in the seat and looked out the cockpit at the landscape rushing by as they bumped their way down a dirt track. "Where are we?"

Tom held up a finger and finished his conversation over the radio. Jean Pierre turned in his seat to look back at Xavier and Emmanuel. They both appeared pale and green at the same time. Emmanuel had one hand over his mouth and the other gripped Xavier's arm. Xavier was blowing out small puffs of air.

"We're down, guys." Jean Pierre chuckled.

Xavier grimaced and pulled Emmanuel's hand off his arm. "I'll never believe man was meant to fly."

"I can't believe after all the air miles you've put in over the years, you're still so squeamish." Jean Pierre settled back in his seat. "I love to fly."

Tom pulled his headphones off as the plane came to a stop on the dirt strip. "Sorry about that. I didn't want to worry you guys, but we were running out of petrol. I had to find a place to put it down when I realized we wouldn't make the airport in Kasama. Seems we were shorted a few litres of fuel and my gauge didn't register it."

Xavier leaned forward to look out the front windscreen. "You mean this isn't a regular landing strip?" As if in answer, a car edged by them, followed by a man on a bike shaking his fist at them.

"No, this was just a long stretch of straight road." He paused. "We may have a worse problem. Seems the customs guys, and the police aren't too happy with us using this road as an airstrip. We're on the Zambian side of the border in a little town called Nakonde. We're supposed to wait here until they send someone."

"How long will that take?" Jean Pierre released his seatbelt.

"African time... could be hours. Who knows." Tom shrugged. "Looks like I may have cost us some time. I'm sorry."

Jean Pierre gave his shoulder a pat. "You tried, mon ami *(my friend)*. That's what's important. It's not your fault some stupid, greedy jerk decided to risk our lives for a few shillings of petrol. We couldn't have gotten this far without you and this plane." He reached for the door handle. "I gotta stretch my legs. Can someone help me out?"

Twenty minutes later, the men crawled out from under the shade of the plane's fuselage as an ancient Toyota Prado skidded to a stop, enveloping them in a cloud of dust.

A distinguished-looking gentleman in a dapper brown-green uniform stepped out and settled a French Kepi-style cap on his head. "Gentlemen, by what authority do you presume to land your plane in my district?" he demanded.

Tom stepped up and extended his hand in greeting. "Jambo, bwana. Jina langu ni Tom McMillian. *(Hello, my name is Tom McMillian).*" He went on to explain why they had landed on the roadway.

The officer shook Tom's hand. "Your Swahili isn't bad, but your accent is atrocious." He replied in perfect English. "I am Captain Kennedy Spweri. You gentlemen must come with me." He gestured to the big SUV with POLICE stenciled down the side. "I will leave one of my men here to guard your plane. I suggest you also leave someone here."

Emmanuel volunteered before it could be discussed. With assurances that they'd be back as soon as possible, the remaining three men gathered their belongings and climbed in.

Anxious to get this over with and get on the road, Jean Pierre used his most persuasive speech—the one he reserved for difficult officials. "Captain Spweri, my name is Jean Pierre Fontaine. I'm an international photojournalist. Six days ago, my wife and children were kidnapped by a known killer. We've tracked him across Tanzania and believe he's headed somewhere in Zambia. We were hoping to pick up his trail in Kasama when we ran out of fuel. The Tanzanian authorities as well as Interpol, are involved in the situation. I can give you their names, if you want to confirm my story."

"And you want me to allow you into my country just like that?" He snapped his fingers. "For your information, Mr. Fontaine, I am aware of the circumstances that have brought you to my border. Regardless, there are still procedures that must be observed and fees paid."

They had arrived at the busy police post. "Please, join me inside. Bring your things with you. They will need to be examined." The men looked at each other. Between them, there were only two duffels. Tom picked up one and Xavier the other.

Jean Pierre's gaze swept the area and landed on a green Toyota SUV turning off the main tarmac onto a dirt side road. A black snorkel snaked up the driver's side. His heart quickened, and he stopped in his tracks. Could that be them? He grabbed Xavier's arm as he walked past. "Look. Can you make out the plate number?"

Xavier followed Jean Pierre's pointing finger and narrowed his eyes. "AAB two seven three, I think. It's hard to see clearly through the dust. You think that's them?"

Jean Pierre ran a hand through his hair. "I don't know. It was green with a black snorkel. Maybe I'm just seeing things, but what if it was them?" He wanted nothing more than to jump back in the Prado and chase after the suspicious vehicle. He started to say something, when the captain effectively cut him off.

"Gentlemen, step inside, please." The officer held the door open and followed them into the gloomy interior. "My office is the first door on the left."

Jean Pierre moved as quickly as his cane would allow. "Sir, you said you already know about the kidnapping. Did Inspector Chenge of the Dar es Salaam police call you?"

Captain Spweri settled behind his desk and removed his cap. "Yes, I have spoken to the Inspector." A clerk followed them into the office, whispered something to the Captain, and handed him a piece of paper. The Captain sat forward in his chair as he read the message.

Jean Pierre leaned onto the desk. "Did he give you the license plate number of Munianeza's Toyota?"

"Yes, but..."

Jean Pierre interrupted him. "Was it AAB two seven three?"

The captain looked through the papers on his desk and scanned one. "No, the number they gave me was AAB two seven eight. Mr. Fontaine, if you'll let me finish..."

Jean Pierre turned to Xavier. "Could that last number have been an eight instead of a three?"

Xavier nodded his head. "Yeah, it could have. There was a lot of dust in the air." A look of shock crossed Xavier's face. "Dear God, it was them!"

CHAPTER 44

Mbala, Zambia

The farther away they drove, the more Cyrus' spirits lifted. It was obvious Betta, and the children, were meant to be with him, where they belonged. If not, why had everything gone so smoothly? No, he'd outsmarted them all, and now he would have a family and a home. Pretty Thing was coming around, and he knew it wouldn't take much to get Freedom to think of him as a father. Mercy would eventually follow her brother's lead. He figured he had several months to solidify the situation before he would have to make a few runs to make some money.

They were heading into the sun toward Mbala. Cyrus pulled the visor down and a picture fell in his lap. He picked it up and held it out to Betta. "I forgot I had that. It's a picture of your new home." Betta took the snapshot without comment. "Well, what do you think?"

"It's nice. The garden needs tending."

Free reached between the seats. "Can I see?"

Cyrus waited for a response, anxious for the kids to like it. He watched in the rearview mirror as the boy handed it to his sister.

"Is there a football field nearby?" Free asked.

"There's one near the school. I'll bet you're a good player. Am I right?" Cyrus watched Free shrug.

"I'm okay, I guess."

"What about you, Mercy, what do you like to do?" He watched the road and waited for her reply. She ignored him. His temper started to rise. He was trying to be nice, but she was acting like a brat. He wanted nothing more than to slam on the brakes, pull the girl from the vehicle, and beat an answer out of her. Instead, he gripped the steering wheel and took slow, deep breaths. "I'm waiting for an answer, young lady."

Betta turned in her seat and reached back. "Mercy's my helper in the kitchen. Aren't you, sweet girl? She serenades me while we make supper for the guests."

The girl remained silent. Cyrus had enough. "You'd better learn to show respect, little girl, or you're going to force me to beat it into you."

"Yes, sir," she mumbled.

The interior of the SUV remained tense and silent until they reached the end of the dirt road, where it joined the paved M2 highway. Cyrus pulled the car off the road under the shade of a flamboyant acacia in full, glorious bloom. "I'm hungry."

A small, roadside eatery advertised the best oxtail soup in the area. A rusty metal sign depicted a bottle of Mosi beer with a picture of Victoria Falls on the label. The place appeared deserted, except for a mangy dog stretched across the doorstep. It was the only place to eat for miles. "Come on. We'll eat inside. I don't want you to speak to anyone. I'll do all the talking."

Betta and the children followed him inside and settled at a discolored plastic table while he talked to the proprietor. Ten minutes later, four plates were set in front of them, along with three bottles of Coke and a replica of the beer bottle on the sign.

Mercy used her fork to stab at the green, slimy pile that was bleeding into a pasty white mound and a dozen tiny, shriveled fish. She made a face. "What's this?"

Cyrus dug in. Around a mouthful of food, he pointed with his fork and replied, "That's nshima *(thick maize porridge),* same as ugali. That's rape *(green, stewed, leafy vegetable),* and the fish are kapenta *(minnow-size fish eaten whole)."*

Mercy gagged and laid down her fork. "I'm not hungry."

Cyrus slammed his palm down, making all three of them jump. "I paid good money for that food and you'll eat it! Understand?"

Betta put her hand over Cyrus'. "She's not a real big eater, but I'm sure she can manage a few bites, can't you, Mercy?"

A glum pout formed on the girl's lips. She mumbled, "Yes, Mama," and picked her fork back up to spear a little fish.

"She acts like she's six instead of twelve. You need to quit treating her like a baby." Cyrus waited while she slowly ate the whole thing. "Be thankful I'm feeding you, little girl."

Her expression changed as she stabbed another one. "These are actually okay, but I like Mama's fish curry better."

Free was diving in, balling his nshima and dimpling it with his thumb like Cyrus. He scooped up a mix of rape and kapenta. "Mmm, not bad."

They finished the meal without further discussion and went back out to the car. He made a show of pulling his holstered gun from under the driver's seat and looked at Betta. "I need to make a call. I'm going to be right outside, so don't think about doing anything funny."

He climbed from the car and pulled out his cell phone. After punching in a number, he listened to the ring and for someone to pick up. "You have reached the office of Dr. Kasmwana. Please leave a message."

Disgruntled that the doctor didn't answer, Cyrus waited for the beep. "Doctor, you may remember me. This is Charles Sharanga. You treated me for a bullet wound a few months back. I need your immediate assistance. Call me back as soon as you get this."

Jamming the phone back in his pocket, he stomped around to the back, opened the hatch, and looked around for the jug of drugged water. Holding it up, he shook the container and frowned. The liquid only covered the bottom two inches. There were no more pills to dilute. He'd have to give it to the children and hope there was enough left for Betta. He stepped around to the passenger's side and opened Free's door. "Drink this and give some to your sister." He thrust the clear plastic jug at Freedom.

"Do we have to? I hate this stuff. It makes me feel strange when I wake up. Besides, I'm not thirsty," Freedom whined.

Cyrus ducked down to better see into the interior and glared at the children. "You're sounding like your sister. No arguments. Do as I say."

His phone chirped. Retrieving it from his pocket, he slammed the door and moved to the front of the vehicle, where he leaned against the hood. "Dr. Kasmwana, I'm glad you called me back. Do you remember me?"

"Yes, I remember. Upper right arm. How can I help you today?"

"Doctor, I have a delicate situation that needs your special attention. You see, I'm married and my wife has become pregnant by another man. I was away and didn't know until just recently.

Rather than throw her out, I've decided she will stay, but the baby has to go. You understand my situation, don't you?"

The doctor cleared his throat and lowered his voice. "So you are looking for someone to eliminate the problem, correct?"

Cyrus could hear the hesitation in the man's voice. "Exactly. I'm willing to pay you handsomely for your service, but it must happen immediately. We're outside of town, but should be able to get to your office..." He consulted his watch. "In fifteen minutes."

There was a pause on the other end, then the doctor announced, "My fee will depend on how far along she is. Less than four months, I can induce with medicine. Over that... well, I'll need to examine her. How does she feel about this?"

"She'll do as I say. We'll be at your office in a few minutes. I'd prefer no one else was there." Cyrus hung up before the doctor could reply.

Almost twenty minutes later, they turned onto Bwangalo Road. Two buildings in from the main pavement, they stopped in front of a small, unimpressive block house with a large sign announcing in bright red letters, 'Dr. Benjamin Kasmwana Modern Medicine Drop-ins Welcome'.

Betta looked at him, terror and panic on her face. "Why are we here?"

Cyrus looked in the back. Satisfied the children were asleep, he pulled his sunglasses off and raised an eyebrow at her. "I told you I won't raise another man's child. Dr. Kasmwana has agreed to take care of the problem. Now get out."

CHAPTER 45

Captain Spweri stood. The sheet of lined paper in his hand. "Gentlemen, please. You need to let me finish."

Tom put an arm on Jean Pierre's shoulder. "We're listening."

"Zikomo *(Thank you)*. What I've been trying to tell you is a young lady brought this note into the station while I was gone picking you up." He handed the page to Jean Pierre. Tom and Xavier pushed in to read it with him.

> Betta Fontaine and two children
> Kidnapped by Cyrus Munianeza-
> wanted for murder
> Contact J. P. Fontaine Lake Victoria
> Lodge Tanzania
> Going to Chila PLEASE HELP!

As one, the three men turned and headed to the door. The stern voice of the Captain stopped them. "Hold it right there. You are in this country illegally. You've managed to leave a plane in the middle of one of my roadways and now you think I'm just going to allow you to chase after a killer. Who do you think you're dealing with here?" he asked indignantly.

Jean Pierre turned back to him. All efforts to control his emotions forgotten, he spoke through clenched teeth. "That monster has my wife and children. We've been tracking him for days and now he's just minutes ahead of us. You can't seriously expect me to sit here and do nothing?"

Kennedy Spweri came around his desk, perched on the corner, and crossed his arms. "I expect you to let the police handle this. My men are trained and they know this country. If I let you leave, you'd head for Chila, correct?" All three nodded. "Well, gentlemen, for your information, there is no such town. Chila is the name of a lake three hours to the west of here. How do you intend to get there? By plane? There is no airport or even an adequate airstrip for miles around. Besides, a fuel truck cannot possibly be here until morning."

"Please," Jean Pierre begged. "I have to get to them. Please."

"I have some medical training. If anyone's hurt, I can help." Xavier offered.

"And I did a stint in the Royal Air Force, so I have combat training," added Tom.

Captain Spweri looked at each man, hesitated, and rubbed his chin between his thumb and finger. Abruptly, he stood to his feet and reached for his phone. "Gibson, how many officers do we have available? Is the truck out of the repair shop? Hmm, that's not good. Well, tell the two of them to gear up and meet me out front, now."

He dropped the old rotary-style phone back onto the cradle, refolded his arms, and lifted his chin. "It seems most of my men are involved in a skirmish between two farmers over a couple of cows. Not that it would matter. I don't have a transport available, anyway.

"I guess you will get your wish. You will remain with me. No heroics. No weapons. You will follow my orders explicitly. Do you understand?" All three nodded in agreement. "When this is done, we will come back here and you will go through customs properly. There will be heavy fines and fees." He abruptly stood. "Let's go." He led them out the door.

They piled back into the Prado while two officers in protective vest and helmets ran up to the vehicle. They each carried a powerful looking semi-automatic rifle with ammo belts criss-crossed over their vests. Without comment, they climbed into the jump seats in the back.

"I hope they know we're the good guys," Xavier commented at their stern expressions.

There were no flashing lights and sirens to warn people to get out of the way. Captain Spweri laid on his horn and shot across the busy highway to the adjacent dirt road they'd seen the green Surf head down. The condition of the roadway only allowed them to travel at an excruciating sixty kilometers per hour *(forty mph)*, when they weren't avoiding the pedestrians, bicyclists, and the giant potholes that threatened to swallow their vehicle. Jean Pierre winced with each swerve and jolt. Even with the pain, he willed them to move faster.

CHAPTER 46

Betta didn't move. Cyrus grunted and got out of the car. Cussing obscenities at her, he jerked the passenger door open. She grabbed the handle and tried to pull it shut. He was too strong and yanked her out. She grabbed the door frame with one hand and pulled against the steel grip he had on her other wrist. "Please, no. You can't do this!"

He laughed and snarled at her. "I can do anything I want, Pretty Thing. Don't you know that by now?"

He wrapped his arm around her, just under her breasts, and wrenched her free of the door. "Don't give me any grief. Once this is over and you settle in, I'll give you another baby. Right now we have an appointment." He lifted her off her feet and carried her to the door.

Panic erupted in a surge of adrenalin. As Cyrus put her down at the door, she broke loose and bolted. Her flight took her across the empty car park toward a small shop on the corner. "Help, someone! Please, help me!" She stumbled in a rut and almost went down. She looked back to see Cyrus thundering toward her, rage on his face. Regaining her feet, she took off again. "Please, someone, help me!" she screamed.

One old man loitering on a bench against the shop front looked up. Even from a distance, Betta could tell he was blind. Just as she was about to shout for him to call the police, Cyrus grabbed her and swung her up in his arms. With one arm around her back, his hand came up to cover her mouth to cut off her plea. Both sandals fell from her feet.

"That was a stupid move, Pretty Thing. Any more like that, and you'll force me to beat some sense into you." He turned and carried her back toward the doctor's office. "Or maybe I'll have to let the children take your punishment. How does that sound?"

Her eyes darted from his cruel face to the car. It appeared empty. The children snuggled down asleep in the backseat. She couldn't let him hurt the children, but she couldn't let him kill the baby. She closed her eyes in silent prayer. *God, I need you! Please rescue me!*

Cyrus must have taken her closed eyes as submission. He eased his hand away and sat her on her feet on the doorstep. Betta didn't try to run. She couldn't risk him taking his anger out on Freedom and Mercy. She looked back. No one seemed to have noticed the commotion she caused. No one was coming to her rescue.

The door opened and a white-coated man stepped back to let them enter. Black-framed glasses perched on a board nose. A bush of steel-gray hair circumvented a shiny brown dome covered in liver spots. He smiled with a nervous twitch at the corner of his mouth.

"Mr. and Mrs. Sharanga. Please, come in."

Cyrus pressed his hand into Betta's back and pushed her into the room. She looked around. It was surprisingly big, with one side sectioned off by a dark gray curtain. An old, rolling office chair squatted behind a well-used desk. A tall, dented metal cabinet, overflowing bookcase, and two tattered chairs comprised the rest of the furnishings. Various posters covered the walls depicting the gestation periods of pregnancy, a call to immunize against an array of diseases, and the importance of clean drinking water.

Betta took it all in. There was another door beside the desk. Did it lead to the doctor's living quarters and possibly outside? Like a caged animal, her eyes sought out the windows and freedom. Her heart dropped. They both sported secure-looking burglar bars painted bright red. She turned back to the doctor and Cyrus. "Please, I want my baby to live."

Cyrus leaned against the door and shook his head. "The doctor here understands the circumstances of your pregnancy. I've explained the situation to him, and he's agreed to take care of the problem. Haven't you, doctor?"

The man appeared ill at ease in the presence of Cyrus' menacing hulk. He chewed his lip and adjusted his glasses. "Well, I prefer delivering babies to aborting them, but when unfortunate circumstances happen such as this, I honor the wishes of the people involved."

Betta reached out and grabbed the doctor's hand. "But that's just it—I want my baby."

Cyrus stepped forward and pulled her away from the doctor. "We need a new start. Remember what I said about Free and Mercy." He turned to the doctor. "What do you need her to do?"

Dr. Kasmwana rubbed his hands together and then ran them down the front of his lab coat. "Well, you're obviously farther along than I anticipated. If you'll go behind the curtain there and change into the examining gown hanging on the hook, I'll just wash my hands and get things ready." He started to turn away. "Oh, and I need everything off please, so I have a clear field to work in."

Betta backed up a step. Out of the corner of her eye, she caught movement at the front window. It was Freedom. His eyes level with the ledge, he looked back at her, confusion and fear in their depths.

Before she could do anything, Cyrus grabbed her shoulders, spun her around, and pushed her toward the curtain. "Do as the doctor says, or maybe you'd like a little help?"

"No, I can do it," Betta responded as she stepped behind the curtain.

Out of sight, she shoved a fist into her mouth to cover the sob that threatened to escape her lips. *I can't let this happen.*

Hoping Free would run for help, she slipped her pants down and undid the knife from the binding on her leg. The weapon gave her a sense of control. Now she would wait for help.

CHAPTER 47

Cyrus paced the room, impatient to get this done and over with so they could officially start their new life together. *I'll fill her belly with my own seed.* "How long will this take?"

"I'll need to sedate her first. Because she's at least four months, I'll have to do what's called a D & C." The doctor turned with a syringe in his hand. "The whole procedure should be over in thirty minutes—if everything goes well."

"Good. I want to get her home as soon as possible." Cyrus turned to the curtained area. "What's taking so long in there?" He whipped the curtain back.

Betta stood with her back to the wall.

"Why aren't you undressed?" Cyrus glared at her. She hadn't removed anything but the kanga. Angry at being thwarted, he started toward her, but stopped short when she pulled her hand out from behind her back. He was surprised to see a good size knife clutched in her hand. "Where'd you get that, Pretty Thing?" He took another step toward her.

Betta pulled the other hand out to steady her knife hand and straight-armed the weapon in front of her. "Don't come any closer. I'm not going to let you murder my baby."

Cyrus chuckled. "Do you really think a little blade like that is going to stop me from getting what I want?"

"Maybe the knife won't, but a bullet will. Don't go any closer to my mama."

Cyrus turned to see Freedom standing in the doorway, his own gun leveled at him. The kid looked pale. Tears welled in his eyes. The gun wobbled in his shaking hands.

"Step back against the wall by the doctor. My mama's coming with me. You're not my daddy. She was right. You're just a mean, hateful killer. I don't ever want to see you again." Freedom's voice cracked with emotion. He wiped his arm across his eyes.

Cyrus saw his opportunity. In three quick steps, he snatched the gun out of the youngster's hand. He couldn't resist backhanding him across the face for his insolence.

Startled, Free cried out and fell under the impact of the blow. He looked up at Cyrus. "I hate you."

Cyrus' jaw worked. His chest heaved as he sucked air in and out between clenched teeth. The sting of the boy's words colored his vision red. He wanted to beat him within an inch of his life, like his father used to pound on him when he was in a drunken rage. The thought stopped him short. *I'm not like my father.* Or was he?

Cyrus pulled the whimpering boy to his feet. "You forgot what I told you. Never point a gun unless you're prepared to shoot it."

"Please, let him go. I'll do what you want." Betta's tone changed from defiance to pleading. She lowered the knife and laid it on the exam table in front of her. "I don't want him here, though. Free, go back out to the car and wait there for us."

Cyrus sneered. "See, I always get what I want." He pulled Free up off his feet and snarled in his face. "You're lucky, boy. Do what your mama says. Get back in the car with your sister and lock the doors. I'll be watching from the window. If you move, your mama's dead, understand?"

Freedom swallowed hard and nodded his head.

Cyrus sat him back on his feet and pushed him toward the open door. "Don't try anything funny, young man, or your mama will pay the price."

The boy backed out of the opening.

The doctor cleared his throat. "Mr. Sharanga, I don't know what's going on here, but I think you need to get a handle on your domestic problems before we consider moving forward."

Cyrus turned and waved the gun at the man. "Doctor, my domestic problems are none of your concern. I'm paying you to perform a service, that's all. Pretty Thing, get undressed—now."

CHAPTER 48

After speaking to the restaurant owner at the junction, Jean Pierre was getting anxious. Munianeza was only minutes in front of them. "How much farther to the lake?"

"It's on the other side of the town, going north. I've contacted the local police post. They have a man watching the place until we get there."

"One man?" Tom questioned.

"You have to understand. This is a small post. There are only three officers assigned here and only one vehicle. Zambia's police force is also military. We are expected to provide law enforcement across a very large country," explained Captain Spweri as he raced down the tarmac road toward Mbala.

They had entered the town proper when Xavier hollered, "Stop, that's it!" The captain pulled to the side of the road, scattering a group of women toting bundles on their heads.

"What?" the other three men up front asked in unison.

"Back there—on that side road—I saw the Toyota parked under a tree." Without comment, the captain backed the vehicle up until the SUV came into view.

"That's it! The license plates match!" Jean Pierre exclaimed. "We've got him."

"You follow my orders, gentleman. No heroics, understand?" Captain Spweri crossed the road and parked on the other side of the adjacent shop, out of sight. "Men," he turned and spoke to the two officers occupying the jump seats in the back. "You two head around back. Leave your walkies on. At my signal, storm the place."

Jean Pierre started to climb out of the front passenger seat when the captain put his hand on his arm. "You're not going. I want you three to remain in the car."

Jean Pierre bristled. "The man has *MY* wife and *MY* kids. You can't expect me to just sit here."

"That's exactly what I expect. My men and I can handle this." Without waiting for a reply, Captain Spweri got out and joined the two officers.

As the three men moved away, Jean Pierre turned to his friends. "We're not really going to just sit here, are we? Look, I'm beat up. I could go in there looking for a doctor. Munianeza doesn't know what I look like. You guys can back me up." Without hesitation, Xavier and Tom opened the back doors.

"Let's get this done." Tom pulled Jean Pierre's door open.

The three slid around the building past an old man sleeping on the bench next to the front door. At the corner, Tom peeked out. The captain had positioned himself along one side of the office, his gun drawn. "Xavier, wait a minute, then follow J.P. I'll go around the back and come in from the other side." He turned to Jean Pierre and squeezed his shoulder. "Are you ready?"

In answer, Jean Pierre stepped out and quick-stepped it toward the building as fast as his bum knee would allow. Nervous sweat popped out on his brow. He had a death grip on the cane in his hand. He wished he had a better weapon. The stout stick would have to do.

He paused at the back corner of the green Surf to catch his breath. His heart pounded. "God, I could use that army of angels again," he prayed and pushed off the bumper.

He stopped as the door to the office opened and Freedom stepped out. The boy looked up. A relieved smile spread across his face. He started to wave and say something. Before the words came out, Tom grabbed him from behind and covered his mouth. He gave Jean Pierre a thumbs up and pulled the boy back around the side of the building.

With Free out of danger, Jean Pierre continued forward until he was even with the back passenger window. Purple and green plaid caught his eye. Mercy Grace lay across the backseat, asleep.

Good, the children are safe.

Captain Spweri motioned for him to back off. He didn't look happy. Xavier scurried to join the officer at the side of the building. Distracted, the captain looked away giving, Jean Pierre the opportunity to hobble toward the front door.

He heard voices through the open window. Leaning toward the edge of the opening, he spied Betta across the room behind an exam table. She looked scared to death. Cyrus stepped in the way, blocking his view.

Captain Spweri and Xavier worked their way down the wall, stopping on the other side of the window. Jean Pierre mouthed, "Betta," and pointed his finger to the left. He pointed straight up and held his fingers like a gun, "Munianeza", then he pointed just right of Cyrus, "Doctor."

The Captain nodded his head once in understanding and whispered something into his walkie-talkie. Before Jean Pierre could stop him, the captain swung around, pointed his gun through the window, and shouted, "Drop your weapon."

Glass exploded, raining shards across the dirt yard. Captain Spweri fired back. "Cyrus Munianeza, you're surrounded! Drop your weapon and come out with your hands in the air!"

"I have hostages. Back off or I'll kill them both," Munianeza shouted back.

Jean Pierre chanced a peek inside. Cyrus had Betta positioned in front of him. One muscular arm wrapped around her. The other held the gun to her head. The doctor was nowhere in sight.

Blood drained from his body, to be replaced by anxious dread. Munianeza would kill her if they didn't do something.

The captain spoke into his walkie.

Jean Pierre wasn't going to chance Betta getting shot. He stepped in front of the window, his hands raised in surrender. "Okay, Munianeza, we're backing off. Let my wife go, and we'll let you get in your car and drive away."

After a moment of silence thick with tension, Betta announced, "We're coming out. Don't shoot. He wants you to back off, and throw down your weapons."

Jean Pierre joined the captain and Xavier, hands raised. Captain Spweri tossed his gun a few feet away. They waited, tense and edgy. The door came opened. Betta stepped out, her back pressed against Cyrus' chest. The gun hadn't moved from her temple. Cautiously, Munianeza eased them forward toward the car, a few steps away.

As they reached the driver's door, Betta clamped her teeth down on the arm across her throat and kicked back, connecting with Cyrus' groin. His grip loosened. Betta swung around with an elbow to his face. Caught by surprise and in pain, Cyrus howled and let go. In an instant, Betta threw herself away from him and ran toward Jean Pierre.

Cyrus swung the gun around and fired. Like something from a nightmare or bad movie, Jean Pierre watched Betta fall forward to the dirt. All the air left his body in one big whoosh. *Oh, dear God! No!* Before he could move, Cyrus fired again and lunged for the driver's door. He wrenched it open and tumbled inside. At the same time, Captain Spweri leaped for his gun and fired from the ground. The bullet pinged off the front fender. His two officers came around the far side of the building, firing as well.

In that instant, Jean Pierre remembered Mercy Grace laying in the back seat. "Stop! Stop shooting!" He waved his arms, frantic to get their attention. "My daughter's in the car!" He locked eyes with Cyrus as the man gunned the car and whipped out of the yard in a cloud of red dust.

CHAPTER 49

Betta coughed and spit the grit out of her mouth. The fall had knocked the wind out of her. She clutched her stomach and rose up on one arm. His face chalk white, Jean Pierre hobbled toward her. He threw his cane aside and fell to his knees next to her. "Oh, my God, Betta! Are you okay? Are you hurt?" He hugged her tight, then held her at arm's length, looking for injuries.

"I'm okay. Help me up." Together, they struggled to their feet.

Freedom shouted and plowed into them. "Mama, Daddy Jean P., I was so scared."

The rest gathered around them, everyone talking at once. Jean Pierre hollered above the din. "This isn't over. He has my daughter." He looked down at Betta. "You and Free stay here with Xavier. I'm going after him."

Betta cried, "Get her back! Get my baby back!" She started to collapse. Xavier caught her from behind. "Go after him. I've got her."

Jean Pierre raced across the dirt as fast as his gimpy leg could carry him. The officers and Captain Spweri quickly outdistanced him. Tom ran up beside him and wrapped an arm around his waist. "Come on or they'll leave us behind."

The two hurried toward the police vehicle and managed to get inside just as the Captain threw the car in reverse and back onto the pavement. Ahead, they could see Cyrus' taillights as he braked for the people running across the street to get out of the way.

"We can't push him. He'll kill her." Tom voiced the thought in everyone's mind. "Where does this road go?"

"He could be heading toward the Tanzanian border or if he turns off to the west, he's making for Lake Tanganyika. Either way, we have to stop him before he crosses out of Zambia." The captain pressed harder on the gas, sending the car flying down the pothole-ridden roadway.

"Can we catch him?" Jean Pierre asked.

"We would have already had him in custody if you hadn't interfered," the captain growled. "I should never have let you persuade me into coming along."

Up ahead, the green Toyota swerved off the road and disappeared behind the scrub that edged the roadway. "He's headed to Tanganyika," announced one of the officers.

Captain Spweri slammed the car to a stop.

"What are you doing? You're letting him get away!" yelled Jean Pierre.

"This road is little more than a track used by bicycles and pedestrians. We're going to need four-wheel drive." He maneuvered the shorter of the two gears into place and shot forward again. "If we're lucky, he doesn't know this road. I grew up in Mpulungu. My father worked at Isanga Bay Lodge. I've walked this road a million times as a kid."

The Prado bucked and swayed down the rutted track. Jean Pierre was pleased to see they were gaining on the Toyota. He wrapped his arms around his waist, trying to ignore the stabs of pains the washboard road sent shooting through him. Nothing mattered but stopping Munianeza and saving Mercy. For a good distance, no one said anything, each man concentrating on the road in front of them.

Tom finally broke the silence from the backseat. "How far does this road go?"

"It's about forty kilometers *(twenty-four miles)* from the turnoff to Mpulungu," Spweri replied. "We've gone maybe three-quarters of that. We're getting closer to the escarpment where Kalambo Falls plunges into the gorge. It's the second tallest falls in all of Africa. We've had a few people die there, either by accidentally falling over the side or going over the edge on purpose."

They rounded a few more corners. On the far side of a dense thicket of bush, Captain Spweri slammed on his brakes. The Prado bucked and settled inches from the rear bumper of Cyrus' SUV. The Toyota's nose was pointed down into a ditch, mucky with rainwater.

"Stay here." Captain Spweri eased out of his door, gun drawn. The two officers climbed from the back and joined him. Cautiously, they duck-walked along the side of the vehicles until they got to the open driver's door. Spweri stood up and aimed at the interior.

Jean Pierre couldn't stand it. "I'm getting out," he announced to Tom and undid his seatbelt.

"Me, too."

The two men moved around the back of the vehicle. The captain and his men were all standing, their guns lowered.

"Where is he? Where's Mercy?" Jean Pierre searched the empty car, his stomach twisted in knots more painful than the pull of the stitches from his surgery or the stab of his broken ribs.

"He's headed toward the falls. Come on—this way." Spweri headed off through the bush.

They followed a meandering path that was little more than a game trail. The scrub on either side stood over their heads. The ground became rocky. Vertical slabs of protruding quartzite kept the men's heads constantly looking down to see where to plant their feet.

In a sudden burst of sound, they rounded a corner of rock to hear the thunder of the falls. Cyrus stood on the precipice. He turned, Mercy pinned against his chest. Bug-eyed and terrified, the little girl clutched at the arm he had across her chest. Her feet dangled off the ground.

"Back off!" Cyrus shouted and raised the gun to Mercy's head.

God, give me the right words and please protect my little girl. Jean Pierre stepped past the others, hands up. He couldn't afford to have one of the officers shoot at Cyrus and risk hitting Mercy—or worse—sending them both over the edge.

"Fontaine, what are you doing?" hissed the captain.

"He's protecting his daughter." Tom edged past the captain and blocked the path.

"Mercy, are you okay?" Jean Pierre asked.

"Yes, Daddy, but I'm scared." The little girl's chin quivered. Tears welled in her eyes.

"Remember what Mommy and Daddy told you when a bad man tries to grab you?" Jean Pierre took another step.

"Stop right there, Frenchman. She's my daughter, not yours." Cyrus took a step back. His foot slipped on the sharp ridge of stone, throwing him off balance and diverting his attention for a split second.

"Now, Mercy!" Jean Pierre shouted as he lunged toward the pair.

The little girl swung her knee forward and sent her foot flying back. It missed Cyrus' groin but connected with his thigh at the precise location of a bloody bullet hole. Cyrus pitched backwards. For what seemed an eternity, he teetered on the edge, Mercy still pinned beneath his arm. He locked eyes with Jean Pierre.

"Please!" Jean Pierre cried out in anguish.

At the very last second, Cyrus pushed Mercy away from him and disappeared over the side. Jean Pierre caught her. He swung her around, away from the danger and fell backwards into Tom. All three crashed to the ground. The officers ran to the edge. It was too late.

The two men struggled to set up and exchanged a look that spoke volume. Jean Pierre wrapped his arms around his friend, Mercy cradled in between them.

"Daddy, you and Uncle Tom are squishing me."

The men laughed in exhausted relief. It was over. Finally.

CHAPTER 50

A beautiful dawn sky had settled into a brilliant shade of blue. The group gathered around the plane were relaxed. A good night's sleep and the knowledge that their ordeal was over had everyone in a cheerful mood. During a late supper, Tom had gotten a call from Gwen. Sikudhani and Taji had arrived without incident. Gwen informed him she was already in love and he would be too as soon as he laid eyes on the children.

Jean Pierre moved his arm more securely around Betta, determined to never let her go. Even though his body continued to protest what he'd put it through, he never felt better. His precious family was safe. He looked at the group of people gathered there. Each had played a part in saving him and getting his family back. He closed his eyes. *Lord, help me to always remember what I almost lost, and thank you, I am so blessed.* He opened his eyes and looked down at his wife. She moved to lay her head against his chest. "You were thanking God, weren't you?"

"Yes, but it doesn't seem like nearly enough."

Tom had a hand on each of the children's shoulders. "Well, we'd better get this plane off the road before Captain Spweri changes his mind and decides to keep us here," he joked.

Jean Pierre dropped his arm and stepped forward to extend his hand to the captain. "Sir, I can't thank you enough for what you've done. I know you've risked a lot by helping us."

The officer accepted Jean Pierre's handshake and harrumphed. "Just make sure the next time you come to Zambia you do it legally. Now you'd better get in the air. I can't keep this road blocked indefinitely, you know." He turned to Xavier. "Mr. Mwena, I'll wait for you and your nephew in the car."

Jean Pierre and Xavier smiled at each other, then came together in a tight hug, hands slapping each other's backs.

"First you saved me, then you saved my son and helped me save my wife. How can I ever thank you?" Jean Pierre whispered, emotion choking him.

Xavier pushed back and looked up into his face. "Just repaying the favor. Guess we're even now."

Jean Pierre leaned on his cane. "Are you sure you don't need me to go with you to Lusaka? I might be able to help you cut through the paperwork more quickly."

"No, my friend. You need to get your family home. If the girl at the orphanage is Precious, I'll move heaven and earth to make sure she is released to go back to France with Emmanuel and me. It may take a few weeks, but Marie's okay if I have to stay. She told me not to come home without her. Besides, we still have to get Emmanuel's papers worked out. That special fourteen-day travel pass we got him in Goma didn't include flying all over the country. I've got Gabe working on getting him a temporary visa to get him out of Zambia and home with me to France."

A car horn honked.

"Uncle, we need to go." Emmanuel stepped up beside Xavier.

"Emmanuel." Jean Pierre stuck out his hand. The young man bobbed his head and laced his fingers into Jean Pierre's in a show of solidarity and triumph.

"Mr. J. P., I hope when you're ready to write your story about the slave labor in the mines, you'll call me."

"I'll do that. Until then, you take care of your family, okay?" Jean Pierre saluted the two men and stepped back toward the airplane where Betta waited beside the open door.

CHAPTER 51

The flight to Lusaka from Kasama was smooth and uneventful. A Zambian Immigration official met them at the airport and took them into the city. They drove down Nationalist Road past UTH, the University Teaching Hospital. The streets were crowded with cars and people, making the going slow. They pulled to a stop at a busy four-way crossing.

Xavier was anxious to get to the orphanage. He'd waited almost fourteen years to see his baby sister again, and now he couldn't stand to wait a minute longer. "Pardon, sir, but will it be much farther?" he asked.

The smartly dressed man in the front seat smiled over his shoulder. "It's just around the corner here. See that green wall?" He pointed to a long stretch of freshly painted mint green block wall. "That's where she is."

It seemed to take an eternity to get to the solid black gate. The driver honked his horn and the steel divider opened to expose a beautifully landscaped yard, abounding with children of all ages. Xavier's eyes traveled hungrily over them, looking for the face that looked like his. Then he saw her standing next to a tall, elegant looking woman.

It was Precious. There was no denying the family resemblance. He could hardly get his shaking legs to support him as he stepped out of the car. Overwhelmed with emotion he'd kept at bay for almost a decade and a half, a gut-wrenching sob welled up and escaped his lips. His eyes clouded with tears as a cascade of excited amazement and wonder flooded him.

"Little Bird!" he cried and held out his arms.

The girl—a young lady of twenty-three now—looked up at the woman beside her. The woman smiled and nodded her head. All hesitation lost, she flew into Xavier's arms and whispered, "You came back."

EPILOGUE

Rwanda

Two Years Later

The reunion took place at the site of the Kamena massacre. Not much was left of the old stone church. A section of the front wall remained standing, including a lovely stained glass window. Although it was no longer white and its edges were charred, the wooden cross still graced the peak above the entrance. The doorframe gaped open—a black-sooted mouth forever screaming the horror that happened inside its walls. The smooth stone steps still led to the front doors, where Father Sebastian once welcomed people to worship and the children to school.

In the mist, Precious imagined she could see him ringing his big brass hand bell, his white robes billowing around him, his jolly face wreathed in a welcoming smile. The image faded as she looked back at the people behind her. There stood Xavier, and Marie with the new baby in her arms. The baby was named Monique, for the mother Precious never knew.

Her nieces, Ann Marie and Margarette, stood side by side. Dressed in identical outfits, each clutched a bouquet of bright, colorful flowers in their hands. The two reminded Precious of Victorine and Venancia, the twins who befriended her at the refugee camp in Tanzania. She often thought of them and hoped their lives were good.

The face of her adopted nephew, Gift, held a somber expression. Was he remembering himself as a little boy, broken and traumatized? His own family lost to the genocide. Gift's story was much like hers—a nightmare neither wanted to relive. The two had become close since she'd moved into the little house in France. Precious felt the teen's pain and understood the jumble of emotions he was dealing with, now that they were standing back on the bloody soil of Rwanda.

Paul, now almost as tall as Xavier, stood beside his father. He looked like a younger version of her dear brother, Phillipe. *I must remember to tell him the story of the time Phillipe saved me from the wild dogs.*

Emmanuel drew up alongside Gift and laid a hand on the young man's shoulder. Gone was the skinny, gawky boy who loved to tease her when they were children. This long-lost cousin of hers now stood tall, confident, and serious. He had become a brother to her over the past two years.

Behind her own loved ones came Betta and her family. In front of them toddled Felicie, named for the baby Precious spent hours caring for under the watchful eye of her Auntie Margarette. This Felicie was chubbier and light-skinned like her father, Jean Pierre, but she had her mother's beautiful golden eyes. A memory surfaced of baby Fellie's sweet face and her toothless smile as she cooed in Precious' little girl arms. Nothing of the tiny girl had ever been found. Now she only lived in the memories of those who loved her.

Jean Pierre wrapped a protective arm around Betta and gave her a loving look. Precious hoped and prayed that someday she'd find that kind of enduring love. For now, in this moment, she would remember her beloved father and brothers, her auntie, uncle, and cousins.

They gathered at the edge of the grassy yard where a plaque listed the names of those who perished on that terrible day in 1994. As Precious read the names aloud, a hush fell over the group. She heard Betta sobbing when she read the name of her father, Andre Nybewe.

After dozens of other names, she came to the names of her own family: Milford Mwena, Theogene Mwena, Phillipe Mwena, Frederic Mwena, Margarette Nzambi, Oscar Nzambi, Victorie Nzambi, Felicie Nzambi. Finished, her eyes blurred with tears, she looked back up at the steps. A crowd, led by the short, round figure of the white-robed priest, seemed to gather in the mist.

They stopped on the top step, their bodies ethereal, their faces familiar. Behind Father Sebastian stood Margarette, with baby Fellie, and Oscar, holding Victorie's hand, her hair ribbons bright against the misty backdrop. Then came her father—her brothers, Frederick and Phillipe on either side. Theo stepped up behind them, his giant form dwarfing the others. He raised a hand in greeting or farewell.

Her father put his hand over his heart and smiled. *Papa!* Margarette blew her a kiss. Her heart swelled with emotion, her mind with memories. The tears that brimmed Precious' eyes spilled over and ran down her cheeks, further blurring the images before her. Xavier's hand came to rest on her shoulder. She looked up at him. His eyes were focused on the doorway.

"You see them too?" she whispered.

"Yes, Little Bird, I see them too."

THE END

Dear Reader,

The story of Xavier, Betta, Precious, and Jeanne Pierre has ended, but only on paper. The people of Africa still suffer horribly at the hands of greedy, power-hungry men. Children are the most vulnerable as they have no voice. We, as a world community, need to be their voice—their advocates for change.

As horrendous as it sounds, the sale and bartering of children for slave labor and sex are big business. Child abduction is a global crisis. Sexual exploitation is a multi-billion business and is considered to be the fastest growing industry worldwide.

The poor, the widowed, and the abandoned are largely the targeted, as they are in dire situations and desperately looking for a way out. False promises of food, security, shelter, income, and even love are the lures these predators of evil use on the innocent. An estimated 21 million people are trafficked worldwide each year, 26% of these are children.

If you think this only happens in third-world countries, you are wrong. Human trafficking in the US is up over 35% in one year, with an estimated 17,000 cases across the country. Imagine if this was your son or daughter. It could happen—it does every day.

How do we stem the tide and save our children? Educate ourselves about this epidemic and help educate communities around the world. Many are sucked in out of a lack of knowledge, and are unable to recognize the truth of what is happening to them until it is too late.

Find an organization you can support with your time, money, and prayers. If you go to my website: www.sonlightpublishing.com you will find a list of organizations who champion the less fortunate in a variety of ways.

I hope you have enjoyed reading *Journey to Sanctuary* and *Journey to Freedom*. Both *Escaping the Darkness* books were written out of a love for the people of Africa and a desire to expose their plight to the world. Although the characters were not real, their stories were based on actual people, events, and experiences and will always have a place in my heart.

As a storyteller, it is my desire to weave a tale that entertains, enlightens, and evokes a desire to change the world around us for the better. I encourage you to share these stories with others, and go out and make a difference.

Blessings,

Debra Shelton

Other books by Debra Shelton

Escaping the Darkness Saga
Journey to Sanctuary

Wild Justice Series
Second Chances
Fragile Reprieve
Final Justice

Rocky Mountain Medley Collection
Price of Grace

Beauty From Ashes *(coming in 2022)*

Debra spent almost 4 years in Zambia working with children at Upeme Hope Children's Centre and those in the neighboring villages. She fell in love with the wild country and the generous people. Escaping the Darkness came from the stories she heard from the people who experienced the genocide and continue to encounter untold tragedies on a daily basis.

Today she lives in Western Colorado, where she continues to write about the human experience. You can reach her at sonlightpublishing@gmail.com or follow her on facebook.

www.ingramcontent.com/pod-product-compliance
Lightning Source LLC
Chambersburg PA
CBHW051431170626
46809CB00006B/2416